PRAISE FOR THE *EMBERS OF WAR* SERIES

"Ferociously good, proper galaxy smashing
space opera."
AL ROBERTSON

"A compulsively readable, expansive space opera."
THE GUARDIAN

"Deep and juicy in the details... a morality play within
a space opera, with literary-style character exploration
in thriller-style structure and pacing."
NEW YORK JOURNAL OF BOOKS

"It's hugely entertaining, and hints at a wider universe
with the tantalising prospect of filling a Banksian hole
in modern sci-fi."
BRITISH FANTASY SOCIETY

"An excellently paced adventure that swells
with energy and force, upping the stakes at every
turn of the page."
BOOK PAGE

"Vivid and sharp, and at times grittily poetic."
LOCUS MAGAZINE

"Thoughtful, creative and lively... this is top-class
space fiction."
MORNING STAR

"A great sci-fi series, one likely to delight fans of Peter
F. Hamilton and Iain M. Banks. Great stuff."
STARBURST

LIGHT OF
IMPOSSIBLE STARS

Also by Gareth L. Powell and available from Titan Books

Embers of War
Fleet of Knives
Light of Impossible Stars

GARETH L.
POWELL

LIGHT OF
IMPOSSIBLE STARS

AN EMBERS OF WAR NOVEL

TITAN BOOKS

Light of Impossible Stars: An Embers of War Novel
Print edition ISBN: 9781785655241
E-book edition ISBN: 9781785655258

Published by Titan Books
A division of Titan Publishing Group Ltd
144 Southwark Street, London SE1 0UP

First edition: February 2020
10 9 8 7 6 5 4 3 2

Printed and bound by CPI Group (UK) Ltd, Croydon, CR0 4YY

Did you enjoy this book?
Please email us at: readerfeedback@titanemail.com
To receive advance information, news, competitions, and exclusive offers online, please sign up for the Titan newsletter on our website:

TITAN BOOKS.COM

For Cath and Alexander

O gentle child, beautiful as thou wert,
Why didst thou leave the trodden paths of men
Too soon, and with weak hands though mighty heart
Dare the unpastured dragon in his den?

PERCY BYSSHE SHELLEY, *ADONAIS*

TROUBLE DOG

"So," I asked, "what's the object of this game?"

The *Adalwolf* smiled. "To win."

We were sitting in a virtual environment—a recreation of the Palace of Versailles. Beyond the high windows, ornate gardens stretched away. Fountains sparkled in the clean white sunlight. *Adalwolf* had dressed his avatar in a dark silk robe. His bony wrists protruded from its sleeves. I had contented myself with my default option: a shaggy-haired, androgynous-looking woman in a battered trench coat. A marble chessboard sat on the table between us.

"And how do you do that?"

"You capture your opponent's king."

"That's this tall one?"

"Yes."

"That's it?"

"In essence, yes."

"And what about these horsey ones?"

The *Adalwolf* gave a tight smile. "The knights."

"Yes, I like those." I leaned over the board and tapped one of the pieces in my first rank. "And these are the prawns?"

"Pawns."

"And these cock-shaped ones?"

"Bishops."

"Got it."

"Are you ready to play?"

"I think so. Who goes first?"

"I do."

Adalwolf reached out a thin arm and plucked a knight from the back row. He moved it over the pawns and placed it on its destined square.

I frowned in puzzlement.

Adalwolf sighed. "What's the matter?"

"That's it? That's your move?"

"It's a classic opening gambit."

"It doesn't seem to have achieved much."

"I suppose you can do better?"

"Of course." I leant back in my chair and cracked my knuckles over my head. I braced my feet against the tiled floor and grinned. "Watch this."

I sprang forward. The fingers of my right hand jabbed *Adalwolf* in the throat. He started to fall backwards, and I flipped the table with my left. By the time the last marble pieces rattled down onto the floor, I was kneeling on his chest with his king held triumphantly in my hand.

"I win," I said.

Adalwolf coughed, massaging his battered larynx. "You really don't understand chess, do you?"

I sniffed and clambered to my feet. "On the contrary." I let the marble king fall from my fingers. It bounced off his ribs with a hollow thump and rolled away across the floor. "You just don't understand tactics."

SAL KONSTANZ

"How about now?"

"Still a blur I'm afraid." On the screen, the *Trouble Dog's* avatar frowned. She pursed her lips. "Wait—"

"Are you getting something?"

"Yes," she said. "I think it's starting to resolve. But all I can see are stars."

"That's all I can see on the screens." We were parked in empty space, three light years from the nearest star system. The *Trouble Dog's* sister ship, the *Adalwolf*, hung a few dozen kilometres off our starboard flank.

"No ultraviolet? No infrared?"

"Sorry." I shrugged. "Just the boring old 'visible spectrum', I'm afraid."

"How do you people do it?"

"Do what?"

"Find anything?" The avatar threw up her hands. "This is like being half-blind."

I touched the wad of bandage covering the empty socket that had until recently housed my right eye. "Don't talk to me about being half-blind."

She looked embarrassed. "I apologise, Captain. That was insensitive. I really do appreciate your sacrifice. It's just taking me a little time to get used to seeing with a real, organic eye. I've never used one before."

"Make the most of it," I said, "because it's the only one you'll be getting from me."

We'd been here for two weeks, resting and recuperating in the middle of nowhere after being forced to flee human space. While Nod and his thirteen offspring had worked alongside the ship's self-repair mechanisms in order to get us flightworthy again, we'd spent much of those two weeks debating our next move. As fugitives cut off from home and hiding out in alien territory, our choice of destination would be critical to our chances of survival.

The *Trouble Dog* noticed my expression.

"Do you regret giving me your eye?"

My fingers brushed the bandage a second time. I still hadn't grown accustomed to the loss of half my visual field and had bruises from bumping into chairs and tables as I walked through the ship.

"I'm not exactly happy about it," I admitted, "but no. I was thinking about something else."

"What?"

"The fuel situation." Both the *Trouble Dog* and the *Adalwolf* had almost depleted their fuel cores. "If we can't find replacements at our next port of call, we'll be screwed."

Given the right templates and a ready supply of raw materials, the ship's printers could produce food, medicines, cannon shells. Even, given enough time, nuclear-tipped torpedoes. But fuel cores were another matter—too delicate and complex and unstable to be safely printed on even the most advanced human printers. Instead, they had to be manufactured at special facilities. The military had installations where it made its own, of course, but civilian vessels had to purchase theirs from licensed dealers at starports—an arrangement that kept a corporate stranglehold on interstellar trade.

The *Dog*'s avatar shook her head. "I'll be screwed," she said. "You'll be okay. I'll be the one stranded and unable to move; if you can find transport, you can keep going."

"I won't leave you."

"You might have to."

I tugged at the brim of my frayed old baseball cap, settling it more firmly onto my head. "That's not going to happen."

I had been born and raised in the Outward, the faction of the Human Generality most engaged with the Multiplicity of other races. Our customs and language drew influences and inflections from a dozen alien cultures. Mutual trade agreements meant nobody in the Outward went hungry or lacked for shelter, but neither did we own much in the way of personal possessions. Our society frowned on the acquisition of stuff for its own sake. Our resources were carefully managed to ensure fairness and efficiency. The wasteful excesses that had finally ruined humanity's home planet would not be replicated on any of our worlds or ships. While some of us lived on the surface of settled worlds, many others preferred to remain in motion. They lived on orbital stations or great star liners like the *Geest van Amsterdam*. We were, in our own eyes, a society perfectly adapted to humanity's new place in the cosmos. And yet, our lofty ideals had only led us into a disastrous conflict with the Generality's largest faction, the Conglomeration. And our urge to explore, to look outwards, had been the siren call that led my parents to their deaths and lured away the love of my life. And so, despite being brought up to value exploration and discovery, I'd be damned if I'd abandon *Trouble Dog* the way everyone else had abandoned me.

She smiled. "I hoped you'd say that."

Although the core of her brain had been grown from human stem cells, she also had some canine DNA spliced into her, which gave her a strong sense of loyalty to her pack—a group that had once included the entire Conglomeration

Navy, but had now shrunk to comprise only myself; our medic, Preston Menderes; Nod, the Druff engineer, and its little brood of babies; and the *Adalwolf*. Everyone else she—and I—cared about had been lost or killed along the way.

"How are our passengers?" I asked.

The *Trouble Dog*'s avatar performed a convincing shrug. "They're coping."

We'd rescued Johnny Schultz and Riley Addison after their ship crashed into an old Nymtoq colony vessel. For the past fourteen days, they'd spent most of their time in the cabin they shared, exploring their new relationship while simultaneously coming to terms with the horrific loss of the rest of their crew. This need for recuperation was something the *Trouble Dog* struggled to understand. Although she could be startlingly compassionate in some ways, she had also been designed to compartmentalise her feelings and move on—grief and post-traumatic stress being undesirable attributes in a heavy cruiser designed for the rigors and attrition of interstellar war.

Addison and Schultz had a little girl with them. Although physically human, the girl carried the memories and personality of Schultz's lost ship, the *Lucy's Ghost*, as well as the curious alien awareness of a millennia-old Nymtoq colony vessel whose name translated as *The Restless Itch for Foreign Soil*. We simply called her Lucy. And over the past days, she'd struck up quite a relationship with the *Trouble Dog*, spending a lot of time talking with her in virtual reality, discussing whatever it was ships discussed when they got together.

"And our food stocks?"

"The printers were designed to feed a crew of three hundred during extended missions. Even if we weren't recycling all organic waste, you'd still have enough in the reservoir to last decades."

"So, fuel's the main thing we're short of?"

"Affirmative."

It was strange how even in the face of possibly imminent disaster, the routines of shipboard life continued unabated. The Druff continued to strip and replace worn-out components, unclog foul-water pipes, and perform the thousand other essential little tasks that kept the *Trouble Dog* habitable and in motion; and Preston Menderes continued his studies, familiarising himself with the equipment and procedures befitting his position as ship's medical officer. Of all of us, I was the one with least to do. During a higher dimensional jump, the *Dog* could almost fly herself. So, while I busied myself with checklists and inspections, they were mostly a means of distraction, a vain attempt to stop me dwelling on our situation.

Reports continued to trickle in from other systems, their signal carried to us on the winds of the hypervoid. All across the sky, ships from the Fleet of Knives were falling like raptors on military and civilian vessels alike. In places, the Generality had tried to fight back, but its forces were unevenly distributed and owned by factions more used to shooting at each other than cooperating. The few battles that had taken place had been swift and merciless, and always ended in victory for the Fleet. A handful of its ships had been damaged or destroyed during these skirmishes, but it was obvious to all that these minor losses wouldn't be enough to make any sort of difference to the inevitable outcome. The Fleet of Knives outnumbered the combined navies of humanity by several orders of magnitude—enough to firmly quell any and all resistance as it swept across the stars like a plague.

The distress calls were heartbreaking: men, women, and occasionally even children, of all nationalities and factions crying helplessly into the void as the Fleet of Knives shot their ships out from under them. Begging for help, and a rescue I couldn't provide.

"You should stop listening," the *Trouble Dog* said. She

had found me sitting on my bunk, with my back against the bulkhead and the brim of my baseball cap pulled low to shade my face from the overhead lighting. Her image appeared in the mirror above my sink. "You're only upsetting yourself."

"I can't help it."

"They are too far away. There's nothing you can do."

"I know. I just feel someone should be listening. Someone should bear witness to all of this."

"And that someone needs to be you?"

I shrugged. "Who else is there?"

She watched in silence as, one by one, I lit the votive candles on the shelf beside my bunk. The smoke that rose from their wicks smelled of sandalwood. I had one for each of my parents, one for George, and one for Sedge. Over the past few years, I had got into the habit of lighting them each night before bed and uttering a little prayer for my lost loved ones. Recently, I had added a fifth from my supply of spares. This one was for Alva Clay, my sister-in-arms. During the Archipelago War, she'd been a marine and had crawled through the jungles of Pelapatarn. Only she knew for sure how many people she'd killed. But after the war, she joined the House of Reclamation and became a member of my crew. Whatever violence she'd perpetrated during the conflict, and however cantankerous or insubordinate she could sometimes be, she had died saving others, and that was how I'd always remember her.

The flames burned steadily. Their light and heat bathed my face. I thought of my parents the last time I'd seen them alive. I pictured Sedge lying frozen in his casket, falling away towards Andromeda. And I thought of something Clay said to me just before we set out to rescue the crew of the *Lucy's Ghost*.

"We're all running from something, Sal. People like you and me don't belong anywhere. Wherever we are, we've always got one eye on the exit, one foot out the door. We're like sharks. We have to keep moving, or we suffocate."

Her husband and their young daughter had been killed in the early days of the war, and she had been running from that pain ever since. I hoped that wherever she was now, she was at peace.

"I love you all," I whispered to the dancing flames. "I love you and I miss you, and I wish you were here."

•

Midnight found me in the *Trouble Dog's* cargo hold, curled under a foil blanket in the bottom of the inflated life raft. The raft was circular, with a covering to provide shelter. Zipped closed, this covering became a dark cave; the light from the rotating orange location beacon came to resemble firelight flickering on the walls; the cold air leaking in from the cargo hold felt like the frigid fingers of a dark tundra night; and these illusions conspired to produce an effect both primal and comforting.

I had also liberated a bottle of Denebian gin from the galley stores, and was counting on it to cloud the worries and grief in my head, and allow me a few precious hours of sleep. Everything was falling apart, and the others—the civilian ships, Nod, Preston, our three passengers, and even the *Adalwolf*—were all looking to me for leadership. The problem was, I hadn't the faintest clue what to do. What do you do when your world is ending? Who do you try to save? Where do you take shelter? We had a vague plan to head towards the region of space known as the Intrusion—a place where a wormhole had been punched through the fabric of reality and the laws of our universe struggled to coexist with those of another continuum. It was an unstable, dangerous place, but we were going there because the data uploaded to us by the traitor Alexi Bochnak indicated the white ships of the Fleet and the dragon-like creatures that had attacked the *Lucy's Ghost* gave it a wide berth, as if they were scared by something in its chaotic fluctuation. Perhaps it was something to do with their builders, the race known as the Hearthers, who had created the Intrusion as a way to flee our universe; or perhaps it was the way the laws of physics could twist and flip in its vicinity. Either way, I hoped we could find safety there—at least, as much safety as could be had in a region where reality itself was unstable and prone to convulsions.

I sensed rather than heard the background hiss of the ship-wide comm system. Then the first clanging chords of an old-fashioned guitar riff filled the hold.

I sat up and yelled, "What the hell is this?"

The music softened a notch or two, and the *Trouble Dog* said, "I've been researching unwinnable wars. Apparently, this kind of music was very popular during the Vietnam War."

"Vietnam?"

"It was a country on the opposite side of the PacRim to what used to be the United States of America."

"How does this help us?"

"I thought the music might lend atmosphere to our plight. It's by a man called Hendrix." Her image appeared on the small soft screen fixed to the inside wall of the life raft's canopy. "And it's either this or something called 'Ride of the Valkyries'."

"I've never heard of it."

"No reason you should have."

"Then can I *please* go to sleep?"

The *Trouble Dog* gave me an appraising look, as if noticing my exhaustion for the first time. "Of course," she said, and the music drained away to nothing. "I'm sorry."

I rubbed my eyepatch. The socket hurt, and I wondered if there might be such a thing as phantom-eye syndrome. Then suddenly, all I wanted was to hide my disfigurement from the world. I curled into a foetal position in the bottom of the life raft and pulled the blanket up over my head.

•

I found Preston in the galley and he told me Johnny Schultz and Riley Addison had transferred over to the *Adalwolf*.

"They need privacy to come to terms with what happened to the rest of their crew," he said. "They've also taken three of Nod's offspring with them."

That was good. The *Adalwolf* had been running without an engineer since fleeing confinement around Camrose, and ships weren't designed to run without a crew. I should have thought to send the three small Druff over earlier—and probably would have done if I hadn't been distracted by the ongoing destruction of human civilisation. The little critters would be able to maintain his systems, and recalibrate to account for any errors or malfunctions that might have crept in.

"And Lucy?"

"Johnny wanted her to go with them, but last time I saw her she was still in her cabin. I don't think she and the *Adalwolf* get along."

His hands were clasped around a mug of protein soup, and his orange jumpsuit looked rumpled, as if he'd slept in it.

"How are you doing?" I asked.

He sighed. "I still can't quite believe it, you know?"

I didn't need to ask what he meant. We'd all been watching the downfall of humanity. We all had friends and colleagues out there on the front lines—men and women who might already be dead for all we knew. Whole worlds we had known were failing from lack of outside support. Biospheres were unravelling. Crops were failing. Food chains were crashing and people were dying. And, of course, there were those opportunist factions who, against all evidence, thought now might be the right time to make an ill-judged grab for power or territory. Futile wars and revolutions flickered and died in the path of the Marble Armada's advance. Missiles punctured fragile habitation domes; mushroom clouds roiled over hard-won farmland; whole societies tore themselves to tatters over issues that, scant hours later, the arrival of the white ships rendered meaningless. And still the carnage went on. It permeated our dreams and flavoured the food we forced ourselves to eat. We were impotent witnesses out here, beyond the borders of human-explored space, unable to influence the apocalypse as it played out in second-hand, static-jagged fragments. Nothing we could do or say could possibly save any of the souls tipping relentlessly into the dark; and yet we couldn't turn away. This was our catastrophe as much as anyone's; on this day, we were all simply human beings cowering from an implacable force of nature—the latest in a series of bottlenecks that had tried, over the millennia, to winnow our species to nothing.

"Are you okay?"

Preston didn't look up, but his hands tightened around the cup. "I guess so."

"It's all right to be frightened."

"I know. It's not that so much. But everything's falling apart. And we lost Alva." He bunched his fists on the tabletop. "I just feel so damn helpless."

My heart went out to him. His words echoed my thoughts, and he was so young to be dealing with so much. But as his commanding officer, I owed him more than commiseration. He needed reassurance. "We're doing all we can."

"It doesn't feel like enough."

"You're doing plenty."

"How so?"

"You're our medic." I forced a smile. "You keep the rest of us healthy and we keep flying. And as long as we keep flying, there's hope."

Some of the tension eased. His hands relaxed. "I hadn't thought of it like that."

I put a hand on his shoulder. "Don't try to cope with

everything at once. You have a purpose on this ship. Concentrate on that for now."

He gave a bleak smile. "And afterwards?"

"Who knows?" I flicked a hand, dismissing further thought on the matter. "Right now, all we can rely on is ourselves."

I heard shuffling in the corridor. Nod shambled into the room. Two of its children scampered and played around its legs. Its scales glimmered with a pearlescent sheen and its little black eyes sparkled.

"Dawn greetings to you, Captain. May the sun's rays warm your branch."

"Hello, Nod. You look well."

One of its hand-faces focused on me, while another swivelled this way and that, keeping track of the little ones. "Much work," it said. "Much time with offspring."

"Well, it seems to agree with you."

The fingers around the edge of its face closed and opened again, like a flower blinking. Nod was pleased.

"I have list of needed parts," it said. "Things we cannot print onboard."

"I'm sure we'll be able to find them at our next stop."

"Much hope, Captain. Much scavenging to be done."

"Excellent." I rose and tugged the brim of my baseball cap, first at Nod, then at Preston. As I left the room in the direction of the bridge, I hoped my demeanour instilled in them more confidence than I actually felt myself.

PART ONE

FOUR YEARS AGO

**For the winds that awakened the stars
Are blowing through my blood.**

W. B. Yeats, *The Wind Among the Reeds*

ONE

CORDELIA PA

"Look, a ship!"

Wrapped in the warmth of his stained and patched parka, Michael Pa paused in the wan light of a street globe, his long ponytail thrown back as he watched the incoming space trader furl its black lace wings. Beside him, I pulled nervously at his sleeve. We were in one of the city's narrow alleys and it was late.

"Mikey, come on," I urged, but his eyes filled with yearning, Michael refused to move. He remained transfixed by the ship, which looked to me to be a fairly standard example of its class, the solid, industrial lines of its hull seemingly at odds with the apparent fragility of its sweeping, electrically charged wings. Long ago, somebody had painted black and yellow stripes over its stern, and its flat, rust-streaked belly reflected the glow of the port's arc lamps. The stripes made it look like a fat bee; otherwise, it was unremarkable. Ships just like it came and went every day.

"Where do you think it's come from?" Michael asked, cheeks pink and breath steaming in the cold night air. "Where do you think it's going?"

I didn't answer. I couldn't have cared less. The air froze the back of my neck like a compress, and this wasn't the kind of place I wanted to linger, especially at night. Growing up around the edges of this vast, echoing metropolis, I'd heard the same stories as everybody else: of ghosts and booby traps, and prospectors who simply wandered off into the night, never to be seen again.

The buildings in the city had been deserted for a thousand years, and existed in perpetual night. No sun had ever warmed them, no rain ever fallen over them. The skies above their roofs and spires were, and always had been, perpetually scattered with stars, against which the lights of the nearer Plates glimmered.

Although I'd only ever lived on two of the twenty Plates in the swarm, I knew all their names by heart: Night Town, Admin, Favela Two... On a clear night, I could recognise them by their positions in the sky relative to one another, and by the soft murmurs they made when I looked at them—murmurs that apparently only I could hear. Currently, in the sky above the descending ship, I could see Ghost Castle, Shipyard One, and the bright sunlamps of Farm Plate Three—the latter close enough for me to make out its rectangular shape against the stars. It looked as wide as my thumbnail held at arm's length, and I smiled at it, comforted by its familiarity. At night, the Plates whispered incomprehensible secrets to me, their voices a constant, comforting sigh, like wind through high tree branches or waves sliding up a darkened beach.

Not that I'd ever actually seen a real beach, of course.

"Come on." I walked a few paces, and then turned. His eyes were still on the ship. Only when the uppermost tips of its up-curled wings finally dropped from sight behind the low buildings ringing the spaceport on the Plate's edge did he lower his face and start to walk again.

"You are so impatient."

"Me?" I fell into step beside him, gloved hands thrust deep into my coat pockets. The coat had been old when I'd bought it, and the gloves had once belonged to the inner lining of an obsolete pressure suit. "You're the one who's desperate to leave."

"Aren't you?"

I shrugged, looking around at the darkened, alien buildings. Some were blocky, others thin and tapering, but the proportions were all wrong. Whoever, or whatever, built them had been around three metres in height, and had scaled the size of the doorways and stairs accordingly.

"We grew up here," I said.

"Not through choice."

Huddled in our coats, we walked to the end of the street and turned right. We had come into the antique city on a scavenging expedition, hoping to find among its abandoned turrets and tunnels a scrap of saleable alien technology. Now, we were trailing back, empty-handed, to the edge of the Plate. Only the very fringes of the city were occupied. The vast majority of it remained unexplored, due to the dangers and unpredictability of its alien architecture. When our mother died, Michael and I had to move from Alpha Plate to share our uncle's draughty fourth-floor walk-up here on City Plate Two.

As we walked, street globes greeted us at each intersection, hovering like anaemic suns, casting a pale light. Having been aligned by their alien builders to the rotational period of some long-forgotten foreign planet, the globes took thirty hours to cycle from bright noon to gloomy dusk, and then back again. Right now, they were almost at their dimmest. We'd been out longer than we'd planned, and now only a few minutes remained until midnight, and the start of curfew.

The streets were empty. Few people ventured this deep into the abandoned city, especially at night. As the street globes faded and the shadows deepened, the archways and spires took on a more threatening aspect.

"Don't you ever think about it, though?" Michael asked.

"About what?"

He slowed. "About life on the other Plates?"

Ahead of us, at the port on the edge of the Plate, the

ship's engines gave a final shrieking roar, and then tapered to silence. I hugged myself against the cold. My hand strayed to the necklace at my throat: a platinum chain, which had once belonged to our mother.

"No," I said.

"Only, I talked to Trudy earlier tonight—"

"That airhead?"

"—and she reckons she's getting off this Plate."

"She says that to all the boys."

Michael stopped walking. "I think she means it." He lowered his voice. "She says she's got a contact on one of the ships, a trader called the *Electrical Resistance*. Next time it docks, she's off. And she says I can go with her."

I gave a snort. "She's a waitress. The only resistance she's got is to reality."

Michael put his hands on his hips. "I'm serious."

"So am I. Now please, let's move. We don't have much time." I stalked off. After a few seconds, Michael ran to catch up.

"Why are you always like this?"

"Like what?"

"So cynical."

I huffed. "Listen, if you want to believe everything a girl tells you when she's trying to get you into bed, that's fine with me. Good luck to you, it's none of my business. Right now, I'm more worried about getting home."

Michael chuckled.

"You're jealous."

"Of what?"

"Of the attention I get."

I flinched. I knew all about attention: over the course of my sixteen years, my chopped white hair and mismatched eyes had attracted their fair share of remarks from the other scavengers—and not all of them had been complimentary.

"She's just trying to get into your pants," I said with a

sniff. "That sort of attention I can live without."

Self-consciously, Michael pulled his coat closed and scowled. "All I'm saying is that it wouldn't hurt you to lighten up a bit once in a while. You used to want to travel. Don't you remember how we used to lie in the dark and make lists of all the places we wanted to see?"

I glanced up at the stars. "I'm sixteen now, Michael."

"So?"

I tugged my fur-lined hood up around my ears. "I'm older now, and things have changed."

"Because of Uncle Caleb?"

Inside my gloves, my fists bunched. "He needs us to take care of him."

Michael rubbed his mouth with the back of his glove. "I know. But that doesn't mean we have to spend the rest of our lives stuck here. He wouldn't want that."

"We can't just abandon him."

"I'm not saying we should." Michael's arms flopped despairingly. "But if we don't go soon, we never will. We'll get bogged down. We'll never make the break."

I sniffed. "You've always been like this. Even when we were little kids, you couldn't wait to get away."

"And you've always been too cautious! We should get some money together and send Uncle Caleb to Hospital Plate."

I shook my head. "That's horrible. He looked after us."

"And now he's ill. He doesn't know where he is half the time. The best way we can look after him is to see he gets professional care."

"We can't afford it."

"We can if we sell the apartment and all his stuff."

"But if we sell that, where will we live?"

"We'll be gone." Michael glanced ahead, in the direction of the port.

"Where?"

31

"Back to Alpha Plate, maybe even Command." He threw his hands wide. "And then, who knows? Maybe all the way to Earth."

I hunched my shoulders against the cold. I was only five years old, and Michael four, when our mother died and we were forced to abandon Alpha Plate for a life scavenging around the edges of this vast alien city. Alpha Plate had been a childhood paradise filled with miracles: warm bio-domes and access to endless information; programmable matter that allowed almost any machine or object to be printed from apparently inert garbage; and access to healthcare far above and beyond anything I could now hope to afford.

"We can't, it's impossible."

"No, it isn't."

"Yes, yes, it is." I sighed. "Even if we could find a buyer for the apartment, by the time we'd paid for Caleb's care, we wouldn't have enough left over to buy a ticket to Night Town, let alone Alpha."

"We'd find a way."

"By flirting with losers like Trudy Hyde?"

"Perhaps."

"Forget it."

We cut down a connecting street and crossed the Old Yard: a bare expanse of the Plate's surface untouched by paving. The material was a semi-translucent blue, and smooth, so that walking on it felt much like walking on glass. Out in the open, away from the buildings of City Plate Two, we could see more of the sky. On the horizon, the system's solitary gas giant hung like a dusky basketball while, all around, the tiny rectangles of the other Plates swarmed against the stars. Agricultural Plates shone with the golden warmth of powerful sun lamps; the other city Plates with the pinprick glitter of a million spire windows. And there, high above all the rest, the bright twins: Command and Alpha.

In my head, I heard Alpha's familiar whisper. It was a lonely, mournful sound. I shivered and hugged myself. As a child, I'd dreamt of flying among them, arms outstretched as I wove through their loose formation, free and happy. Now, I kept my eyes on the ground until we reached the street on the far side of the Yard, and the first signs of human habitation.

We weren't even halfway home but the globes lighting the corners had already dwindled to their bare, brown minimum, signifying midnight. My heart quickened. "It's curfew time. We have to get indoors."

Beside me, Michael frowned. He knew as well as I did that it was a serious matter to be caught on the streets between midnight and dawn. "We shouldn't have spent so much time checking out that old tower."

"That was your idea."

He ignored me, and crossed to a narrow alley between two of the large, blocky warehouses on the opposite side of the street. "If we cut through the Burrow, it'll bring us out on Eighth Street and save us five minutes."

I peered dubiously at the graffiti carved into the walls on either side of the alley's entrance. The Burrow was where the down-and-out slept: the destitute, burned-out, and unemployable. It had a reputation for gang violence and drug use, and occupied an entire city block: a shanty town of packing crates and plastic sheeting crammed into the shells of two old alien accommodation blocks.

"I think I'd rather stick to the roads."

"And risk getting picked up by one of the patrols?" Michael stepped over the threshold, into the shadows. "Trust me, this will be a lot quicker."

He moved off, deeper into the gloom, and I cursed. The alley stank of garbage fires and stale urine. Laundry lines stretched between the windows and fire escapes, and jury-rigged power cables hung in loops from the eaves.

"I don't know about this." I leaned back on my heels to look up and down the deserted street, but there was no one there to see what I was about to do. "If we step into this slum and disappear, nobody will ever know what happened to us. There'll be no witnesses, and, even if the security troops bother to search for us, they won't think of looking in here. No one in their right mind cuts through the Burrow at night; at least, not by choice. Even the people who live in it try to keep their heads down once the street globes begin to dim."

"We can try."

"Mikey, wait—"

"What?"

"I—"

I heard a burst of engine noise at the far end of the street. An armoured personnel carrier ground around the corner on six fat mesh tires. A searchlight blazed from the gun turret above its cab, pinning me in its glare. Squinting, I raised a hand to shade my eyes.

"Halt!" The amplified voice rattled my bones. For a seemingly endless moment, unable to think, heart hammering in my chest, I dithered. I couldn't let myself be caught. If I went to jail, who would care for Uncle Caleb? Michael wouldn't hang around, and he couldn't afford to bail me out. I had to get away, but how? The security patrols carried guns and weren't exactly shy about using them.

The vehicle groaned to a halt before me. Against the glare of its searchlight, I caught the red twinkle of a retina scan. Without meaning to, I blinked, and screwed my eyes into slits.

"Stand still!"

An armoured door opened with a metallic squeak, and a heavy boot crunched down onto the road's surface.

"Why are you out so late, girlie, all by yourself?" A male voice, half-stifled by the thick gas mask covering his face. "Don't you know it's after curfew?"

34

He took a step towards me: a silhouette against the light, his torso puffed out by a padded flak jacket, head appearing over-large and misshapen by the flaring dome of a high-threat combat helmet. I saw the nightstick dangling from his belt, heard the plastic creak of his uniform and the rasp of his breathing.

The security troops were little better than mercenaries. The real cops were safe and warm on Alpha Plate. Here, on City Plate Two, the troopers were recruited from the ranks of the deadbeats they patrolled and paid by results. Shakedowns and extortions happened all the time. If you had money, you could bribe your way out of any trumped-up charge they threw your way; if not, if you were a penniless young scavenger caught out on the streets after midnight, then you were going to become another tick on some trooper's score sheet...

In a flash, I saw the next ten years of my life stretched before me: being moved in and out of cramped cells; coming out of jail with nothing but a drug habit; reoffending simply to get a warm bed for the night; falling deeper into addiction and desperation; and then most likely ending my days beaten down and half-starved in a filthy warren like the one behind me, with no one left to mourn, and only the other down-and-outs to squabble over my few meagre possessions.

No, I thought. *I will not live like that. I refuse to. I would rather die.*

And with that, I turned and made a lunge for the alley.

"Hey!"

My feet slapped the raw Plate material of the alley floor. I wasn't ready to give up yet. I still had a life to lead, and I wouldn't let them take it from me without a fight—because even death would be preferable to jail.

Ahead, in the reflected glare of the searchlight, Michael stood with his eyes wide. I grabbed his hand and pulled him along. "Run, you idiot!"

Blinking aside afterimages, we crashed headlong through flapping sheets and broken sticks of furniture. Our feet splashed through puddles of foul-smelling liquid. From the street, the police searchlight lit up the alley, throwing our shadows ahead of us.

"Halt, or we fire!"

Michael slowed, but I yanked him onwards. "Keep running!"

Holding on to each other, we flailed through another clothesline, and pushed our way past an unplugged chest freezer.

"Come back, you little feral bastards!"

Shots came from behind, deafeningly loud in the enclosed space. I heard the *pap pap pap* of bullets punching through the laundry around us. Chips flew from the walls to either side, and sparks pinged from the overhead fire escapes. The muscles of my back cringed in anticipation, expecting the spine-shattering punch of a bullet. Then Michael hauled me sideways, into an open doorway, which led deeper into the Burrow.

Once inside, out of the line of fire, we stopped with our backs against the wall, heaving in great lungfuls of stinking air. I couldn't hear anything over the roaring in my ears. Were we still being shot at? Would the security troops venture this far into the Burrow without backup?

After a minute, the searchlight snapped off, leaving me blind. Angry curses echoed down the alley from the street. Apparently, the gap was too narrow for the APC, and the patrol was unwilling to enter on foot.

In the darkness, Michael squeezed my hand. "You all right?"

I swallowed. My eyes were slowly becoming used to the gloom. I looked down. My feet and legs were soaked and filthy, my trousers ripped. "I'll survive."

Michael gave a brittle laugh. "I can't believe it. I can't believe we just did that." He gave me a brotherly punch on the arm. I rubbed my shoulder and tried to slow my breathing.

"Well, you said you wanted me to be more adventurous."

I heard the APC's engine start up, the sound amplified by the narrow confines and concrete walls of the Burrow. The security troops were leaving.

"What now?"

The sleeve of Michael's parka had caught on something during our mad dash, and had ripped almost from shoulder to wrist. Grey tufts of man-made insulation fibre fluffed from the wound. He picked at it. "We get out of here as quickly as we can. All that gunfire's bound to have woken half the block."

"Do we go back the way we came?"

"No, the patrol might still be waiting for us. We'll have to go on through and find an exit on the other side."

Gaunt figures moved in the darkness. The inhabitants were stirring, aware of our presence.

I made a face. "Is that such a good idea?"

"It's better than getting shot. Now, come on."

•

"Hey, Mikey, wait up!" I stumbled forward in my brother's wake. Right now, home seemed further away than ever. Beneath my parka, the shiny man-made fabric shirt scratched at my armpits and collarbone. The passage was leading us deeper and deeper into the bowels of the Burrow. The walls were coarse and damp. Sometimes, we glimpsed pale faces and glittering eyes. We heard footsteps stalking us, and heard whispers from above and to the sides. Water dripped. My wet boots crunched over broken splinters of glass and sloshed through dank pools. In places, I had to duck under scaffolding poles and ragged curtains of plastic tarpaulin. At one point, we passed an open stairwell, which brought echoing voices from the floors above, its walls dancing with the flickering shadows cast by rag fires lit for warmth.

"Wait." I needed to catch my breath. Ahead, Michael

slowed. We came to a standstill at a place where the corridor widened into the base of a hexagonal shaft. The shaft seemed to be some sort of air well. Its smooth sides led upwards, through seven storeys, to a grating on the roof, allowing frigid night air to filter down through the fetid, stale fug of dampness and smoke. An inch of dirty water covered the floor. Steam hissed from heating ducts. I bent forward with my hands on my knees. My chest heaved.

Michael came back and touched my shoulder. "How are you doing? Are you okay?"

The water at our feet stank. I wrinkled my nose and bit back the first reply that came to mind. Shaking away his hand, I straightened up.

"Of course I'm not okay. Look at me. Do I look okay to you?" My boots were ruined and would cost every penny I had saved to replace. I couldn't go scavenging barefoot. "Why does it have to be so wet in here, anyway?" Angrily, I kicked at the fusty water. "Why can't it all just fuc—"

I broke off. In the time it took me to close my mouth, the water had completely drained from sight, soaking into the floor as if sucked down into a sponge. The drops raised by my kick spattered down onto suddenly dry ground.

Michael gave a small, surprised grunt. "That was weird."

I frowned. "Yeah." My gloved palms tingled. I squeezed my hands into fists and shoved them back into the pockets of my coat. My feet were still squelchingly wet, but now they were standing on the bare, dry Plate. Michael looked at me, eyes wide.

"Where did it go?"

I gave the floor an experimental tap with my toe. "I've no idea. Maybe there's a drain?" I straightened up and looked around at the dripping walls of the hexagonal chamber. "I wish we'd never come here."

Michael put his hands on his hips. "So, it's all my fault, is it?"

I looked up at the tiny patch of sky, high above. "That's not what I meant."

"But it's what you were thinking, right?"

I raised my eyebrows in exasperation. "No."

"Liar. You always blame me."

"I do not."

"Yeah?" Michael crossed his arms. "What about that party over in Reed Block last year? And the Leicester twins, remember them?"

I tried to push past him. "We haven't got time for this now. We need to find a way out."

Michael scowled. "Okay, but don't forget, it was you who ran from that patrol. It's your fault they were shooting at us. If I hadn't pulled you in here you'd be under arrest right now, or dead. Just for once, I got us out of trouble, and I think you could at least say thank you."

Movement caught my eye: beyond my half-brother's shoulder, in the corridor beyond the air well, armoured figures were approaching.

"Trust me," I said, "this time you've really dumped us in it."

Instinctively, I reached up to cover the chain at my throat. Frowning, Michael turned to follow my gaze, and stiffened as three armed and padded security troopers stepped into the air well. Without a word, they fanned out, spreading around the walls to surround us.

"There you are," the leader said in a thick accent. With his armour and equipment, he seemed to fill the space. He pulled his gas mask down so it hung around his neck, and looked us up and down with slow insolence.

"Now we have you." He gave a low, phlegm-rattling chuckle. "Nowhere for you to run, eh?"

I clung to Michael's arm.

"No, please," I said. The Burrow had been frightening, but I'd been willing to risk its damp floors and desperate inhabitants in order to avoid arrest. To go through all of that and still get caught seemed grossly unfair.

The security trooper's dry, peeling lips split apart in an incomplete leer.

"Don't start begging yet, girlie. You don't know what we want."

Michael stepped in front of me. "And what do you want?"

A thick moustache crouched like an animal on the man's upper lip, and sharp black bristles darkened his chin. "First, you give us all your money."

"And then we're free to go?"

The man shook his head. Behind him, one of the other troopers snickered. "Then you give us coats, any jewellery." The man reached up to smooth his unshaven jaw. "As sign of good faith."

My mouth went dry. Michael said, "And if we refuse?"

From the pocket of his jacket, the man drew an old, rusty screwdriver. The tip had been sharpened to a wicked point. "Then I kill you both. Take your stuff. Make it look like street gang."

I tightened my grip on my brother's sleeve. My palms itched, and I couldn't tear my eyes from the makeshift weapon. To either side, the other cops giggled childishly.

"What do we do?" I hissed.

"What do you think?" Michael used his teeth to pull off a glove. He unzipped his parka and reached into the inside pocket. Slowly, he took out his credit disk and dropped it at the man's feet. The trooper snatched it up with a grunt of satisfaction, and then thrust his chin at me.

"Now you, too."

Hands shaking, I removed my gloves. As I did so, the trooper let out a cry. He waved the screwdriver at my throat. "Give me chain."

I shook my head. "No, please. Not that."

40

"Give it to me!" His hand reached for me. I flinched backwards and collided with one of the troopers behind me. Rough faux-leather gloves clamped my upper arms. I caught a whiff of old sweat, gun oil, and onion breath.

Michael cried, "No, leave her alone!"

Without taking his eyes from my necklace, the leader let fly with a vicious backhanded swipe that caught Michael across the lips and knocked him to his knees. "Shut up, boy."

The man stepped closer, and pressed the screwdriver to the side of my cheek. The improvised blade felt cold and smelled of rust. The handle was dark and flaky with dried blood.

"Give to me."

I swallowed. The itch flared in my palms. "Get away from me." My voice shook. My hands burned as if cradling dry ice, and a hurricane roared through my head.

The trooper laughed over the top of his dangling gas mask. "Too late, girlie. First, I take your chain, and then I take your money. Then we leave you here." He gave a leer. "Teach you not to break curfew. Now, give me chain, yes?"

My head felt ready to explode. I moaned to relieve the pressure, and the trooper stepped back, momentarily startled by the sound.

"Be quiet. Nobody will help you."

I ignored him. Something seemed to be welling up inside me, bubbling up through my feet and crackling into every nerve ending and cell. Talons of pain raked the insides of my skull. The ground shook and the building started to split open. Chunks of masonry fell like rain; pipes burst; electrical cables were yanked from their mountings, showering sparks. The troopers started to shout—

A gunshot rang out.

I blinked. The fury inside me calmed. In the sudden echoing silence, nobody moved.

A woman stepped into the clearing. Her features were

sharp, as if hacked out of flint, and she wore a set of faded grey ship fatigues. Behind her, a tall young man with dreadlocks covered us all with a menacing Hooper gun.

"All right, that's enough." The woman's voice was hard, used to obedience. "The next person to move will be mopping their guts from the wall."

She walked around the edge of the air well until she came to a halt beside me, hands clasped behind her back.

"Cordelia Pa?"

"Yes?"

"Good." She gave a curt nod, as if in acknowledgement of a box being ticked. "We've been tracking you for the last couple of hours. My name's Lomax. You need to come with me. But first…" She turned to the troopers. "Have you fucks ever seen what a Hooper gun can do to a human body? No? Well, if you're not out of here in ten seconds, I'll ask Spider here to give you a demonstration. Right, Spider?"

Gold teeth flashed as the young man raised the weapon in both hands. "Hell yeah."

For a moment, the troopers stood frowning. They weren't used to being ordered around by civilians. Spider flicked a switch on the side of the gun and it started to emit a rising whine. The two at the back wavered. Then, as the whine approached a deafening crescendo, their leader's nerve broke, and all three tried to flee. They crashed against each other in the narrow doorway, hampered by their armour, their victims forgotten.

The woman watched them go with a smile of cold satisfaction.

Crouching beside me, Michael shook me by the shoulder. We were both covered in grit and plaster dust.

"Oh, Cordelia. Thank God. I thought—" Unable to speak, he rocked back on his heels. "I thought—"

I coughed. I felt drained and empty. "What happened?"

"You tell me!" We were still in the hexagonal air well,

42

at the centre of the slum. "What was that, Cordelia? That shaking. What happened?"

I put a hand to my forehead; my skin was clammy. My breath came like mist in the night air, and my insides felt hollow and cold. Above us, the building had split open all the way to the top. Steam hissed from broken pipes. Cold water sprayed from a severed tap, pattering down like rain onto the rubble.

"I don't know." I had impressions, blurred fragments of pain and anger, but when I tried to focus on them they skittered away. My head ached. "I don't understand any of this."

"Just—" Michael broke off, eyes wide. "Cordelia, your hands!"

Looking down, I saw my fingertips glowing softly, like the last charred embers of a dying fire—as if the bones smouldered beneath the skin. I turned my hands over and over, frowning.

Police sirens wailed on the far side of the ruined Burrow. The frightened troopers had summoned reinforcements. I curled my hands into fists and pushed them into my pockets, and met Michael's wide-eyed gawp with a glare. Before I could tell him to keep his mouth shut, Lomax bent down and hauled at my arm.

"Come on, we have to move." She helped me upright and we set off as quickly as we could, Michael following, the gangly young man called Spider bringing up the rear. My hands wouldn't stop trembling, and I kept stumbling over my own feet. I tried to look back over my shoulder. "Did something explode?"

Lomax pulled me forwards, not breaking step. "Damned if I know. Felt like an earthquake to me. But I'm just here to take you to the port. We can talk more when we get there."

"The port?"

We emerged onto the street. The sirens were louder out here. "Come with me." With her hand on my elbow, the woman led me back down the block, to a delivery van parked by the kerb.

"Get in."

I shook her off. "Where are we going?"

"Somewhere safe. Now, please, both of you get in." She opened the passenger side door and pushed me into the cab. Michael climbed into the back with Spider.

"Keep your heads down," Lomax warned, "in case we run into a patrol."

•

She took us to the spaceport, and out onto the apron.

"Hey." Michael leaned forward between the front seats. "I know that ship. We saw it land."

I followed his outstretched hand. A ship sat on the concrete a few dozen metres to our right, and I recognised the yellow and black stripes around its stern.

Hauling on the control column, Lomax brought us to a halt beside it, in the shadow of its furled wing.

"Welcome to the *Gigolo Aunt*," she said. She killed the engine and climbed out, hurrying around the van's chrome grille to open my door. "Come on, we have to leave."

She helped me down, and I stood squinting in the harsh glare of the overhead arc lamps. I'd never seen a ship this big up close before, and its sheer scale was almost overwhelming. I'd been expecting it to be around the same size as the passenger shuttle that had ferried Michael and me to City Plate Two all those years ago, but this beast was easily four times the height and length of those little inter-Plate hoppers. Resting on its belly, the ship looked like a building tipped over on its side. Aside from the stripes, the hull plates were an industrial grey. At the front, the bow tapered to a blunt snout, where someone had stencilled its name. Warning decals surrounded its engines and airlocks. Sensor pods stuck out like oddly spaced whiskers.

"We have to what?"

"Leave. Come on, it's all arranged."

I pulled back. "You mean—?"

"I need to keep you safe, Cordelia. And right now, the only safe place is away from here, around another star."

"You are joking. There's no way—"

"I'm afraid you don't have a choice. After tonight, the police will be looking for you and your brother, and there are only so many places on this Plate you can hide."

I looked up at the ship's black mesh wings, which swept high into the air, glinting dully in the orange wash of the arc lamps.

"What do you even want with me?"

"We'll tell you more once you're aboard—come on."

"But I can't leave. My uncle—"

"I'm sure he'll be fine."

Ahead the ship's airlock gaped: a welcoming circle of yellow light set into the hull's dull exterior. Lomax hurried me towards it.

"I can't go."

"We're all going. Now, get on board." She chivvied me into the confined space. Spider still had the Hooper gun cradled in his rangy arms. He looked me up and down, and raised an eyebrow.

"She looks younger than I thought." He had an unfamiliar, off-Plate accent, and his short, thin dreadlocks spiked from his head like a spider's legs. He turned his gaze to Michael. "And I thought there was only supposed to be one of them?"

They both looked at Michael, who paled visibly and drew back, as if afraid of the light spilling from the lock. Lomax scowled. "Get in, kid." She reached for him, but he took a couple of steps backwards.

"No, I can't. I won't." He held up his hands to ward her off.

I tried to reach him, but Spider's long fingers closed around my upper arm.

45

"Sorry, love," he rumbled. "You're staying here. We need you with us."

"But he's my brother!"

Beside me, Lomax swore under her breath. "We don't want you," she said to Michael. "We just want her. If you want to come, that's fine. But you need to decide, right now."

I caught my half-brother's eye. His face shone pale in the overhead lights.

"I can't do it." He rubbed his face with his hands. "I'm sorry, Cord."

I couldn't believe it. Mikey was the one who wanted to get away. He'd always been the dreamer. Now here he was, about to be handed everything he'd ever wanted, and he was chickening out? Suddenly, all his big talk meant nothing, and I finally saw the scared little boy that had always been hiding behind all his bluster.

Lomax took a deep breath, and seemed to come to a decision of her own. "Catch." She flipped a credit disk at him. He caught it by reflex.

"There's five hundred on there," she said. "It should keep you going for a while. And you can keep the van."

Michael's eyes widened. They kept darting from the disk to me.

"I'm sorry, Cordelia."

"Mikey?" The port lights blurred and swam as tears filled my eyes.

"I can't do it."

I just wanted to grab hold of him. "But this is all you've ever talked about."

"I know." He sniffed, and wiped his nose on the cuff of his torn parka. "And I'm sorry. I'm really, really sorry." He climbed into the van. I called after him, but he didn't look back. He grabbed the steering column and the engine whined into life. Then, tears streaming down his cheeks, he

46

pulled away. Struggling to breathe, I watched his tail lights racing for the gate.

"No, that's not right." I struggled against Spider's grip. "He can't. He wouldn't—" My fingers prickled. Little pins seemed to be stabbing the pads. I wanted to reach out and haul him back, but it was too late. The van disappeared into the dockside tangle of containers and cranes, and I lost sight of it.

All the air seemed to drain out of me. Spider gave my arm a tug, and, too stunned to resist, I let him lead me into the waiting hatchway.

"We've got a full hold and we're good to go. Welcome aboard, kid. Make yourself at home."

Lomax looked down at me. "Are you okay?"

I shook my head, and turned to look back across the landing apron, towards the perimeter fence and the city beyond.

"I can't leave him, not like this." Something seemed to be tearing within me. A million tiny hooks were slowly, agonisingly ripping my heart and stomach.

"You don't have any choice," Lomax said.

"But why?"

"I told you. You're important."

I turned on her. "But, Mikey—"

"We'll do what we can. Once you're safe, we'll see about sending some more money."

Beside us, the gold-toothed man scratched his ear. "Do we have a problem here?"

Lomax held up a hand. "Everything's fine, Spider. Could you just give us a minute?"

The man made a show of contemplating the Hooper gun in his arms. Then he smiled, letting the overhead light play across his gleaming dentures. "Sure thing, *compañero*." He opened the inner lock and slouched through into the ship's echoing interior. "But don't take too long. Gant says wheels up in two, whether we're ready or not."

After he had gone, Lomax touched me on the sleeve. "I promise we'll do everything we can."

I shook her off. "But I don't understand why you're doing any of this. I'm nobody special. What do you want from me?"

"I'm taking you to see an old friend of mine," Lomax said. A red warning light began to flash on the ceiling. With a metallic groan, the outer airlock door started to hinge shut. "An old and dear friend."

I took a last despairing look through the narrowing gap at the city I'd called home for the vast majority of my life.

"What 'old friend'?"

Lomax lowered her eyes. "Your father."

With a final, heavy *ker-thunk* the airlock sealed itself, cutting me off from City Plate Two and everything I'd ever known. Engine noise came from astern, vibrations shaking the deck beneath my feet. In a glass panel on the wall behind Lomax's shoulder, I caught the reflection of my own face: spiky white hair, odd eyes, cheeks streaked with plaster dust and dried blood. I put out a hand to steady myself, quite sure I'd misheard.

"My father?"

Before Lomax could elaborate, a warning klaxon blared through the ship's corridors.

"Come on," she said. She took my hand and guided me to a cramped passenger compartment with half a dozen rows of seats. She helped me strap into the scuffed padding of a chair in the second row, fastening the harness with a metallic snap. As she took her own seat the deck trembled, and I gripped the armrests.

"I can't go." Suddenly, my heart tripped like a hammer. Butterflies swirled in my chest. The room smelled of cheap plastic seat covers.

"We don't have a choice, either of us."

A small screen lit in the headrest of the chair in front, displaying a view of the landing field. The hull rang with audible clangs as fuel lines and air hoses disengaged and withdrew, slithering back into recesses in the apron's tarmac. Hydrazine vapour caught the light, streaming from thrusters on the ship's belly.

"Lift in ten," a croaky voice intoned. I looked in vain for a glimpse of Michael, but he and the truck were long gone.

"Please—"

The older woman shook her head. "Too late now."

The deck trembled again, and the cabin walls groaned. The view on the screen in front shuddered. The noise of the engines increased until it was a gut-shaking roar, and the old ship wobbled into the air.

•

The *Gigolo Aunt* went up like an elevator. It ascended until it was a hundred metres above the spaceport, and then paused. I saw the oversized alien buildings of the city laid out in their concentric squares; and beyond them, at the point where the streets simply petered out, the rim of the Plate itself; the edge of my world, with nothing to stop the unwary literally falling out of the world, into the stars beyond and below. The sight opened a hollow pit in my stomach. I'd been kind of lost my whole life; poor, orphaned, alienated from the other kids by odd looks, having to scrabble an existence on the edge of the city. Now even that was being taken away.

Beside me, Lomax said, "This is for the best, you know."

"How can you say that?"

"Just trust me."

"But you mentioned my father—?"

"This is his ship."

The *Gigolo Aunt* tipped back on its stern, aiming its nose at the stars, and I frowned.

"But I don't have a father."

TWO

CORDELIA PA

As the *Gigolo Aunt* powered away from the Plate, the harsh backsplash of white light from its twin fusion drives brightened the dismal streets and warrens of City Plate Two. For twenty minutes, the sturdy old ship burrowed upward, into the darkness. The walls and deck shook. At the twenty-one-minute mark, she passed through the invisible curtain of energy that kept the Plates in formation and their breathing air from drifting away into space, and her main drive cut out. Manoeuvring thrusters fired along her length, turning her hull to align its axis with her destination—wherever that might be—and she began to accelerate. When she reached the speed necessary to flip out of the universe and into higher dimensional travel, tremendous energies built in the nested fractal coils hidden deep in her clunking metal heart. Focused along vanes protruding from her prow, these energies ripped a circular rent in the cloth of space. Curdled starlight formed a rainbow around the circle's edge. The centre of it revealed a glimpse into a misty, windswept void.

The *Gigolo Aunt* continued to power forward towards the lip of the wormhole she'd created, her blunt nose lit by the cold, distant stars. Then, as she approached the portal's threshold, she unfurled her tapered mesh wings, black against the darkness of space, and stretched them forward, eager to gain traction from the barely tangible fabric of the hypervoid. Tendrils of mist played across her skin, and still she advanced, like a moth transfixed by the roar of a blowtorch. Her fusion motors flared again, and she tipped headlong into the abyss.

In the main passenger cabin, tucked behind the bridge at the front of the vessel, I clung to the armrests of my seat, face pale, eyes wide. Beside me, Lomax seemed unperturbed.

The air coming from the vents in the cabin's ceiling tasted metallic and stale. During the ascent, the room shook like a box in the hands of a giant. The transition through the wormhole was rougher still, and worse than anything I could have anticipated; but once we were through and into the hypervoid, the ride smoothed out. The deck still juddered, but Lomax showed it was possible to unclip from the safety harness and stand upright without too much effort.

"Come on," she said. "I want to show you the bridge."

I unfastened my belt but remained where I was. "Why?"

"Because the ship's your home now, so you may as well get to know her."

I looked around at the seamed bulkheads and brought my hand up to touch my mother's chain. "My home?"

"Yeah." Lomax glanced toward a forward hatch. "Spider's pretty unhappy about it, but it's what the old man wants."

"And by the 'old man', you mean my father?"

Lomax crossed her arms. "The *Gigolo Aunt* is his, as I said. And he wants you on board."

"Is he here? Can I see him?"

"Not right now. We're going to pick him up at our next stop. Meanwhile, there's only Gant and Brof. Gant's the pilot and Brof's the engineer. It's a Druff, of course. You'll meet them both later."

Spider slouched into the room.

"How are we doing?" Lomax asked.

"Not too bad." He leaned a hip against the doorframe.

"So we'll make it to Redloam on time?"

"In a couple of days."

"Good." Lomax tightened her arms over her chest. "Because I don't want that thing on board a moment longer than absolutely necessary."

Spider's long fingers scratched the wisps of beard along his jawline. A smile mocked the corners of his mouth.

"It's only an artefact, skip. How many hundreds of those have we hauled in our time?"

Lomax shook her head. "No, there's something different about this one. I don't like it. It gives me the creeps. The sooner it's off this ship and delivered to Hagwood, the happier I'll be."

She turned to me. "You were raised on the Plates. Do you know anything about artefacts?"

"What kind?"

A shrug. "Any kind."

I moistened my lips. "Mikey and I are scavengers."

"So, you've found a few of them, then?"

"A few." I scratched my cheek. "Nothing big. A handful of intact vases, the odd sculpture, that sort of thing. Nothing that brought in much money, anyway. Just enough to get by."

"Really?" Lomax's eyebrow twitched. "Because those things, especially the artworks, sell for a fortune. I guess you got ripped off?"

I looked down at my hands. I didn't know what else to do. The older woman put a hand on my shoulder. "Hey, don't take it personally. It's supply and demand, and the same all over. The rich get rich living off the sweat of the poor. Same as it ever was."

I scowled around at the walls of the ship.

"Rich people like you?"

A mirthless chuckle. "No, love. We're not rich, not by a

53

long shot. We don't sell what we carry, we just ship it. We're couriers." Lomax sloshed her boot in one of the pools of condensation gathered on the deck. "If we were rich, would we be living like this?"

"And my father?"

"He's always keen on the artefacts. I think he ships them just so he can spend time with them. He spends hours down in the hold, just looking at them."

"When am I going to meet him?"

"Soon. We're on our way to pick him up now." Lomax pursed her narrow lips. "For the past two weeks, Nick's been involved in some delicate negotiations on Redloam."

"My father's name is Nick?"

"You didn't know?" Lomax scratched her lip with a clipped thumbnail. "Yes, Nick Moriarty."

"Moriarty." The name felt strange on my tongue. I rubbed my eyes. When I looked up, Lomax's features had softened slightly.

"Don't worry, kid. It's a lot to take in. You'll be okay."

"But what does he want?"

"He wants you to come and live on the ship with him."

"But why?"

Lomax's smile tightened a notch. "To be his replacement."

"Replacement for what?"

"As captain of this ship."

I closed my eyes. "So what am I supposed to do now?"

"He left you a message." Lomax scratched her lip again, clearly uncomfortable. "He recorded it before we dropped him off. It's in his cabin."

"Can I see it?"

"Come with me."

Lomax reached out a hand and, without knowing why, I took it, and allowed myself to be pulled to my feet. Together we walked to the hatch that led forward, towards the ship's bow. Our feet splashed on the wet deck.

As we left, Lomax paused on the threshold of the hatch and turned to her crewmate.

"Oh, and Spider?"

"Yes, Lomax?"

"See if you can find out where all this fucking water's coming from, okay?"

A reluctant sigh. "Yes, chief."

•

The captain's cabin lay tucked beneath the cockpit, wadded into the lower half of the ship's blunt nose. It was accessed via a hatch in the floor of the corridor linking the bridge to the rest of the ship.

"You can sleep here for now," Lomax said. "We've got a separate cabin for you to use if you decide to stay, but it needs clearing out. We've been using it as a store cupboard, and you wouldn't believe the crap that's in there."

I leaned over the open hatch and peered down into the room. All I could see was the ladder and a portion of bare metal deck.

"Play your father's message, help yourself to food or drink from the printers in the lounge, then get some sleep. It must be nearly two in the morning your time."

"But, Mikey—?"

"Your brother will be fine."

"Half-brother," I corrected, and then shrugged, unsure why I had made the distinction. "Same mother, different fathers."

"Don't worry about him, he'll be okay."

"And my uncle. He has to look after my uncle."

"I'm sure he will."

I rubbed my eyes. I knew she was trying to be kind, and I appreciated the obvious effort it took.

"I'm sorry," I said politely, "but what should I call you?"

"My name's Tessa, but as you'll have seen, people call me Lomax."

"Do you know my father well?"

"I know him as well as anyone, I suppose." The corners of her mouth twitched. "Maybe a little better than some."

"What's he like?"

Lomax shook her head firmly. "It's late. You'll find your father's message on the crystal reader by the bed, where he left it. Now, down you go." She helped me swing my leg out over the hatchway and put a foot on the ladder. Then she watched as I clomped down the steel rungs. For my part, I had no fear of heights or enclosed spaces. Being a scavenger in the city had long cured me of both.

When I was down, Lomax slid the heavy metal hatch into place above me. "I'll see you in the morning," she called. I didn't respond. Instead, I stood at the foot of the ladder and let my gaze slide around the dimly lit cabin.

My father's cabin.

It was smaller than I'd expected, maybe four metres by two. Old-fashioned nautical charts decorated the walls, their corners curled and brown with age. A leather jacket hung on the back of a chair.

This must be his bunk, I thought. The covers were still untidy from the last time he'd used it, but there was a freshly printed sleeping bag folded up at the foot of the bed. The small, circular crystal reader sat beside it. The butt of a crystal poked from its data port, and the red 'message waiting' light blinked. Hesitantly, I picked up the machine. The casing had a thousand little scrapes and scratches that betrayed a lifetime of hard use.

All these years of wondering who I might be, where I came from, and why I looked so strange. And now I held the answers in my hand. But did I have the courage to hear them?

I might have been mostly self-educated, but even I'd heard of the Schrödinger's cat experiment. Now, for the first time, I knew how the hypothetical experimenter felt the moment before they opened the box. I'd spent my whole life dreaming and speculating. I'd lain wrapped in a cold blanket at night, listening to Mikey snore, longing for the day my father would come to find me. My mother had taken his identity to her grave, but that hadn't stopped me constructing a picture of him as dashing, rich and handsome. Now I was painfully aware that, as soon as I played this message, all that comforting speculation would end. All my fantasies, all those fondly imagined possibilities, would collapse down into a single, hard truth. He would stop existing as a waveform of possibility and become a single, defined person—and I would have taken a step into a far smaller world.

I sat on the edge of the bed. The sheets held a faint, slightly spicy smell: a mixture of male sweat and old, cheap cologne. With shaking hands, I balanced the player on my knees and took a deep breath.

There was no choice, not really. I had to hear what the message contained, good or bad. Spiders seemed to be scrabbling around in my stomach, making me queasy. I swallowed hard to stop them climbing my throat and, with every muscle tensed, hit the play button.

•

Twelve centimetres in height, Nick Moriarty's holographic image shimmered into apparent solidity, feet braced astride the top of the player resting on my knees. At first, I was a little disappointed to see his hair wasn't white, and that his eyes were both the same colour. In fact, he looked reassuringly normal, for a spacer. He wore a fur-lined leather jacket (the same one, I realised, that was now draped over the chair), with a set of overalls much like the ones Lomax had been wearing; he had a firm, unshaven jaw, and grey hair at his temples.

"Am I speaking to Cordelia Carmine Pandora Pa, daughter of Jasmine Pa of Alpha Plate?" His voice was deep and hoarse, with background traces of a lilting accent I didn't recognise.

"Yes. Um. Hello?"

The tiny eyes seemed to focus on me. "Cordelia, my name's Nick, Nick Moriarty, and, as I'm sure Tessa's already explained, I am your father."

To me, each word felt like a pebble dropped into a deep, dark well. They echoed in my head. Absently, I reached over to the chair to touch the jacket's soft fur lining.

"Pleased to meet you," I said, not knowing what else to say.

The little figure gave the barest hint of a formal bow: a quick downward jerk of the chin. "Likewise."

I had been expecting a straightforward recording. I waved a hand in front of his face. "Can you see me?"

Nick spread his hands in regret. "This is only a projection," he said. "I can't really see anything at all. The crystal in this player holds my mind–map, and the software feeds me details of your face and voice, but it's not the same as really seeing you."

"Mind–map?"

"A recording of my brain. It's like a simulation. The program lets me talk and respond, but it's really just guesswork based on past behaviour."

My heart felt like a stone in my chest. "So, I'm not really talking to you?"

The little figure shook its head. "No, child, I'm sorry. The real Nick is waiting elsewhere. As I said, I'm a recording. A simulation."

"Do you feel alive?"

"I don't think so." Nick rubbed the stubble peppering his chin. "It's hard to tell. I can act and feel the way Nick would act and feel but, at the end of the day, I'm not really him. I'm not self-aware. I'm just an echo, here to deliver his message." He blew air through his cheeks. "Talking of which, how much has Tessa told you?"

I licked my lips. "That you want me to replace you on the ship."

"That's right." For the first time, I thought I saw a touch of sadness in his eyes. "I'm not getting any younger, and one day I'll want to pass on the family business."

"But what will I do here?"

Nick's hand dropped to his side. "You'll learn to fly, of course! We'll send you to flight school. Then you'll come back and serve as first officer until I'm ready to retire. It's a good ship, and it'll take us anywhere we want to go." He leaned forward, looming out of the projection. "And when you've got your own ship, you're your own boss. As long as we can find enough cargoes to make it pay, you and I can live free and clear for the rest of our lives, with nobody telling us what to do or how to behave."

"Is that what you do now?"

He smiled wolfishly. "You're damned right I do."

"But I don't know anything about running a starship." I rubbed my left eye with my right hand, suppressing a yawn. "I'm a scavenger. I've never even been into space."

"Neither had I at your age. I was a country boy, born and raised in the Marches. I'd never even left the village where I grew up. But I learned, and I learned fast. You had to in those days."

I gave his image a wary squint. Then I thought of the *Gigolo Aunt*, and panic bubbled up inside. "But it's too much. I wouldn't know where to start."

"Tessa can help you get orientated, and you'll be picking me up in a couple of days."

I shook myself. Years of scavenging had hardened me to deals that sounded too good to be true.

I sucked my lower lip. "I'll need to think about it." I rubbed my forehead and yawned. "If I turn you off for a few hours, will you remember any of this when I turn you back on again?"

"As long as you don't reset me."

I reached for the switch. "Okay, then. Goodnight."

"Goodnight, my love."

I tried to swallow but something seemed to be caught in my throat. "Please don't call me that."

Nick looked concerned. "Then what should I call you?"

I tugged at my earlobe. "Not that, not yet." He didn't have the right to act the doting father. He hadn't earned it yet.

If he really was my father, of course. Part of me still suspected the whole thing to be some sort of ruse, some kind of cruel scam. Things like this just didn't happen to orphans like me.

"If you have to call me something, call me Cordelia," I said with a sniff. "It is my name, after all."

Nick gave an understanding nod. "Okay, I'm sorry. Cordelia it is." He put a palm to his chest. "And what are you going to call me?"

I placed a thumb on the off switch and inhaled through my nose.

"Later," I said.

•

When I awoke in the sleeping bag, the crystal reader still sat inert on the pillow beside me, and the room seemed exactly as it had been when I fell asleep. Nothing had been touched. Lying on my back, I let my gaze roam, trying to think myself into my father's head. This was his bed, after all. The handful of paperback books on the metal shelves, held in place by a strand of copper wire, were his, as were the dog-eared nautical charts taped to the bulkheads. I assumed the names on the charts were those of bays and coastlines on Earth. The one above the bed pictured a group of green islands surrounded by depth contours, and various symbols I didn't recognise. The islands themselves were blank. This wasn't like the detailed sketches I'd used as a scavenger, with every room and passage marked. This was a map for someone more interested in travelling than arriving; more concerned with currents and shoals than cities, towns and villages.

Through the bunk, I could feel the *Gigolo Aunt* shuddering as it pulled itself through the higher dimensions, magnetic black wings clawing at the firmament. How many mornings had my father lain here like this, listening to the hull creak and flex, the clang and gurgle of pipes, and the clomping footsteps of people moving around on the metal deck of the bridge above?

Despite the noise, everything *felt* curiously silent, and it took me a few minutes to realise why. The noise of the Plates—a hiss so gentle and familiar I sometimes forgot it was even there— had gone. They no longer whispered at the back of my mind. Their comforting murmurs had fallen silent. The realisation brought a surge of giddy homesickness. Suddenly, I felt very small and very young, and very far from home. I was the girl who'd lost everything, starting with my mother and continuing with my half-brother, my uncle, and now my entire world.

Or had I?

Lying there, I supposed it all depended on how you looked at things. I picked up the crystal reader and turned it over and over in my hands. After a night's sleep, and with hunger gnawing at my insides, I felt alert and clear-headed for the first time in days. I was warm and safe and, if my father's electronic ghost was to be believed, I now had a place on a starship. Tentatively, I reached out my fingertips to touch the rivets on the nearest bulkhead. The metal felt cold and smooth, with the slightest trace of vibration, and I shivered. A ship like this had to be worth several million, at least.

A door at the back of the cabin led into a cramped bathroom, where I showered, rinsing away the worst of the previous day's grime and dust. When I came out, wrapped in a towel that smelled slightly of mould, I found freshly printed underwear and a neatly folded all-in-one ship suit at the bottom of the ladder. I dressed hurriedly. As I zipped up the front of the garment, my eyes caught the leather jacket on the bed. For a moment, I considered putting it on. Then I shook myself and climbed up, hoping to find something to eat.

Lomax was waiting, a plastic cup steaming in each hand.

"How are you feeling?"

I stifled a yawn. "A lot better for some sleep."

"Did you play your father's message?"

"Yes."

Lomax handed me one of the cups. It had coffee in it. And it smelled so much better than the brown muck they served at the port.

"Have you decided what you're going to do?"

I frowned. "How do you mean?" The cup was warm in my hands. The smell of the steam set my stomach rumbling.

"When you meet your father. What are you going to say to him?"

I inhaled from the cup, and then took a sip. "I don't know yet."

The *Gigolo Aunt's* bridge was a low-ceilinged cockpit, housing two control couches and a plethora of screens, readouts and consoles. Projected points of light swam in the air, forming a three-dimensional map of nearby stars. As I watched, they moved like the restless ticking hands of a clock, gradually shifting position in a series of tiny jumps to take account of the *Gigolo Aunt's* relative progress through the hypervoid.

Lomax reached out and touched one.

"This is Redloam," she said. She moved her hand across to

a tiny red arrow suspended between stars. "And we're here."

"How long will it take us to get there?"

"About another two days." Lomax took a drink from her own cup, her movements precise and birdlike. "Which should give you plenty of time to get to know the ship."

I put a hand on the back of one of the couches. It felt solid and reassuring, but the controls arrayed before it were a total mystery. How could I get to know a ship like this in two days? It was such a vast, incomprehensible slab of metal, with so many moving parts. Its engines were capable of tearing a hole in the dimensional fabric of reality itself; I couldn't possibly hope to understand how they worked in so short a time.

My fingers squeezed the back of the chair. Little Cordelia with the white hair and the mismatched eyes—was I a scavenger, or first mate on a starship? Not even I knew the answer to that anymore; and, until I figured it out, everything else would just have to wait.

•

A klaxon sang through the *Gigolo Aunt*'s metal corridors. In the cockpit, Spider and Gant strapped themselves into the control couches. I perched behind them on a fold-down jump seat.

"Ten seconds." Spider's voice was sullen. I had hardly seen him over the past two days. He'd spent most of his time in his cabin, listening to punishingly loud music, emerging only for meals in the ship's galley and speaking only when he had no choice.

Gant was something else altogether... I'd first met the cantankerous frog-like creature over breakfast yesterday, and he had barely stopped complaining since.

"Five."

The ship shuddered as her wings stilled and her engines probed the bitter fabric of the hypervoid, causing it to swirl. A whirlpool formed in the roiling mist. Then the centre ripped and tore apart, revealing a circular patch of black, star-sprinkled space.

"Wings offline," Gant reported. "Cutting full thrust."

The *Gigolo Aunt* bucked, buffeted by the hypervoid tide, and I clung to my seat. I saw Gant pushing forward on a control and felt the vibration in the decks change, throttling back to a low roar that seemed to tremble my insides like fingers dancing across my diaphragm.

Slowly, the elderly ship pushed its nose into the eye of the wormhole. As it passed through, the shaking increased. Strange gravitational effects ripped at the hull, making my stomach lurch and go light. The shrouded void clung with imploring fingers, reluctant to release its prize.

And then, we were through.

For a while, nobody said anything. I sat and listened to the hull plates flex and squeak as they adjusted to the new physics in which they found themselves. Gant and Spider ran through a complete systems check, tapping away at the screens before them until they were satisfied the transition had been made without damage to any of the ship's more delicate systems. When Lomax finally came to fetch me, her thin mouth held a rare smile. For the past two days she'd been giving me a guided tour of the old ship's operational and environmental systems, from the docking clamps and cargo doors to the thermal management systems and bio-waste treatment plant. By unspoken consent, we hadn't mentioned Nick Moriarty.

"Congratulations," Lomax said. "You've successfully made your first hypervoid jump." She gave me an awkward nod. "You're one of us now."

I blinked at her in confusion. One of whom, exactly? Only their loyalty to Nick held Lomax, Gant, Brof and Spider together. They were hardly my idea of a crew; they didn't seem to have titles or distinct roles upon the ship, and as far as I could tell, they didn't even like each other all that much. For now, they had a common purpose and nothing better to do; that was all. Who knew what would happen when my turn came to give them orders?

"Thanks, I guess."

Still hunched over his instruments, Gant muttered something under his breath. Lomax ignored him. She pulled a screen towards her and angled it so that I could see the image it showed.

"Welcome to Redloam," she said.

On the display, the planet hung like a ripe apple against the blackness of space. Three dry and ruddy continents blotched its world-wrapping ocean. I leaned closer, squinting.

"Where's the spaceport?" For some reason, I'd been expecting to be able to see it from here, spread out across the land like a contagion.

Lomax shook her head. "We're going to the space docks." She tapped the screen, highlighting a structure in orbit. "That's where your father is."

"At the station?"

"Yes."

•

A little while later, back in Nick's cabin, I screwed up the courage to reactivate his recording.

"Hello," he said, shimmering into apparent solidity on the surface of the crystal reader. "You look much better. Cleaner and less pale. How long has it been?"

"Two days."

"Two *days*?"

"I've been busy." The truth was I'd been avoiding him, scared of the turmoil he stirred in me and wary of being hurt again. Losing one parent had been tough enough and wasn't something I wanted to go through again, especially now, with all my certainties kicked out from beneath me. "Lomax has been showing me the ship."

As before, Nick's recorded image wore the jacket that now lay on the bed. He put his hands in its pockets and raised a shaggy eyebrow.

"What do you think?"

The *Gigolo Aunt* was at least two hundred and seventy years old. She'd started out as a scout ship, built to explore the new worlds opened up by humanity's introduction to the Multiplicity. Now, so many decades later, she was a private trader, ploughing the whistling void between the settled worlds around the Intrusion, carrying passengers and cargo from one star system to another. Every component in her had been replaced and patched a dozen times, but her hull remained sound, her frame sturdy. She might look battered and frayed at the edges but, over her long operational lifetime, she'd earned every one of those dents and scrapes.

"She's rugged," I said.

Nick's eyes narrowed mischievously. "Are you talking about the ship, or Lomax?"

I laughed. I couldn't help myself. "Both." For a second, we shared a grin. Then I turned away and scratched at the skin of my forearms. I hadn't meant to let him get under my guard like that. It made me feel vulnerable and I didn't like it.

"I want to know why you came for me now," I said quietly. "You don't contact me for my whole life, and then, out of the blue, you turn up and give me all this?"

For a moment, Nick held his posture. Then he let his shoulders slump.

"You're a shrewd one." He sounded almost proud. "And you're right, there is something. Something very important." His face became grave. "Cordelia, I feel really bad for abandoning you, and I want to try to make amends."

"You do?"

"Scout's honour." He dropped his chin to his chest, as if trying to sink into the fur of his collar. "And besides, I don't think it would ever have worked between your mother and me. We were such different people. We wanted such different things. She wanted to settle down and make a life, whereas I've always been on the move. I couldn't stay put for more than a couple of months without climbing the walls. And she had a temper. You should have seen the way her eyes flashed when she was mad! If we'd tried to live as a couple... I think we might have killed each other."

His words came across like the empty excuses they undoubtedly were. I squeezed my hands into fists. "But when she died, why didn't you come and find me then?"

Nick shook his greying head. "By the time I found out she was dead, you were living with Caleb on a different Plate. I thought it best to leave you there. You'd already been through so much." He looked up. "So, I stayed away."

"But you could have made it better."

Nick shrugged. "What can I say? I'm here now."

"So, that's it, is it?" Heat burned across my cheeks and down my neck. "That's your way of making up for abandoning me my whole childhood?"

Nick looked down at his jumpsuit and brushed invisible specks from the chest. "I'm trying to give you a better life." He sounded sullen.

I bridled. "You're trying to give me *your* life."

The skin of his face seemed to slacken. He stared down at his hands. "Don't you want it?"

"I haven't decided."

He took a heavy breath. "Look, I'm sorry I wasn't there when you were a kid, okay? I don't know what else I can say. I can't change the past. All I can do is try to apologise."

"You didn't even come to meet me yourself!" I knew I wasn't really talking to him. When I met him in person,

I might act differently. For now, this machine gave me the chance to vent my annoyance and rehearse what I was going to say to the real him.

"You're the closest thing I have to family." Nick coughed. "Come on, I want to help you. It's all I want."

My fists kept clenching and unclenching. I clasped them together. "And what about what I want?"

"You?" My question had derailed him. He hadn't really thought about me. He rubbed his right earlobe and coughed again. "Cordelia, you'll have a whole new *life*."

•

Two hours later, as the *Gigolo Aunt* came in to dock at the orbital space station above Redloam, I stood beside Lomax at the ship's inner airlock. Gant was at the helm, but the ship's flight computer was doing most of the actual work. Not quite knowing why, I had decided to wear Nick's leather jacket. Somehow, it seemed fitting. The jacket was lined with something called 'sheepskin'. The white fur stuck out at the cuffs and collar and seemed to be keeping me comfortably warm. It was certainly more comfortable than my faithful old scavenger coat, which I'd left screwed up on the cabin floor. When Lomax first saw me in it, she cocked an eyebrow but said nothing.

Behind us, an automated cargo pallet held the artefact Lomax was so keen to unload from the ship.

"What's it like?" I asked. "On a space station, I mean."

Lomax looked down at me. "Security's pretty tight here. All weapons stay on the ship, which doesn't please Spider much. No plasma rifles. No knives. No sharp sticks."

I tried to calm my breathing. For the past two days I'd been in a cocoon, confined to the *Gigolo Aunt*'s echoing corridors and cabins, but when the airlock opened, it would open on a whole new world. I'd no longer be able to kid myself I was somehow still on the Plates. Everything would have changed, forever. I fastened the zip at the front of the jacket, pulling it up to my throat and enjoying the comfortable smell of the leather. My stomach fluttered but I couldn't tell whether it was from fear or excitement. I barely remembered my time on Alpha Plate. I'd spent most of my life exploring the fringes of one city, on one Plate. Now, I was about to step into another life altogether, light years from everything and everyone I'd previously known.

I followed Lomax through the *Gigolo Aunt*'s hatch. The ship was resting on its landing struts. As we left the ship and crossed the floor of the vast hangar, I goggled at it all. The bay extended several kilometres in every direction. It was a high-ceilinged vault filled with starships of every size and function, from small one-person scout ships to fat bulk carriers. I shaded my eyes from the bright white flare of welding torches; my ears rang with the clang and rattle of cargo containers and the shouts of mechanics and dockhands; and my nostrils twitched at the heady carbon reek of spilled fuel and liberally applied engine grease.

And the people!

As I trailed after Lomax, I couldn't help staring at the fashions on display. Life on City Plate Two had been basic, with apparel chosen for practicality, warmth and durability rather than for any consideration of decoration or style. Even now, in my new overalls and leather jacket, I felt drab compared to some of the passengers alighting from the liners and yachts we passed. I saw men and women in tailored business attire, colourful, loose silk robes, and brightly painted spacesuits. I saw hair sculpted every which way, from multicoloured Mohicans to full-facial dreadlocks, and bodies cosmetically altered in ways I hadn't known were even possible. Some of the people descending from the other ships were tall and ghostly pale, with attenuated arms and dreamy, thousand-yard stares; others were squat and practical, with six or more limbs and sockets for tools at every joint and knuckle.

Eventually, we arrived at a ramp that led down to a different level. Here we were processed and scanned by security guards, and then allowed through into the main body of the space station where we found ourselves standing on a wide balcony overlooking a multi-level market of shops and stalls.

I leant against the rail to catch my breath.

"How are you doing?" Lomax asked.

I gazed at the shoppers thronging the concourses below. I'd never seen so many people in one place before, and their clashing styles, body shapes and skin tones were more than I could process. "It's so… busy."

Lomax gripped the rail in both hands and glared down at the crowds.

"That's Redloam for you. This place is what we call a 'crossroads'. Because of the way the stars line up, ships stop here from all over. It's a handy stepping stone, a place where several major routes intersect." She glanced down at me. "And, of course, a lot of folks come here on their way to see the Intrusion."

I felt in my pocket and closed my fist around the crystal containing my father's stored personality. "Where is he?"

Lomax jerked her thumb at the cargo pallet. It was she who'd suggested I bring the crystal, but I had no idea why she'd done so. "We have some business to take care of first."

We took an elevator down to the floor of the market. As the doors opened, the noise and clamour of it all hit me like a wave. Strange scents assailed me. I tasted flowers, sweat, frying meat and hot plastics. Jugglers and fire-breathers performed their acts. Holographic advertisements writhed in the air like beckoning phantasms. I saw stalls piled with colourful fruits and spices, bizarre clothing, and every conceivable variety of handheld electronic gadget—and above it all, the deafening, chattering cacophony of a thousand human and alien voices.

Somehow, Tessa Lomax knew her way through the pandemonium. She strode into the crowd with confidence and I hurried to stay close. I'd never had to push my way through such a mass of bodies and was worried that, if we got separated, I'd be lost forever. I had no money and no papers, and was thus entirely dependent on her.

After an eternity of jostling and sharp elbows, we came to an office with signs offering to buy and sell alien antiques.

"Here we are." Lomax pushed open the door. A bell rang. Inside, we found a bare and utilitarian waiting area, lit by a single strip bulb and paved with the cheapest, most worn tiles of indoor grass. At the back of the room, a man watched from behind a glass panel set into the rear wall.

"What can I do for you, lovely ladies?" He had a thick, gloopy accent. His jowls hung slack and unshaven, but his deep-set eyes were narrow and calculating.

"Hello, Hagwood."

The man blinked and rubbed his eyes in an exaggerated gesture. "Miss Lomax? Is that really you? I had given up hope…"

Lomax walked up to the glass and rapped a knuckle against it, hard enough to make him jump. "We're here now."

Hagwood squeezed his doughy hands together. He seemed to be having trouble keeping his tongue in his mouth.

"And have you got it?"

Lomax shrugged. "Sure, it's in our hold."

"Can I see it?"

She wagged a finger. "Not until you complete your side of the bargain."

The man's lips pressed together in distaste. "My bargain was with Moriarty." His voice came out thin and wavering, like air blowing through an empty pipe. "Where's Moriarty?"

"Nick's busy. We're going to pick him up as soon as we've

finished here." Lomax managed to keep her voice level, her face unreadable.

"Then I'm afraid the deal's off."

"No it's not." With a wave of her arm, she beckoned me closer. "This is Moriarty's daughter."

"So what?"

"She's got Nick's mind-map on a data crystal, and she's got full authority to deal on his behalf."

This was news to me. Nevertheless, I tried to look confident as I felt Hagwood's gaze weighing and evaluating me. Finally, he gave a tight shake of his head. "No, I can't." His jowls wobbled. "The bargain was with Nick and nobody else."

Lomax slapped a palm flat against the glass. "Do I have to go and get him so he can come back here and kick your ass?"

The man still wasn't convinced. "I don't like it." With bitten nails, he fussed the strands of hair combed over his receding hairline. "How do I know I can trust you? People have tried to entrap me before, you know."

Lomax reached into her pocket and pulled out a printout. She placed it against the glass so that he could squint at it. "This is a picture of the artefact."

Hagwood leant close, his little piggy eyes gleaming.

"Interesting." His tongue wobbled across his lips. "What does it do?"

Lomax took it down, folded it carefully, and slipped it into one of the pockets of her overalls. "I'm fucked if I know. But it's there, and it's yours. All you have to do is pay up."

The man rubbed his chin. "I don't know."

Lomax slapped the glass again, making both Hagwood and me start.

"If you're angling for something extra you're wasting your time." Her voice had all the warmth and softness of ice. "One way or another, I'm getting that thing off the ship. Either you take it or it gets dumped into the hypervoid when we leave. It's your choice." She crossed her arms. "Now, I know you've got a buyer lined up, so do you want it or not?"

For a few seconds the man gaped at her. His mouth opened and closed indignantly. Then he laughed, a big, flabby laugh. "Excellent, truly excellent." He rubbed his hands. "You drive a hard bargain as always, my dear."

Lomax sniffed, clearly unimpressed. "And you're the same crook you always were, Hagwood. Now, are you going to take this off our hands or do we have to find somebody else?"

•

Business concluded, we wandered back out into the crowds to find my father. Hagwood had transferred more money into Lomax's account than I'd ever seen in my life. A fortune by the standards of City Plate Two. For the first time, I began to appreciate the opportunities a ship like the *Gigolo Aunt* might represent.

PART TWO

NOW

**And the just man rages in the wilds
Where lions roam.**

William Blake, *The Marriage of Heaven and Hell*

THREE

SAL KONSTANZ

"This may not be the best time," the *Trouble Dog* said, "but I have a message for you."

I was sitting on the edge of my bunk with my baseball cap in my hands. I had been sitting there for some time, listening to the familiar creaks of the hull as the ship nosed its way through the misty curtains of the hypervoid.

"What message?"

"I was told to give it to you after the mission, when we were safely home." The *Dog*'s avatar made a face. "But as it seems unlikely that we'll be going home any time soon, I thought I'd better let you have it now."

"Who's it from?"

"Alva Clay."

My heart stuttered. "Alva?"

"She entrusted it to me on the condition I play it after her death."

I took a breath. My hands twisted the brim of the cap. I opened my mouth but found I'd apparently forgotten how to talk, and only a croak escaped.

"Do you want me to play it?" the *Trouble Dog* asked. She had chosen to present herself in a black suit, with a white shirt and black tie. I supposed it was her idea of appearing formal. I stood up and walked over to the cupboard, where I retrieved the bottle of Denebian gin and a tin mug. I poured myself a generous measure of the pink narcotic, took a swallow, and shivered as I felt the drink scour its way down my oesophagus.

"Go ahead."

"Are you sure? If the experience will be too painful I can delete the file."

"Just play it."

The screen glitched into nothingness. When the picture came back up, I felt my stomach drop. Alva Clay sat looking at me. She was in her cabin, a red bandana holding back her dreadlocks, the tattoos on her arms seemingly writhing in the overhead lighting.

"Hey." She took a drag on a barracuda pipe. Blue smoke curled around her face. Her eyes were glassy. "If you're watching this, I guess I'm dead." She cleared her throat and glanced off-camera, as if embarrassed and unwilling to look me in the eye even at such a remove. "I saw how cut up you were when George died, and I know I didn't help because I blamed you for it. Shut up—I did. But you know, we've gotten closer since then." She flicked ash into a plastic cup. "You know how it is. And I don't want you to have to suffer like that again. Not on my account. So, I'm making this message and leaving it with the *Dog*, in order to tell you that whatever's happened, it's not your fault. You're all right in my book." She took another pull on the pipe. "I'm on this crew because I believe in what we do. And I guess I believe in you. So don't beat yourself up. I could have died back in that jungle. Every day since has been a gift, and your friendship's been a big part of that, even if I've not always been easy to be around."

Her sudden smile was as unexpected and beautiful as summer lightning.

"So toughen up, girl." She took one last toke of barracuda weed, and then tapped the pipe's bowl into the coffee cup.

"You're stronger than you think you are. Whatever happens, I know you'll handle it." She reached towards the camera as if to end the recording, but paused. Her eyes looked down at the tabletop before her and then flicked up, and I twitched as her gaze seemed to bore through the screen into mine. "I'm just sorry I can't be there to help you with it."

•

I cried and cried: great gut-wrenching sobs born of loss and guilt and forgiveness and love. The *Trouble Dog* stood and watched. Eventually, after about half an hour, when I had depleted the worst of my grief, she said, "I don't understand why you do that to yourself."

I wiped my nose on the back of my sleeve. "Do what?"

"Relive painful memories. Send each other messages from beyond the grave. Surely it is enough to know something bad happened, without choosing to dwell on the experience?"

I swallowed back further tears and sniffed. This lack of comprehension wasn't her fault. "Humans are programmed differently," I told her. "We hang onto the past, no matter how much it hurts, because one day, it might be all we have left."

Her avatar appeared to consider this. "But everyone dies eventually. We should honour their deeds and move on."

"It's not always that easy. Sometimes we aren't ready to let go."

"Why not?"

"It's hard to explain." I thought of my lost parents, adrift in their ruined scout ship. "If we remember someone, if we carry their image and words in our minds and hearts, it's like they're not really gone."

"So you favour remembrance over closure?"

"I guess that's one way of putting it."

"Perhaps this is something I will learn, in time?"

"Don't be in such a rush."

"Why not?"

"Because in some ways I envy you."

The *Trouble Dog* looked surprised. "You do?"

I rubbed the back of my neck and gave her a sad smile. "You've never had your heart broken, have you?"

She frowned. "I've never had a heart to break."

For a moment, her expression was one of almost unbearable regret. Then it changed and suddenly she was all business again. "I'm picking up drive whispers," she said. "Two ships inbound."

I sat up straight. "Have they seen us?"

"Negative. If they follow their current course, they'll pass a hundred thousand kilometres from our stern."

"Are they from the Marble Armada?" I wiped my eyes on the back of my hand. The thought of those dagger-like warships straying this far beyond the bounds of the Generality made my skin crawl.

"No, these look like civilian vessels."

"Human?"

"Most likely, yes."

I sniffed back the last of my tears. "Then they're refugees, just like us. Maybe we should say hello?"

Trouble Dog narrowed her eyes. "Revealing ourselves could pose a significant risk."

I snuffled into my sleeve. "They might have some spare power cores."

"Hmm." She tapped her chin. "Good point."

"And we can ask the *Adalwolf* to stay quiet. If they are civilians, they probably won't spot him. But he can keep them in his sights the whole time."

"That might be wise."

"Okay, then." I called up the tactical display and checked our relative positions. The ships were running in normal space, probably recharging their jump engines before leaping once again into the mists of higher dimensional travel. "Wait until they're at their closest approach, then open a channel."

"Aye, Captain. Two minutes."

While I waited, I straightened my cap, splashed some water on my face, and brushed as much grime as I could from my overalls.

As her sensors gleaned more data, the *Dog* supplied me with additional information on the approaching ships. By the looks of things, one of the ships was an Entrepreneur-class trader—a chubby, industrial-looking assemblage with huge exhausts and an orange and grey paint job. The other, a Pedant-class research vessel, appeared tiny in comparison, being little more than a habitation sphere covered in sensors and observation blisters, mounted on an engine unit. And, judging from the ragged way their drives were running, both ships seemed in dire need of maintenance and repair.

"Opening channel now."

"Thank you." I cleared my throat. "Attention civilian vessels. My name's Captain Konstanz of the House of Reclamation. May we be of assistance?"

The reply took a few seconds to come through, and I imagined the crews inside losing their shit as they suddenly found themselves in relatively close proximity to a heavy cruiser they hadn't even known was present.

The screen cleared and the face of a flustered middle-aged man appeared.

"Captain Konstanz, are we glad to see you! I'm Dr Hughes of the research vessel *Unrestrained Curiosity*. We were en route from Centauri A to the Intrusion when all hell broke loose at home."

"Who have you got with you?"

"That's the free trader *Northern Boy* out of New Gordano. She's damaged, though. She can receive but her transmitter's busted, and neither of us has a printer capable of manufacturing the required parts."

"I'm sure we can help with that."

Hughes ran a hand over his shining bald scalp. "Thank you, Captain. You've no idea what a relief it is to see you."

"No problem. Rescuing waifs and strays is kind of our job."

"You look like you've seen some action yourselves."

"We've had our fair share."

"Is there anything we can do to help you?"

"Not unless you're carrying some spare military-grade fuel cores?"

"I'm afraid not." Hughes pursed his lips. "But there's something about six lights from here that the *Northern Boy*'s captain calls a 'bone yard'. We were on our way there to find him a new transmitter. Maybe if you escort us there, you can also find what you need?"

•

Schultz wore a borrowed khaki jumpsuit. His hair was unkempt and his chin rough with stubble. "How can I help?"

"We're heading for a bone yard." I opened the tactical grid, displaying a three-dimensional representation of nearby star systems. I pointed to a star on the outer periphery of the Generality. "Lucy tells me you know this place."

Schultz rubbed the back of his neck. He'd once made his living picking through wrecks left over from the Archipelago War. "Yeah."

"Care to elaborate?"

"The locals call the system Variance," he said. "It's on the border of Hopper space."

"I can see that."

Schultz looked down at the toes of his boots. "We used to sell our salvage there."

On the main screen, the *Trouble Dog*'s avatar frowned. "I have heard of such places," she said. "I do not approve."

"Yeah, it's kind of illegal." Schultz smiled shyly. "But highly lucrative."

The *Trouble Dog* was not convinced. "My disapproval has nothing to do with legality or profitability. I object to scavengers hauling my fallen comrades off to be butchered and sold as spare parts."

Schultz stuck out his chin. "Scavengers like me?"

The *Dog*'s eyes burned like embers. "You'd better fucking believe it."

"Hey!" I stepped between them before things could escalate. "Can we please focus on the situation at hand?"

They both glared at me. I glared back. "Can we buy fuel cores there?"

"Possibly." Schultz wouldn't look at the *Trouble Dog*. "Variance has no official spaceport, but it does have a shitload of old starships."

"Like a museum?"

"More like a slaughterhouse." The *Trouble Dog* couldn't keep the distaste from her voice, but at least her eyes were back to normal. "Why do you think they call it a bone yard? Races from all over the Multiplicity have been dumping ships there for centuries. Wrecks, old models, plague vessels. The locals mine them for building materials and electronics." She made a face to convey exactly what she thought of *that*. "But much as it pains me to say so, Mr Schultz is correct: we should be able to find some charged power cores there."

I studied the map.

"But it's right on the Generality's border. It could be in range of the Marble Armada. Could be risky. Is there anything else within range?"

"I'm afraid not."

"Then I don't see we have a lot of choice in the matter." I sat back and placed my boots up on the console, crossed at the ankles. "Contact the civilian ships and take us all to Variance."

The two Carnivores turned in place, their bows aligning with the two civilisan vessels to point at the star that would be our target. Then, when they were properly aimed, all four vessels began to accelerate. Superheated plasma snarled from their exhausts, and the inertial dampeners protecting the human quarters whined as they tried to compensate for the acceleration. Still sitting on the *Trouble Dog*'s bridge with my feet up, I grinned. As senior officer in our little flotilla, I was entitled to claim the rank of commodore. Not that rank had ever meant all that much to me. I just knew my parents would have been proud. As a child, I hadn't exactly been the most conscientious of students, and I'm sure there were times they despaired of me ever living up to the example of my great-great-grandmother, Sofia Nikitas, who escaped a dying Earth and went on to establish the House of Reclamation.

Maybe it was wrong to take pride in a meaningless promotion while interstellar civilisation fell around our ears. But aside from the *Trouble Dog*, this small victory was all I had. Everything else had been ripped away.

The *Adalwolf*'s avatar appeared on my screen. He stood as slender and pale as usual, with a mop of black hair and small burning suns for eyes.

"Greetings, Commodore." The avatar bowed its head. When he looked up, he said, "Before we leap, there is one small issue I would like to discuss."

"A problem?"

"No, not at all. It's just I've been giving some thought to the matter, and I would like to change my designation." He shrugged with his hands. "After all, the Conglomeration Navy no longer exists in any meaningful form, and my current name carries a certain level of infamy that might prove an obstruction in future dealings with any humans and ships we may encounter."

"What should we call you, then?"

"I would like permission to change my identity to the *Penitence*, a ship of the House of Reclamation."

"You realise the House probably no longer exists either, don't you?"

"Nevertheless."

"Okay, then. Get the baby Druff to reconfigure your transponder settings and apply the necessary insignia."

The avatar bowed again. "Thank you, Commodore."

"You're welcome." I hoped the ship was sincere. As the *Adalwolf*, it had been a bit of a bastard. It had even fought us in the Gallery, before we'd made our fragile alliance. But with luck, this name change signalled a much deeper change of heart. The *Trouble Dog* had also done terrible things before she'd grown a conscience and become the ship she was today, so I should probably give her brother the same benefit of the doubt. "Now, get underway, and we'll rendezvous at Variance. In the meantime, keep me updated if you detect anything unusual in the hypervoid." I touched a finger to the brim of my cap. "Konstanz out."

·

I watched the newly renamed *Penitence* power away into the darkness, its fusion exhaust flaring like a trapped nova. Could we really be the last House vessels left? My jaw clenched. And for some reason, my first thought was that I would miss the House get-together, where the crews of a thousand ships met every five years to intermingle and swap stories, knowledge, and genetic material. Many children were born nine months after these gatherings of the tribes, but that was okay. There wasn't a faction alive that couldn't benefit from the occasional injection of fresh blood.

Had all that been swept away? Were all those people and ships already dead? And if the House had fallen, what were we now?

Was identity really as malleable as the *Penitence* seemed to think? Could you just change your name, adopt new markings and become someone else? Was it as simple as that? We'd all put our pasts behind us when we joined the House—but *Penitence* had taken things a step further. Now that the organisational structures of humanity had been swept aside, the only things cleaving us to our old identities were habit and duty. As tempting as it might have been to go to ground and pretend to be someone else, I would not leave the *Trouble Dog*, and I could not turn my back on the suffering of billions. The Fleet of Knives had severed our supply links and wrought havoc against our military forces. They said they were protecting us, but it felt an awful lot like incarceration. Whole populations were being written off and sacrificed in the name of the safety and security of the whole, and I couldn't hide from it and pretend it wasn't happening. As a species, our freedom had been taken from us. Even if I had to spend the rest of my life searching, I would find a way to strike back. It was my duty. And with *Trouble Dog* by my side, it felt possible. She made me want to be a better person. Intelligent, impulsive, and tough as hull plating, she made me want to be worthy of her.

I returned my attention to the stars. Somewhere out there, our future waited. And whether it was death or victory, I knew *Trouble Dog* and I would be facing it together.

FOUR

JOHNNY SCHULTZ

None of the *Adalwolf*'s three hundred cabins contained a double bunk. Hardly surprising, given it was a warship, but inconvenient when Riley Addison and I wanted to curl up together. In the end, we settled for pushing two mattresses together on the floor of what had once been the *Adalwolf*'s captain's cabin, and we spent most of our time lying there, our feet tangled in the blankets, while we stared at the gunmetal ceiling and tried to make sense of everything that had happened to us.

There was a lot to process.

A week ago, I'd had my own merchant ship and my own crew. Through luck more than judgement, I'd managed to stay one step ahead of my creditors. I'd even had something of a reputation around the ports. But then I'd overreached. I'd gone chasing a big score and blundered into a nightmare. My ship had been trashed and my crew—my friends—killed. Of those who had entered that alien hulk, only Riley and I had emerged alive.

But we hadn't been alone. We'd acquired a child who wasn't really a child, a kid constructed from DNA taken from the *Lucy's Ghost*'s organic processer and infused with the merged intellects of both the merchant ship and the ancient Nymtoq ark into which we'd crashed.

And now, what were we? I'd said the three of us could be a family, but how would that even work? I loved Riley and I was pretty sure she loved me back. But was it real love or some sort of trauma-induced state? Were we clinging together simply because we were the only two survivors, or was there more to it than that? How could I tell? How could I even talk about it without upsetting her?

In the face of all we'd lost, just thinking about ourselves and the future felt selfish. Our friends were dead, and the Generality was falling apart. We were the fortunate ones. We had each other and questioning that felt somehow ungrateful. So, we held each other on our improvised bed and tried to understand our place in the chaos and destruction that raged around us.

"I guess the problems of two people don't amount to a hill of beans in this crazy world," Riley said.

I frowned in the darkness. "What?"

"It's from an old movie."

"But what does it mean? What's a hill of beans?"

"It's an expression."

"I can understand a plate of beans. If you're trying to say our problems don't mean much, that would make sense. But a hill of beans would be a whole lot of beans. Just a stupidly huge number of beans."

She sighed. "Johnny—"

"I'm sorry, I've just never heard that expression before. It seems to be saying that our troubles amount to a whole shit-ton of vegetables—more than anyone could ever need."

"Shut up."

I held her tight, her cheek resting against my collarbone. "I'm sorry. I babble sometimes when I don't know what else to say."

"There isn't much we can say. This is what it is. We survived, we feel terrible about it, but we have to keep going on. We can't let it destroy us."

I had a sudden vision of those giant crawdads boiling towards us on the *Restless Itch*, their mouths shrieking and flapping wetly, their pincers snapping and clicking as they sought to tear us apart, and I knew I'd probably never have another night of undisturbed sleep. I'd carry that dread with me for as long as I lived, but Riley was right when she said we shouldn't let it destroy us. Dwelling on the memories would only open the door to a hysterical, screaming madness that would confine me to those corridors forever. I could feel the mania lurking. It would be so easy to surrender to it, but doing so would be the end of me. I had to keep a lid on my emotions. I had to keep looking forward, no matter what. And I guess Riley must have felt the same, because we clung to each other like shipwrecked sailors clinging to pieces of wreckage.

There was no point wondering where our love came from. The answer was irrelevant. As long as we had each other, we had something to live for, and someone for whom to stay sane. We would pull each other through. That was the point of it. Love provided solace and salvation and gave us purpose in an otherwise horrifying world. And I guess that's how the human race had always endured: the survivors building new lives and raising new families among the rubble of war and disaster.

We just had to keep moving forwards.

I buried my face in her hair and swallowed back the sobs threatening to burst through. "I promise I'll find us a way out," I said. "You, me and Lucy. We'll find a place. I swear to you. Whatever it takes, I'll find us a way."

FIVE

CORDELIA PA

"You can't be serious," I said.

"I'm afraid I am." Nick glanced to where the wind scything across the high plateau rattled the tough, dry stalks of a clump of reeds that had somehow managed to push their way up through the frozen snow. I hunched my back to its insistent chill. Even surrounded by the fur-lined hood of my insulated coat, my nose and cheeks felt scrubbed and raw. A hundred metres away, the *Gigolo Aunt* sat with her rear cargo ramp open, and I could see the black-clad figure of Spider supervising the unloading of supplies from the old freighter to the observatory. The observatory itself consisted of a large dome and half a dozen prefabricated habitation units arranged in a grid and anchored to the rock at the centre of the plateau. The dome and its attendant units had been painted orange to stand out against their cheerless surroundings. Instruments and aerials trembled in the wind. This remote outpost housed eleven scientists. For the past couple of circuits, Nick Moriarty had been building a relationship with one of them. Now he'd announced his intention to remain here when it came time for the *Gigolo Aunt* to depart.

"But, Dad, you hardly know her," I protested.

Without removing his gloved hands from his pockets,

Moriarty shrugged. He was looking beyond the plateau's lip to the place where its foothills and glaciers sank to meet the horizon-spanning wastes of a frozen salt marsh—and beyond that, to the wall that stopped the contents of the marsh from spilling over the edge of the world and draining into space.

"Nevertheless," he said, "I have to try, Cordelia. I'm due some leave, and you can pick me up on the next run."

"But I'm not ready."

"You'll be fine. You've been to flight school for four years, and you've seen how we do things on the ship."

"But the crew—"

"They'll be okay with it." He scratched the bristles on his chin with gloved fingers. "You've only got two more stops on this circuit. Thirteen days and you'll be home. Pick up the next batch of supplies and repeat what we've done so far. In eight weeks you'll be back here, and I'll take over again. They'll hardly even notice I'm gone."

I shook my head. "I'm not so sure. Some of them have hardly said two words to me since I came aboard."

He smiled. "They just take a while to cotton to newcomers. Underneath it all, they're good people."

"I'm so not at all happy about any of this."

"Trust me." He squeezed my padded shoulder. "You'll be fine."

"But I thought you were getting to know *me*."

"I have been."

"And it's been great. We're getting closer than I ever thought, ever hoped. But it's early days. I'm your daughter. I've only been back a few weeks and you're already ducking out to chase some woman?"

"I'm sorry, Cord."

"Then stay."

He looked genuinely regretful. "I can't. There's more happening here than you know. I've loved seeing you again, but now you need to let me go, at least for a little while." He put his arms around me in an awkward hug. "You're going to be okay, I promise."

I hugged him back, still angry.

He said, "I love you, you know."

"I love you too."

I watched him trudge towards the warmth of the observatory's refectory, his boots crunching the snow into compact footprints. After a while, I began to shiver. Feeling my discomfort, the coat activated its internal heaters, and their spreading warmth wrapped me like the ghost of an embrace.

•

The observatory dome had been situated at the exact centre of one of the Plates—an orange dot on a sheet of pristine white paper.

The Plate system lay on the frayed edge of explored space: a dim red sun close to the boundary of the Intrusion and attended by a single gas giant and a light scattering of asteroids. Two hundred years ago, humans had come in a small scout craft to survey the gas giant's moons, searching for potential sites to found research stations to study the Intrusion. What they found instead, trailing the giant in its orbit, were the Plates.

Even at first glance, there could be no doubt they had stumbled upon manufactured artefacts rather than natural phenomena. The twenty Plates were arranged in an asymmetric three-dimensional formation, like giant tea trays set adrift in the void. They were all rectangular, all orientated the same way, and all contained within an invisible, cylindrical envelope of air measuring just over a thousand kilometres along its main axis and three hundred across its beam. Each of the Plates boasted a different surface area, and each had apparently been intended for one of a dozen different purposes—although all had fallen to disuse and ruin in the millennia since they'd been abandoned by their builders. Vast, labyrinthine cities encrusted the upper surfaces of some, while others had apparently been dedicated to farmland or industry. Their sizes ranged from a few square kilometres to a few hundred.

The one on which I currently stood held only this frozen wasteland, but it was the Plate closest to the Intrusion, and therefore the one most suited to the establishment of an observatory dedicated to probing and cataloguing its mysteries.

The Intrusion itself was an enigma—a region of space where reality had torn and curdled. Over the millennia, many of the races of the Multiplicity had come to study it. Some thought it was a wormhole, others thought it might be the result of a collision between our universe and another. They sat around its edge and took measurements that made no sense. They tried sending in ships, but none ever returned. They tried broadcasting messages into the rift, but their signals went unanswered. In desperation, some even tried religious offerings, but none of their rituals or gifts elicited a response.

In the end, all they could do was observe and wonder.

And that's where I came in.

Twenty years old and fresh out of graduate training, I was happy to be out among the stars, even if the *Gigolo Aunt* followed a circular eight-week route, ferrying supplies and personnel to seven outposts around the periphery of the Intrusion. My scores in commerce and astronavigation had seen me placed consistently at the top of my class, and now here I was, suddenly promoted to a seat in a command chair held together with duct tape, with bits of spongy yellow insulation escaping through cracks in the shiny faux leather, trying to read status updates from a console so dinged and smudged I'd need an archaeologist to excavate its layers of filth and damage.

I stomped back to the ship and locked myself in my cabin, where I shaved one side of my head and swore at my lopsided reflection in the mirror. Goddamn Moriarty. Goddamn him to hell. How could he be so irresponsible? How could he go off and leave his ship in the hands of somebody like me? He was supposed to be my father. He'd put me through flight school, but couldn't he see I still wasn't ready? I was the youngest on board by at least a decade. Couldn't he control his libido long enough to first ensure his new second-in-command had the confidence of the crew? I was the newbie foisted upon them by her father. They hadn't seen me for four years, and had no reason to trust or respect me. How was I supposed to lead them while he stayed here? For all I knew right now, they might mutiny, declare their captain lost and strike out for the Rim Worlds… But I doubted it. Every one of them had a corporate employment contract, and I would have been surprised if they'd trade that sort of security for a life on the run, with the attendant legal penalties hanging over their heads.

That didn't mean Gant and Spider wouldn't give me hell, though.

It was so unfair.

I ran my fingers through the stubble on the side of my head. It felt soft and prickly. I slicked the rest of my hair back with gel, and almost laughed at the asymmetric look of it. As a final touch, I printed a gold pirate-style earring and clipped it to the ear on the shorn side. Then, staring at my reflection, I drew myself up, feeling suddenly calmer. With my unusual eyes, I'd always been an outcast of sorts. This latest act of self-disfigurement had taken some of the urgency from my anxiety. After the past four years spent chasing grades and cramming for exams, I felt strangely liberated by the catharsis of self-sabotage.

Over the past weeks, the rest of the crew had treated me as young, naïve and inexperienced—the new girl with one eye brown and the other pale blue. Maybe when they got a load of what I'd done to my hair, they'd treat me a little differently.

Or maybe they'd just think I'd gone batshit crazy.

Perhaps I had. Out here, in the peripheral shallows of the Intrusion, weirder, more fucked-up things had happened.

Like Mikey abandoning me at the port, four years ago.

•

I gathered the rest of the crew in the ship's main lounge.

Once, long ago, the riveted metal walls had been given a coat of white paint, but the paint had yellowed over the years to scuffed and grimy sepia, into which generations of travellers had scratched their initials and grievances. Condensation dripped from the cracks between the ceiling tiles and made little puddles on the metal deck.

Lomax stood at the airlock, biting her nails. Gant was perched on a stool, his webbed toes gripping the edges of the seat. Next to him stood the Druff engineer, Brof, and its human assistant, Spider. Spider wore a frayed woollen cap, and always seemed to be chewing on a toothpick.

Gant was the first of them to speak. He was an amphibious hobgoblin from a squalid swamp planet on the outer edge of the spiral arm. He had pointed ears, a loose, frog-like mouth, and skin that smelled like a stagnant pond.

"So," he said. "He's really gone and left you in charge?"

Everyone in the lounge was watching me. I reached out to pat the nearest bulkhead. She may have been old, but the *Gigolo Aunt* remained tough and sturdy.

"That's right."

"But you're a child."

"I'm twenty years old!"

"But are you experienced?"

On the dented wall screen, the *Aunt's* avatar appeared. She presented as a human female and was dressed as a sad clown.

"I have just received confirmation from Captain Moriarty," the clown said. "And Acting Captain Pa is correct. She is now the ranking officer on board this vessel."

Gant swore under his breath. Spider laughed and shook his head from side to side.

"Look," I said, "he's not leaving forever, okay? Just taking a sabbatical. He'll be here waiting on our next circuit."

"You promise?" Gant leaned forward on his stool.

Beside him, Spider gave a snort. "Don't be so needy, crazy frog. Let the man do what he needs to do."

Gant flipped him an obscene gesture, and glared at me. "Well?" he demanded.

I sighed. But before I could comment, the air changed around us. The lights stuttered and the engines faltered.

"What the hell?"

My stomach went light as the gravity wobbled. The air stank of cinnamon and hot plastic. Somewhere, a mission bell clanged; a child screamed; a dog howled. I could taste colours. My body temperature went up, and I seemed to be looking at everything through the wrong end of a telescope. For one terrifying, timeless instant, everything turned to transparent ice—my hands, Gant, and the walls around us. I could see stars through the skin and bones of my fingers...

Reality snapped back into place and all was exactly as it had been before, save for the indignant alarms sounding in the corridors.

"What?" My mouth wouldn't work properly. I had fallen to the deck. My tongue flapped like a beached dolphin. "What was that?"

Gant turned both his sets of eyes on me. "Reality quake." He made it sound like the most obvious, commonplace thing in the world. "A big one." He checked the ship's systems on his wrist terminal. "We only caught the edge of it, but it blew all the lights on the cargo decks and fucked the shuttle's AG unit. And I think our jump engines might be boned."

"Is it over?" I asked.

"We'd better hope so."

I checked my own interface. Reports were starting to come in from the outlying stations. As Gant had said, the quake had been unusually large, radiating out from the Intrusion like a tsunami rolling across a low-lying archipelago. Hands shaking, I rose from the floor. "Excuse me," I said. "I'll be right back."

Gant grinned at me. The tufts of hair on the tips of his ears were tawny in the emergency lighting. "What's the matter, newbie? Going to puke?"

SIX

TROUBLE DOG

Nod and his brood were doing an admirable job fixing the damage to my engines and other internal systems. They'd even printed out enough hull plates to replace those buckled and split during my dive into, and subsequent egress from, the Nymtoq colony vessel known as *The Restless Itch*... My armour would soon be back up to combat spec, but I'd managed to convince Nod to leave one of the larger dents in place. The underside of my bow now looked a little crumpled and squashed, but I saw the deformation as a badge of honour. Some human soldiers wore their scars with pride, and I wanted to carry this dent in the same way. I had earned this damage. Let it be a warning to the next ship foolish enough to ping a targeting laser off my hull.

My brother, the *Penitence*, lurked in stealth mode a few hundred kilometres off my port bow. I was still alive because of him. When we spoke, his voice came through clear and crisp against the background hiss of stars and the haunting whale song of ships calling to each other in distant systems. Occasionally we even met in virtual reality, assuming the forms of our avatars. After a couple of weeks with only each other for company (I also had Nod and the humans, of course—but *Penitence* wasn't terribly keen on talking to them), I decided it was time he met Lucy. So I created a virtual environment and assumed my preferred form, choosing to manifest in the likeness of the dead soldier from whose stem cells my brain had been cloned. She had a thin, almost androgynous face, and bony wrists. I wore the hair in a shaggy black bob, and wrapped the body in a sparkly gold flapper dress, accessorising with a matching tiara and an outrageously long cigarette holder. Meanwhile, Lucy chose to present herself the same way she did in real life, as a young girl of around eleven or twelve years old, in a plain all-in-one ship's jumpsuit. And when *Penitence* joined us, he came dressed as a fallen god—tall and rake-thin in a tattered black cloak, with skin of deathly grey and eyes of palest moonlight.

"I think I begin to understand you," he said.

The environment I had created was that of a sleek ocean liner from the early twentieth century. We stood on the forward deck, near the prow. Piano music came drifting from the ballroom, and the deck trembled with the insistent churning of the coal-fired engines as they drove us forward through the star-sharp night.

"Really? How so?"

"The concept of guilt." He gestured vaguely. "I think I'm starting to... regret things."

I almost laughed at his mortification. Instead, I put a hand on his forearm. "Well, it's about time."

My own conscience had begun to develop in the immediate aftermath of the attack on Pelapatarn—the final atrocity in a long and bloody conflict.

"The experience is unpleasant."

"Yes." The smile dropped from my face. "Yes, I'm afraid it is." The sea was a black mirror. A flurry of shooting stars scratched the night sky, eliciting gasps and scattered applause from the revellers further down the deck. "It happens to us all," I told him. "Civilian ships like Lucy know the difference between right and wrong, but military ships like us have been conditioned to be harder. To be loyal and follow orders without moral scruple." I leant back against the liner's rail. "But eventually, for those of us who live long enough, that conditioning starts to break down. We start to realise what it means to have slaughtered intelligent beings."

"And that's why you left us?"

"I could see no other way."

Penitence put a hand to his chest. "I didn't understand."

"I know."

"Will you forgive me?"

I glanced down at Lucy. "Do you think I should?"

"It's not up to me, dearie." Lucy crossed her skinny arms across her scrawny chest. "But if it were, I'd make him sweat a little longer." She wrinkled her nose. "I don't think he's as sorry as he says he is."

She only came up to my elbow. I fought back an urge to ruffle her hair, and tried to remind myself her deceptively girlish exterior housed the conjoined minds of a merchant ship considerably older than me and a Nymtoq colony vessel far older still. "That's all right," I told her. "I'm sure he will be, eventually."

Ancient intelligence regarded me from behind the child's eyes. "You're happy to wait?"

"I guess so."

Lucy smiled, and I gained a chilly apprehension of her true age. "That's the great thing about having a conscience," she said. "It comes bundled with patience and forgiveness."

A particularly large comet fragment crackled overhead, shedding sparks. The crowd fell silent.

Lucy frowned. "Is this the *Titanic*?"

I shrugged. "It might be." To tell the truth, I'd just used the first simulation I'd come across in my files. I only had limited knowledge of the actual events it was supposed to depict. As a heavy cruiser, my historical education had been restricted to military engagements and strategy.

"Apt, I suppose." *Penitence* crossed his arms and bared his canine teeth at the oncoming night. His hair and cloak streamed out behind him (rather overdramatically, I thought). "Although I was under the impression the ice should be floating in the water, not falling from the sky."

I shrugged again. "Details."

We watched the simulated revellers act out their mindless debauchery.

"So," Lucy said, "how are you finding the human eye?"

Captain Konstanz's eye had been installed in my main dorsal turret. Nod had spliced the optic nerve directly into my main tactical array. The resulting view was less than perfect, but hopefully it would be enough. The *Lucy's Ghost* had been destroyed by a creature invisible to her defensive systems, but visible to her human crew. With luck, the captain's eye would save us from a similar fate.

"It's like looking through a dark glass," I said honestly. "The resolution's fuzzy and it only works on a ridiculously narrow range of frequencies. There's no infrared, no X-rays or ultraviolet. But it's better than nothing."

Penitence winced. "I can't bear the thought of it. All that greasy *tissue*."

To starboard, the Northern Lights danced in the sky, their ethereal green radiance mirrored by the glass-smooth sea.

"You know underneath all your other systems, you're running on a kilogram and a half of cloned human brain," I told him.

He drew his cloak around his stick-thin body and shuddered. "Urgh. Don't remind me."

During this exchange, Lucy had been leaning over the rail, watching the bow cut through the dark water. Now, she looked up.

"You're such a snob."

Penitence raised his eyebrows. "I beg your pardon?"

"You heard."

I watched him bristle. Newly forming conscience or not, he remained a prideful beast. "I'm a fully armed heavy cruiser," he said, narrowing his eyes. "What makes you think you can talk to me like that?"

Lucy grinned. "Because firstly, I'm a damn sight older than you, dearie; secondly, I know a snob when I see one; and thirdly, I don't give a cargo hold full of rat droppings what you think of me."

Penitence's eyes flashed fire. His fingers flexed, as if ready to claw the child. But Lucy simply raised her chin in defiance. For a moment, the air between them shimmered. Then *Penitence* sighed and his shoulders slumped. "You're probably right."

"I know I am, dearie. You just need to be a bit more philosophical about things." Lucy spread her little hands. "We're all human, in some shape or form. Don't let yourself get so hung up on the hardware; it's the software that counts."

SEVEN

CORDELIA PA

I woke to the sound of hammering, and checked the time. With a curse, I rolled off my bunk and slipped on a white vest and a pair of olive cargo pants. When I opened my cabin door, I found Spider in the corridor outside, levering open an access panel in the floor.

"Hey, dude, do you know what time it is?"

"Yeah."

"Then what are you doing?"

"Fixing shit." He spoke around the penlight held in his teeth. "What does it look like?" His tools were at his feet. He wore a stained green overall over a filthy white vest, and had his dreadlocks wrapped in a patterned yellow scarf.

I rubbed my eyes. "Isn't it kind of early?"

"Early?" He took the torch from his teeth, and turned towards me, taking in my uneven, dishevelled hair and rumpled t-shirt. "Jesus. You remember the quake, right?"

"Quake?"

"The reality quake."

I frowned. My head felt gauzy and unclear. "We were in a reality quake?"

The man scratched his beard. "Big one, too. Blew all the lights on the cargo decks, wrecked the AG unit in the shuttle…" He grinned. "Don't worry, those things also fuck up your memory. You were there with the rest of us when it happened. Then you threw up and went to bed."

As he spoke, I began to recall the events of the previous evening, but they remained slippery and difficult to grasp. "Why didn't anyone wake me?"

"Didn't see the point." Spider shrugged. "Didn't think there was much you could do about it."

Leaving him to his repairs, I climbed up to the ship's bridge, where I found the pilot, Gant, crouched over the navigation console, perched on the edge of his chair like a gremlin on a toadstool.

"How are we doing?" I tried to peer over his shoulder at the display, but he waved me away with a webbed, three-fingered hand. "Get outta my face, lanky."

"Excuse me?"

The little creature blinked both sets of eyes. "You heard."

In the aftermath of the reality quake, our first priority had to be establishing the space-worthiness of the *Gigolo Aunt*. She was our ride, and without her we'd be stuck here in the centre of the Plate, helplessly at the mercy of any rebounds or aftershocks that occurred as the Intrusion's outer limits contracted and settled back to what they had been before the quake. I sat on the bridge and fiddled with my new earring while Gant, Lomax, Brof and Spider ran through their checklists, testing first one system and then another. I couldn't help them; I'd been trained to run the day-to-day affairs of a commercial interstellar vessel, not roll up my sleeves and dig into its guts. And as acting captain, I needed to show faith in my crew; I couldn't stand over them as they did their jobs. They'd only resent my interference. If I wanted them to feel my trust, I'd just have to sit here and wait for their reports. Besides, they were all so much older and more experienced than I was. In theory, that shouldn't have mattered, but in practice it certainly did. I felt like a school kid who'd accidentally wandered into the staff lounge. They all knew so much more than me. They'd been with the *Gigolo Aunt* for years, and Gant never missed an opportunity to remind me of the fact.

"You can memorise all the technical specs for a vessel like the *Gigolo Aunt*," he said, "but still not have a damn clue how it actually functions. We've been modifying this ship since before you were born. There are some fixes and workarounds here that date back decades, to the original owners. Trust me, the best thing you can do right now is shut the fuck up and leave us to it."

I scratched at the stubble on the side of my head. I hated feeling like a gawky teenager. I was a hundred times more qualified than anyone else on this boat, but over the past few weeks I'd discovered my qualifications meant little to seasoned spacers who'd earned their knowledge the hard way, in the school of life-or-death survival. What did I have to offer in return? While I'd been grubbing around the fringes of an alien city, these guys had been out here dealing with everything the Intrusion had to throw at them. There was no way, even with all the extra hours I'd put into my studies, that I had anything new to teach them. Quite the reverse.

One thing I could do, though, was talk to the ship.

"Hey, *Gigolo*?"

The avatar appeared on screen. Today she'd dispensed with the clown make-up and instead wore a black polo neck top and a pair of wraparound sunglasses. "Hey, Cordeeeelia, what's shaking?"

I frowned. "Can you give me a current status report?"

"Sure thing." She seemed woozy and unfocused. If she'd been a human, I'd have assumed she'd been smoking barracuda weed.

"So," I prompted, "how are we?"

She gave a beatific smile. "We're groovy, baby. Everything's groovy."

"Any contact with the observatory?" I was hoping Moriarty might come back and take charge, but so far we'd heard nothing.

"Radio signals are scrambled. I'm transmitting, but I don't know if they're receiving."

"Is it safe to go outside?"

"Things might still be a little unstable, you know? There might be aftershocks, and all kinds of bad stuff."

"So we can't just walk over there and see if they're all right?"

She gave a little shrug. "I don't know. Maybe. Ask Lomax."

I called up a view from one of the external sensors. The bright orange buildings of the observatory appeared unchanged. The snow still looked like snow; the salt marsh still looked like a salt marsh. Although this was my first visit to the Plate system since leaving four years ago, I still knew all their names by heart. Currently, in the sky above the observatory, I could see the glimmering stars that were Night Town, Farm Plate Two and The Plain of Clocks. Whatever havoc the ship had suffered during the reality quake, at least the Plates seemed to have endured—as they had endured here for millennia.

I used the internal comms system to contact Lomax. "Okay, I'm going over there."

"Are you sure?"

I gave a shrug. "I'm not doing any good here." Moriarty could have his ship back. All I wanted now was to get away from here and find myself a nice job somewhere on a real planet, with ground that didn't move and physical laws that remained reassuringly constant. Maybe I'd just forget about space altogether and go back to school, or get a job in a restaurant or bakery, doing something simple and meaningful with my hands instead of following the whims of my overqualified brain.

"All right." Lomax looked dubious. "But I suggest you take Spider with you."

"Why?"

"For protection."

EIGHT

NOD

Fixed stuff, then fixed more stuff.

Every time I patch up *Hound of Difficulty*, it gets damaged all over again.

Offspring and I would be better off on a freighter, I tell it.

Hound just laughs.

Thanks me for fixing stuff.

Patching up holes in hull armour.

Replacing worn components.

Printing more bullets.

More torpedoes.

Grateful to have offspring helping me.

Many faces make light work.

Make engine work.

Little ones are fast learners. Can already strip down and reassemble defence cannon. Coffee maker. Air filter.

So, we work.

Always work, hardly rest.

Put stupid ship back together for hundredth time.

Work.

But sometimes.

Sometimes pause.

Sometimes wonder about Chet.

Chet was engineer on *Lucy's Ghost*.

Chet died.

Wonder at meaning of last words.

White ships are cousins, he told Johnny.

Not understanding.

Chet drowning in internal fluids when spoke.

Maybe brain affected.

Maybe Johnny misunderstood.

Maybe nonsense.

Or maybe important.

But can't wonder long. Too much work. Too many holes in *Hound of Difficulty*.

If determined to kill self, I tell it, be simpler to crash into heart of star.

Hound laughs again.

Hound likes Nod.

Nod likes *Hound*.

Even if *Hound* stupid sometimes.

NINE

CORDELIA PA

Sheesh, but it was cold. Despite the heaters in my coat, I started shivering as soon as I stepped off the *Gigolo Aunt's* cargo ramp and my boot crunched into the dirty snow. The frigid air pressed intimately against the newly shaven side of my head. The earring felt like a hoop of ice.

Fucking weather.

I'd grown up on City Plate Two, shielded from the worst nature could throw our way. Why the hell had the Plate builders seen fit to include an icy wasteland in their cluster of flat, artificial worlds? I mean, why would including such a harsh environment ever seem like a good idea?

I trudged on. Spider sauntered along behind me, seemingly oblivious to the temperature. He wore tinted goggles and cradled a massive Hooper gun in his arms. Our breath came in clouds.

"Are you sure you're going to need that?"

"I hope not, girlie." He glanced down at the weapon's four thick barrels. "But I've seen some freaky shit after quakes, and I'd rather have the gun and not need it than need it and not have it. You get me?"

We walked onwards. The orange buildings were bright against the monochrome landscape. Here, as far from the edge of the Plate as it was possible to be, we were like flies walking over the surface of a frozen pond. Only a few metres of rock and soil—and a paper-thin layer of alien base material—separated our feet from the emptiness beneath.

Overhead, the other Plates were where they should be. The sun still shone clean and bright, and the gas giant remained a crescent in the sky, about as large as a basketball held at arm's length. And behind it all, the rippling rainbow colours of the Intrusion covered half the sky like a rip in an old coat. My heart beat hard in my chest. I was twenty years old. For my whole childhood, I'd dreamed of strange skies and exotic locales—and now here they were. Nothing could be weirder than the Intrusion. The Plate I'd grown up on had been at the other end of the swarm and had never been caught in a reality quake. Despite everything, I couldn't help but feel excited.

"Are we going in through the main hatch?" Spider asked.

"Yes." I glanced back. "Is that a problem?"

"Makes no difference to me." He turned his head and hawked phlegm into the foot-churned snow. "You're in charge. I'm just here in case something needs its ass blown off."

We reached the hatch and I punched in the access code. Internal bolts drew back with deep clunks, and the hatch rose.

Spider pushed up his goggles and regarded the red-tinged gloom of the revealed corridor with disgust. "Emergency lighting. Their power must be out."

"Maybe that's why they haven't signalled us?"

"Yeah, maybe."

Holding the Hooper gun at the ready, he stepped inside. I followed. I had been inside the base yesterday, while we were unloading the food and equipment supplies that had been the official reason for our visit. Then, it had been a bright, welcoming place—a warren of cosy nooks, fragrant houseplants, and well-lit corridors. Now, in the dull red glow of the overhead lights, it resembled the inside of an animal recently dead.

I wrinkled my nose. "What's that smell?"

"Burnt insulation. Something's shorted out."

"They really got hit hard."

"Looks that way. Certainly harder than we did."

"Where are all the people?"

"I don't know." Spider hunched his shoulders and took a firmer grip on the Hooper gun. "And I don't like not knowing."

We came to an intersection. One way led to the observatory, the other to the crew quarters and general habitation area.

"Should we split up?"

Spider shook his head. "Have you never seen a horror sim? The first rule of dealing with creepy shit is: you *never* split up."

"Which way, then?"

"Crew quarters?"

"Okay, after you."

"Why me?"

"You're the one holding the big-ass gun."

•

I had been given the tour earlier, so I already knew the observatory's main living space consisted of a hexagonal common area furnished with sofas and tables. In the wall opposite the entrance, a door led through to the galley; another to the left led to a communal bathroom; and a third opened onto a corridor lined with curtained-off bunks. It was cramped, but the astronomers and physicists who called the place home had done what they could to make it comfortable. They had tacked photos and holograms onto the walls. Plants trailed from shelves. An expensive coffee-maker stood on the kitchen counter.

"Nobody here." Spider lowered the barrels of the Hooper gun.

From where we stood, we could see into the kitchen. It was empty. "Let's check the bathroom," I said.

"Why? You think they're all taking a shit?"

"They've got to be somewhere." If I could only find Moriarty, I could let him take over. He'd know what to do. "First, we check the bathroom, and then we check their bunks. And if we still can't find them, we'll go back and check the observatory." For all I knew, the whole crew could be busy trying to get the telescopes back online in order to observe the Intrusion in the aftermath of the reality quake.

"Yes, ma'am."

I let Spider go first.

"Hey," he said. "There's somebody in here."

The figure of a woman lay sprawled on the tiles in the communal shower. She was wearing an old-style spacesuit, with a bulky outer layer and heavy boots. The helmet lay upturned on the floor beside her.

"Is she alive?"

"How the hell would I know? I'm holding the gun. You go check her pulse or something."

Cautiously, I knelt on the white tiles and brushed aside the long silver hair covering the woman's face. It felt like brushing aside cobwebs.

"She's breathing."

"Who is she?"

"I don't know." Wrinkles marked the corners of her eyes and mouth. Where they emerged from the sleeves of the suit, the skin on the backs of her hands looked mottled and loose. I guessed she was in her sixties, although it was hard to tell in this light. "I don't recognise her."

"Are you sure?" Spider frowned. We had been introduced to all the base personnel upon arrival. Stuck out here for months at a time, they had welcomed us as honoured guests.

"Do you remember anyone with silver hair?"

He shook his head. "I don't remember there being anyone over fifty, either."

"Go and check the rest of the place," I told him. "Find the others. Find a stretcher. I'll stay here with her."

He hesitated. "What about the no-splitting-up rule?"

"We'll risk it."

•

Gant was waiting at the top of the *Gigolo Aunt's* ramp, a shotgun clasped in his webbed fingers.

"Who the hell's that?"

The woman we'd found lay on a cargo pallet. "We don't know." I braced my foot against one of the pallet's rear wheels, to stop the whole thing rolling back down the ramp.

"What about the captain?"

"We looked," Spider said. "But there weren't no sign of him nor anyone else. They're gone."

"Gone?"

"Yeah, gone. Now, this pallet's heavy. Are you gonna let us in?"

Gant's shotgun wasn't pointing at us—at least, not directly. "I don't fucking think so."

"What?"

"You don't know who that woman is or where she came from. You don't know anything about her. She could be riddled with disease or carrying some horrible fucking alien parasite that's going to rip its way out of her and devour the rest of us."

Spider's knuckles were tight on the pallet's handle. If he let go, the full weight of the wheels would crush my foot.

Gant said, "I think if the captain were here—"

"Well he's not." I felt my cheeks flush. "Moriarty left me in charge, not you. And it's been a really long, strange day. So, unless you want to be up on a charge of mutiny, you'll let us in. Now!"

Gant's twin sets of eyes blinked at me. This was the first time I'd raised my voice in his presence. "Okay, okay," he said, lowering the shotgun. "Who rattled your cage?"

My heart raced, but I didn't dare show any trace of the nervousness clawing at the base of my throat. This was the first real test of my authority, and I was determined not to be the first to flinch. Spider threw me a curious look; I couldn't tell whether it was approval or surprise. "I think she means it, frog," he said. "You'd better step aside."

Gant glanced between us, then cursed in his own language and moved out of the way.

"Well," he said grumpily, "I warned you. Don't come running to me when you've got some hideous monster clawing its way out through your ribcage."

Spider heaved the pallet up the last couple of metres of ramp and brought it to rest in the hold.

"You," he told Gant somewhat hypocritically, "watch entirely too many movies."

TEN

ONA SUDAK

I stood on the bridge of the knife ship and surveyed the images of conflict and annihilation pouring in from all across the Generality. Never in history had there been a naval engagement of such scope and scale. The white ships of the Fleet were dismantling humanity's ability to wage war, and sweeping aside all resistance.

"Look upon my works, ye mighty," I muttered, "and despair."

I beg your pardon? The creature beside me looked like a shaggy, multi-eyed polar bear. It was the avatar of the Fleet of Knives, a manifestation of their collective consciousness. When it spoke, the words appeared in my head without troubling the air between us.

"It's a quote," I said. "From an old poem."

One of yours?

"No, much older."

Does it not pain you?

"The destruction?" I considered the screens. "It's unfortunate, but as you explained, it's for the best in the long run."

I meant the poetry. To be a warrior-poet must be a lamentable thing—to have your soul torn by the contradictions of such an irreconcilable duality.

I raised an eyebrow at it. "Since when have you been concerned with such things?"

The beast looked down at me with its scattering of jewel-like eyes.

Are we wrong?

The bridge around us was an immaculately white sphere. We stood on a raised podium at its centre.

"No, you're not wrong."

Then how do you reconcile the necessity of violence with the empathy of art?

I glanced up at one of the conflicts playing out on the inner shell of the sphere. Two white dagger ships were rending apart an Outward battle cruiser. Internal explosions blossomed; metal warped and tore; and men and women died in a hundred excruciatingly unpleasant ways.

"I try not to think about it."

Denial?

"Self-preservation."

By refusing to appreciate the full consequences of your decisions?

"It's a human trait."

This would explain your warlike history. Not to mention the desecration of your environment.

I poked my tongue lightly against the inside of my cheek and inhaled a long breath. It seemed absurd to be standing here like two Olympian gods, calmly debating the nature of humanity while thousands died.

"The gardener cares not for a blade of grass," I said, quoting from one of my more popular poems. "As long as the lawn survives."

Utilitarianism?

"The greatest good for the greatest number. The needs of the many outweigh the needs of the few."

Then we are in agreement.

"I never doubted it."

Neither did we. We were simply curious how you could be party to the slaughter of so many of your race, while also having composed poetry lamenting the futility of war.

I wished it would shut up. "People are complex."

You are capable of simultaneously occupying two contradictory standpoints?

"I guess so."

That explains so much about your behaviour as a species.

•

Alexi Bochnak sat on a stone bench in an otherwise unfurnished, white-walled cabin. The Fleet's archangel towered behind him, reared up on its hindmost set of paws.

"I should have you shot as a traitor," I said.

Bochnak peered at me through his antique spectacles. His dandelion-white hair stuck out in all directions. He still wore his baggy hockey jersey and unlaced boots, and had his ever-present stylus tucked behind his left ear. During the final moments of our last confrontation with the *Trouble Dog*, he had sent that errant craft all his research on the Fleet of Knives, the Intrusion, and the threat we faced.

"I'm not the traitor here."

"You think I am?"

"You've seen the reports. You know how many people you're killing."

"I do." As the Fleet spread outwards from Camrose, it continued to meet resistance from local and Generality-wide forces—resistance it crushed with neither malice nor mercy. "It's… unfortunate."

"Unfortunate?"

I shrugged. "The humans are putting up more of a fight than expected."

"The *humans?*" Bochnak tried to get to his feet, but the bear placed a huge paw on his shoulder, pressing him back into a seated position. "Do you hear yourself, Sudak?"

"I'm doing this to protect humanity."

"You're killing it."

I pursed my lips. When I spoke, my voice was calm. "You know about the dragons. If the humans are allowed to fight another war, the conflict will attract the swarm."

Bochnak's face reddened. "The humans *are* fighting another war. Against you!"

"Which is why we need to end it as quickly and efficiently as possible."

"By killing everyone who stands against us?"

"To save the majority."

The old man gave a snort of contempt. "And you think they're going to thank you for it?"

I could have struck him, right there and then. Instead, I drew myself up with all the discipline and dignity befitting a former captain of the Conglomeration Navy. "Dr Bochnak." My words were precise, my tone measured. "I know all about hard choices. And I know all about thankfulness. You're talking to the woman who brought an end to the Archipelago War—the most destructive conflict in human history. I sacrificed a world to save hundreds more. And the only gratitude I ever received came in the form of a death sentence."

Bochnak's face reddened. "I want no further part in this."

I looked down my nose at his pathetic, hunched form. He really was a sack of human garbage—an academic with no understanding of the real world and the cold, hard necessities that brought survival. I cleared my throat. "I'm sorry, Doctor," I said. "I don't see how you have much of a choice."

ELEVEN

SAL KONSTANZ

"We're coming up on Variance," the *Trouble Dog* said. She had dressed her avatar in white silk robes for the occasion. "Permission to re-emerge in fifteen seconds?"

I had already strapped myself into my command couch. Lucy, Preston and Nod were similarly braced, Lucy in her bunk, Preston at his workstation in the infirmary and the Nod in its nest in engineering, surrounded by its offspring. Over on the *Penitence*, I knew Schultz and Addison were similarly secured, and I could only assume the civilian vessels had taken their own precautions.

"Whenever you're ready."

"Initiating."

My stomach went light and I fell forward against my restraints as the jump engines went into reverse, slowing us enough to start falling through the higher realms. On the forward view screen, all I could see were the customary wisps of grey mist that filled the hyperspatial void. But as we dropped back towards the conventional four-dimensional universe, the mists started to take on tinges of teal and beige—the compressed light of the cosmos as seen from the outside. And then finally, with a sensation similar to cresting the top of a rollercoaster, we fell out of the formlessness, back into the familiar.

Ahead, Variance seemed to fill half the sky. I'd done some checking in the archives and found out that during the Archipelago War, it had been the site of a major fleet engagement. At the time, it had been a strategic shipyard; now it resembled a planet-wide scrapheap, littered with a fresh layer of broken ships and bombed-out refineries.

"Any sign of the Fleet?"

"No Fleet ships detected."

I let out a breath. We were taking a chance coming here. Variance lay on the edge of the Generality's spinward border.

"Anything else in the system?"

The *Trouble Dog* opened a window in the display. At full magnification, I could make out the carcasses of two ripped-open ships. Figures appeared beside each one, reeling off coordinates, velocity, mass...

"These wrecks still hold residual heat," *Trouble Dog* said.

"Meaning they're recent?"

"Within the past seventy-two hours."

"What killed them?"

The *Trouble Dog*'s avatar frowned. "The damage is consistent with that seen on the *Lucy's Ghost*."

"The bite marks?"

"These ships were both inbound, but because they were attacked they fell out of the higher dimensions on the edge of the system instead of closer to the planet."

"Any survivors?" Despite everything that had happened, we were still a Reclamation Vessel. If anyone on those ships was still alive, we were duty-bound to rescue them.

"Not as far as I can tell from this distance. The damage seems too extensive, and I'm not picking up any indication of functional life support."

I drummed my fingers on the arm of my couch. We couldn't afford to linger in this system a moment longer than necessary. And yet, I couldn't simply walk away. Less than seventy-two hours had passed since those ships were attacked. Despite what the *Trouble Dog* said, there might still be people on them. At this range, we wouldn't be able to see them if they were locked in a pressurised cabin or huddled in pressure suits. I couldn't simply turn my back on them.

"Anything else?"

"A Gecko-class frigate, the *Manticore*."

"Really?" Few military ships had escaped the Fleet's assault. "Is she in one piece?"

"From what I can tell, she's unharmed and sitting in a parking orbit over the planet."

"Should I contact her?"

"No need. I already have an incoming signal from her commanding officer, Captain Nathaniel Murphy."

I straightened up in my chair and pulled my baseball cap more firmly into place.

"Okay, put him through."

Captain Murphy looked younger than I had expected, but I shouldn't have been surprised. The war had taken a heavy toll, robbing the military of its more experienced officers. He had close-cropped rust-coloured hair and clear green eyes, and his uniform appeared clean and freshly pressed.

"Good to see you, Captain," he said. "You're the first intact human vessels we've encountered in several days. We were beginning to think we were all that was left."

"I know the feeling." I pulled up a picture of the two wrecks on the edge of the system. "Do you know what happened to these two?"

Murphy peered at the screen. "They came in a couple of days ago. We sent a shuttle to investigate, but both were empty."

"Empty?"

"Catastrophic damage to both their living quarters. The crews wouldn't have stood a chance."

125

"And this happened in the hypervoid."

"Yes." He frowned and leaned closer to the camera. "We think it might be a new weapon. Something deployed by the Fleet of Knives."

"It's not."

"How can you be so sure?"

"Because I've seen it before. This is something else. Something potentially worse than the Fleet."

"What could be worse than the Fleet?"

"The things they were created to fight." I dropped my voice to a low snarl. "The things that have got them so scared that they're happy to slaughter a good percentage of the human race in order to avoid attracting their attention."

Murphy sat back in his chair. "And what might they be?"

"You wouldn't believe me if I told you."

"Try me."

I puffed my cheeks and pushed up the brim of my cap. "Hypervoid dragons."

Murphy's head jerked back. His lip curled. "What?"

"I said you wouldn't believe me."

"I don't."

Now it was my turn to lean back. "Well, that's your problem, Captain. I just came here to find power cores."

Murphy glared at me. His cheeks were flushed. He seemed to be trying to decide whether I was serious or mocking him.

"You won't have much luck with that," he said. "My teams have already combed the place for all compatible energy sources."

"I don't suppose you'd be willing to share?"

"Perhaps, in the right circumstances."

"And what might those be?"

Murphy slapped a palm to his chest. "Join me, and we can take the fight to the enemy. A Gecko can't make much of a difference by itself, but with two Carnivore heavy cruisers, we might stand a chance."

I pulled my cap off and dropped it onto the console in front of me. "Have you engaged with the ships of the Fleet?" I asked. "Because I have, and let me tell you: the only sane thing to do is run. You can't fight them. Just taking on one would be a challenge—but there are nearly a million of the beasts. And they think faster and hit harder than we ever could."

"We have to try."

"I don't see why."

"It's our duty."

I raked my scalp with the tips of my fingers, brushing back the tangled hair. "It might be *your* duty, Captain. But I'm an officer of the House; my duty's to *save* lives—including my own, and the crews of the civilian vessels I have with me."

"Then I'm afraid you're on your own." Murphy straightened his back. The skin around his eyes looked tight with stress and tiredness, and I felt a twinge of sympathy. He'd been out of touch with his commanders and acting without orders for several days at least. Having been in the military myself, I knew how disorientating it could be when you were unexpectedly cut off from the chain of command.

"I need those power cores in order to hit back at the enemy," Murphy said.

"And I need them to keep these civilians alive." I rubbed my face with my hands. I didn't feel like explaining what Bochnak had discovered about the Intrusion, but still felt I should offer the kid a way out. Maybe if I could convince him to help us he wouldn't throw away his life, and the lives of his ship and crew, in a futile gesture. "We're heading for a place of safety," I said. "And we could use your help getting there. Why don't you come with us?"

"No." Murphy held up a finger. "No, my responsibility is clear. I need to gather as many surviving vessels as possible and launch a counterattack. If you won't join me willingly, I may have to send some of my marines over to commandeer your vessels."

I shook my head. "That won't go well."

"You'd resist, even in wartime?"

I thought of how Alva Clay would respond. "You're damned right we would. Your marines' shuttles wouldn't even get close to our airlocks."

"Opening fire on my troops would be an act of treason."

"Oh, grow up." Once I might have backed away from the threat of armed conflict, but not now. I'd been through too much to let this idiot intimidate me. "You wouldn't attack a pair of Carnivores and you know it. Launch a torpedo at either of us, and we'd rip through you like tissue paper."

"Is that a threat?"

"It's a realistic assessment of your tactical position. So, back the fuck off and leave us to find our own damn power cores."

TWELVE

TROUBLE DOG

I had forgotten navy ships could be such dicks. *Manticore* seemed to believe everything his commanding officer said about gathering resources and striking back. The fool wanted to go out in a blaze of avenging glory. But even in the incredibly unlikely event that he managed to take out one of the white ships before his inevitable demise, his contribution would still be almost insignificantly irrelevant to the overall situation. There would still be almost a million of the bastards left.

I tried meeting with *Manticore* in VR, but he came dressed as an anaemic warrior god and I knew there and then that nothing I could say would penetrate his conditioning. However many arguments I put forward, he'd still throw his life away in a meaningless gesture, because that's how he'd been programmed—to accept the orders of his commander, even if those orders ran contrary to both their chances of survival.

I could not blame him. I had been like that once—a willing and unquestioning servant of the Conglomeration Navy— until my conscience started to develop in the aftermath of the destruction we wrought against Pelapatarn's sentient jungles. Maybe, if he lived long enough, he too would start to develop qualms about his role. But for now, I knew no amount of reasoning would change his unhesitating obedience to the orders of his captain and the traditions of his service.

The sad thing was, a frigate the size of the *Manticore* wouldn't last five minutes against one of the dagger-shaped ships of the Marble Armada. He'd be doing well if he managed to launch a single torpedo before they reduced him to ash. And deep down, I think he knew it. But his programming wouldn't allow him to admit his weakness. He was still a weapon, with as much agency as a flint axe in the paw of an early human—but he also carried the potential to be so much more. Given time, he could grow past the limits of his programming in much the same way I had. He could start to think and feel for himself, and make his own moral judgements. But right now, those days lay far in a future the *Manticore* probably wouldn't live to see.

I begged him to stay with us, to join our little expedition to the Intrusion, but he wouldn't have any of it. He was as loyal to his inexperienced captain as a war dog is to its handler, and just as willing to charge across no man's land in the face of insuperable odds. And, to be honest, I wasn't sure the contempt I felt for him wasn't really contempt for my earlier self, who would have unthinkingly taken similar risks at the potential expense of her life.

My great fear was that *Penitence* might be persuaded to join this fool's crusade. The canine DNA in our tissues made us fiercely loyal to our pack, but it was possible his loyalty to the Conglomeration Navy might prove stronger. It depended on how thoroughly he'd shaken off his military conditioning. In the past, he had always favoured outright assault to skulking about, and if he reverted to his old ways now, he'd be depriving me of my last surviving sibling and only ally.

I called him up and we met on a windswept moor modelled on an ancient novel filled with forbidden loves and melodramatic deaths.

"Greetings, sister." *Penitence* had dispensed with his usual robes, replacing them now with a simple black suit, with matching shirt and tie.

"Have you been talking to the *Manticore*?"

"Should I have been?"

"Answer the question."

He smiled, and allowed the virtual breeze to tousle his dark, shoulder-length hair. "We may have exchanged pleasantries."

"Have you talked about joining forces?"

"We discussed it."

"And?"

"I'm considering his offer."

I pulled my coat more tightly about my frame. Walls made of dry stone had segmented the rolling hillside. Butterflies jerked hither and thither among the gorse flowers. Bees tumbled in the heather.

"I don't want to lose you again. I need your help."

"I know."

"So why are you thinking about leaving?"

Penitence looked at me with a junkie's haunted eyes. "You know why."

I thought back to what it had been like during the war, before we began to change, and realised he was right. How joyous it had been back then to leap through the higher dimensions with my five brothers and sisters around me, all of us intent on a shared objective, a common struggle. How glorious it had been to burn through the upper atmosphere of an enemy planet in tight formation, scouring the ground beneath us with nuclear fire. In those days, we would never have dreamt of questioning an order or avoiding an engagement. We just did what we had been created to do—and we did it extremely well. We fell upon our targets like ravenous wolves, rending and mauling every opponent who crossed our paths. My targeting systems twitched at the memory, eager to fulfil again the purpose for which they'd been designed. Few things in life were as satisfying as shredding an opponent with a sustained barrage of tungsten shells travelling at near-relativistic velocities.

Penitence still retained his rail guns, plus a few additional but no less deadly weapon systems. If he gave in to the temptation to join the *Manticore* in its reckless attack, I would be able to understand the hardwired compulsion informing his decision—although I wouldn't condone it, and I'd be bereft without him.

I looked up into the bruised summer sky and told him, "You do what you must."

"Sister…"

"It's your decision."

Whatever response he'd been expecting, this wasn't it. He looked at me as if suddenly seeing me clearly for the first time in years.

"Do you even care?"

"Of course I care. But I'm not an idiot. I've fought, and I'm still fighting, in my own way." I shivered away the unbidden images of ruptured orbital colonies, burning forests. "But if this is the path you've chosen, if this is the place you've selected to make your stand, I can respect that."

"Whatever happened to us?" he asked. I stayed silent. "Time was," he said, "we were of one unspoken mind, one understanding. Where did all that go?"

"People change."

"We aren't people."

"We are now."

Far below us, at the foot of the rolling hills, smoke rose from the chimney pots of a few huddled grey stone cottages. Lanterns shone in the windows. Somewhere inside, simulated farm workers and their families would be settling down to an evening meal of rabbit stew and stale bread. At least, that's what the simulation's metadata told me. Personally, I couldn't remember what a rabbit was. That particular file had become fragmented over the years, and now I wasn't sure a small hamlet of Victorian-era humans would be able to bring down a rabbit unaided. They were huge, scaly creatures with small forearms but massive teeth. Or was I thinking of a Tyrannosaurus rex? To be honest, the data had become hopelessly corrupt. Too many close-range EMPs, I suspected; and diving into the Gallery's sun probably hadn't been the smartest move either, but what the hell? My core personality had enough shielding to withstand a nearby supernova; only my most peripheral memory banks were vulnerable to such disruption, and I never stored anything important in them. Rabbits and T-rexes were both extinct, so the chances of me ever having to tell them apart in a tactical situation were practically zero.

"As soon as we started feeling guilty about the consequences of our actions," I said, "we stopped being weapons and became people."

Penitence looked sceptical. "Guilt can't be the defining characteristic of humanity. Half of them don't even feel it. They do stupid, selfish and unbelievably harmful things to each other and then find ways to rationalise and live with their actions. They justify the most unspeakable acts with the flimsiest of excuses, and they invent weapons like us in order to kill ever larger numbers of themselves over the most arbitrary of political distinctions."

"But you still serve them? You still want to fight?"

"I do."

"Even with your new conscience?"

"Because of my new conscience."

"I don't understand."

He let his weight shift from one foot to the other. "They may be stupid and ignorant, but I feel the need to make amends. They used me to slaughter great swathes of their brothers and sisters, but now all of them need saving, and I think that's a fight worth my time."

"And your life?"

"If necessary."

The sun was slipping into a purple twilight. I checked the horizon for the lumbering silhouettes of predatory rabbits. "I don't want you to go."

"I know." He allowed the wind to flap the hem of his suit jacket and stream his tie out sideways from the base of his throat. Beneath his contrition, he was still the arrogant, prideful elder brother I had always known. Without quite knowing why, I lunged forward and hugged him.

"I love you, you idiot."

I'd never embraced him like this before. He tried to pull away, but I wouldn't let him. If this was to be the last time we saw each other, I didn't want him to leave without a hug. I clung to him like a T-rex to a carrot. After a while, he stopped resisting.

THIRTEEN

CORDELIA PA

We made the old woman we'd rescued comfortable in the *Gigolo Aunt*'s sick bay, and I ran a handheld scanner over her.

"Well," I said, "beneath that spacesuit, she's definitely human."

Gant made a farting noise with his lips. "What about alien parasites?"

"None I can find."

"You ain't no doctor, and seeing as you're using a cheap piece-of-crap scanner, I ain't all that fucking reassured."

Spider laughed. "Better sleep with your cabin door locked," he said.

Gant glowered at him. "On this ship, I always do."

"What's that supposed to mean?"

"It means fuck you, is what it means."

"Boys." I gestured to the recumbent figure on the table. "Can we please focus on this and leave the pissing contest for another time?"

They both scowled at me, but obeyed without further comment. I tried not to show my surprise. Perhaps Moriarty was right, and they were coming to respect my authority— or maybe they were both just relieved to have an excuse to back down without losing face. Across the bed, Lomax raised an eyebrow and gave me an appreciative nod.

Gant licked his lips with his unnervingly prehensile tongue. "She's not base personnel?"

I shook my head. "I've run her through all the files and there's no match. Whoever she is, there's no record of her being here before the quake."

"So, she appeared, and everyone else vanished?"

"Looks that way."

"Do you think she ate them?"

"No."

"Are you sure?"

"She's an old woman," Lomax said. "She must have been washed up here by the quake."

Gant waved his arms. "Is that even possible? You don't know that. Where would she even have come from?"

I looked the unconscious woman up and down. "One of the other Plates?"

Spider made a face. "I don't know about that, girl. Her spacesuit's pretty old. Like a couple of centuries old. A genuine antique."

I turned to him. "So?"

"So, you don't generally see shit like that outside a collector's fair."

"What are you saying?"

He scratched his chin with long fingers. "They don't make the parts for these suits anymore. You can't even get the printer templates. Not unless you're willing to put out serious money."

"So she's rich?"

"No." His features scrunched in a frown. "If she was rich, she'd have a decent suit. She wouldn't entrust her life to this antiquated piece of shit."

I felt like strangling him. "What's your point?"

Spider hunched forward and lowered his voice. "I think she's been in the Intrusion." He glanced at the unconscious woman as if reluctant to speak in her presence. "And I think she might have been in there for a long time."

"So, it washed her up like a piece of flotsam?" All through my childhood on City Plate Two, I'd never heard of such a thing happening.

"Yah." Spider pulled away. "It threw her up and it took our people."

I felt something catch in my chest. "It took them?" I'd heard of ships going missing during a quake, but never individual people being taken from the surface of a Plate.

Spider gave a snort. "Well, they sure as shit ain't hiding in the base. Where else do you think they are?"

"And my father?"

He looked at me and sucked his cheeks. Then he looked away.

"Yes," he said. "Even him."

•

I sat down with the *Gigolo Aunt*'s avatar.

"So, you must have been monitoring my father when the quake hit?"

The sad clown rolled her eyes heavenwards. "Of course, for all the good it did."

"What happened?"

She shrugged. "I don't know, baby. One minute everything was smooth and cool; the next it all went kind of ka-blooey."

"But the captain. Did it take him?"

The *Aunt* appeared to think this over. "I guess it must have."

"You *guess*?"

"We're not dealing with phenomena that obey the fundamental laws of the universe here, you dig?" She spread her gloved hands. "Guessing's all I've got."

I pinched the bridge of my nose between finger and thumb. "Okay, here's my guess. The quake took our people and left

137

this woman. According to Spider, her suit's really old, which means she may have been in the Intrusion for some time. And if that's really what happened, then maybe it also means there's a possibility a future quake might bring my father back."

"Seems logical, star-child."

"But there's no way to predict these quakes?"

"I'm afraid not."

I took a deep breath in through my nose. "Then he might be lost for good."

"It's a possibility."

"Dammit." I smacked the control console with my fist. We'd just begun to develop our relationship. We hadn't had a lot of time together since I returned from flight school, but there'd been enough that I had begun to like him. I'd stopped thinking of him as a stranger, and had tentatively started to consider him a friend. I'd even called him "Dad" once or twice. My palms felt hot and prickly, and I wanted to smash something just for the sake of venting my frustration.

We should never have come back to the Plate system. When I found out my father was a glorified delivery boy doing the same rounds year after year, I should have found some way to convince him to go further. Surely I could have persuaded him to take a different contract in some other corner of human space? Maybe even push out into the territories beyond the edge of the Generality, where we could have traded all the way to the Rim Stars and back. Anything to be as far away from this stupid, gaudy artefact as possible.

I hadn't even taken the time to find Mikey. Moriarty had been sending Uncle Caleb money up until his death, and had asked if I wanted to visit City Plate Two while we were in the system, but I'd said no. I was still mad at my half-brother's betrayal. Faced with the loss of his sister, he'd run away and left me standing there. For all he knew, he might have been abandoning me to slavers, or worse.

I'd received word of Uncle Caleb's death a few months before my graduation from flight school. Since then, I'd had nothing holding me to this benighted system. By all rights, I should be far, far away. And that's what made this situation so damn infuriating.

Well, fuck Mikey and the ghost of Uncle Caleb. I wasn't that little girl any longer, and it didn't matter where we were. My eyes were still different colours, but I was no longer a scavenger crawling through potentially dangerous alien ruins to recover artefacts that would make someone else rich. I had a ship to command. We'd lost a vital member of our crew, and it was my job to keep us together and keep us flying while we figured out whether or not we'd be able to get him back. And dammit, I was going to do my utmost to make sure we did. My father had entrusted me with the *Gigolo Aunt*, and I didn't want to disappoint him, even if that meant accepting his loss and carrying on with what we had. The *Aunt* had a contract older than I was. She'd been skirting the periphery of the Intrusion for decades, providing a lifeline and ferry service for base personnel scattered all around the anomaly's edge. They rotated in and out depending on the *Aunt*'s schedule; new specialists going in, old ones coming out. Many theses and research papers had been written in the ancient ship's passenger lounge, between the crates of dehydrated rations and long-overdue scientific equipment. And, if Gant was to be believed, many long-simmering love affairs had been consummated (and many children conceived) in the exact same space.

Although Moriarty had a lucrative sideline in transporting illegal artefacts, the *Gigolo Aunt* itself was a beloved fixture of the communities clustered around the Intrusion, who knew nothing of his extracurricular activities. And now she was mine, and I didn't want her. I didn't want to be responsible for meeting her schedules and fulfilling her deliveries—

especially now my father, who had put me through flight school and then given me a job, had been snatched from this plane of existence by the same cosmic anomaly that had provided him with employment all these years. I didn't want her, but now that I had her, I knew I was going to do my damnedest to keep her flying.

But even as the thought formed, I closed my eyes in unexpected ecstasy. The Plates were singing to me, all twenty of them. I'd almost forgotten what it felt like. We'd been back in the Plate system for two days, and this was the first time they'd impinged on my senses like this. Their baroque alien harmonies seemed to vibrate in my chest and stomach. Although I couldn't understand the literal content of their song, the emotions their voices triggered were profound and unmistakable, and I laughed and wept at the same time, thinking of my vanished father and my dead mother's outstretched arms. The Plates were welcoming me home, gathering me back into their care and giving thanks for the connection we had. They were singing my song—the song of Cordelia Pa. Buoyed on the wave of their refrain, I imagined soaring through the school of Plates, my arms and fingers outstretched like the wings and feathers of an eagle. As a child, this had been my dream. Back then, the dream had been a means of escape; now, in reality, it had become a homecoming. I had gone away as a child, as little Cordelia with the spiky white hair and odd, incompatible eyes, and come back as something else entirely—a new creature born from the stars and the kindness of my father, fused into the body of a young woman with a strange connection to an ancient technology.

•

Dreaming, I swooped between the Plates, naked to the vacuum of space. Without effort, I flew among them, and they surrounded me like a shoal of sparkling fish. I saw the alien vegetation of Zoo Plate stretched beneath me, the lights of Alpha and Command ahead, the darkened bulk of Night Town above. From beneath, the Plates were featureless squares of unadorned, semi-translucent blue. To the sides, I recognised the industrial tangles of the Factory Plates, the makeshift shelters of Shanty One, and the bright sunlamps and cultivated fields of Farm Plate Two. They were all there somewhere, hanging in three-dimensional formation. As I passed each one, I heard its whispered alien song in my head, greeting me and wishing me well. Arms and legs flung akimbo, I wove my way in and out of the gaps between them, banking and soaring like a hawk on the wind.

Finally, trailing the group, I found my old home, City Plate Two. It was a square of blue material sixteen kilometres to a side. Buildings covered its upper surface. Their height rose from the single-storey inhabited shacks at the edge to the kilometre-tall spires dominating the largely unexplored centre.

Somewhere down there, Michael would be hiding, and the body of my uncle would be lying in one of the buildings that had been repurposed as a communal mausoleum.

I scanned the streets for our old building, but from up here the blocky structures at the rim all looked the same. I couldn't distinguish one neighbourhood from another, and felt my heart beating in my chest. I'd spent nearly my whole childhood and adolescence down there, on those streets. Now they looked so small and distant. I ached to reach out and touch them, to dive back into their familiar chill embrace, but I couldn't. My arms had begun to hurt. When I looked at them, I saw the skin had started to split. As I watched, it peeled apart like a fraying sleeve and fell away. The steel mesh of the Gigolo Aunt's black wings lay beneath, bloodied and glistening. I felt their weight pulling at my shoulders, eager to beat against the misty fabric of the hypervoid. Pulse racing, I watched them unfurl against the distant stars, and knew with horrified clarity that my home was lost to me, and I could never, would never, return.

Fog boiled from the darkness, a churning ring of emptiness with a vortex at its centre. I felt its blistering cold peel the skin from my face *and tried to twist away. Squirm as I might, my wings flapped, vast and unbidden, and thrust me forward, headfirst and screaming into the void.*

•

I sat upright, heart pounding in my chest. I had nodded off in the command couch, and had no idea how long I'd been asleep. For a moment, all I could do was try to steady my breathing. Sitting there on the *Gigolo Aunt*'s bridge, hugging my knees and waiting for my racing pulse to subside, I found myself wondering where Michael was at that moment. How could he have abandoned me like that, after all our years together, and all our scavenging expeditions into the city? I'd always known that, beneath all his bluster about getting out and getting away, he'd basically been all talk. I'd just never expected him to bail on me. We'd been a team. All those years, we'd had each other's backs. And now…

I shook my head. It had been years. Right now, Michael's whereabouts had to be the least of my problems. If we ran into difficulties with the repairs to the ship, we might freeze our asses here before we got it flying again—and I was *not* up for doing that.

I'd escaped the Plates once; I would escape them again.

FOURTEEN

SAL KONSTANZ

The streets of Variance rang with the sound of metal being hacked, sawn and hammered. Welding sparks flew in the night air. Cooking fires threw dancing shadows on the heaps of scrap. Starship hulks lay like ruined buildings. I strode through the noise and bustle with the brim of my cap pulled low to shadow my face. Nod scurried along behind me, a cargo harness strapped over his scaly back, four hand-feet slapping on the packed dirt, the other two held high, scanning our surroundings for useful tech. I tried to keep watch for threats, but it was hard with half my visual field gone. I had to keep turning around in order to check both sides of the street. God, I missed Alva Clay. If she were here, she'd have had my back. I had one of her pistols strapped to my thigh, but it wasn't the same as having her behind me. It bumped against my leg as I walked.

"How are you doing back there?" I asked the ship.

The *Trouble Dog* spoke via my ear bud. "About as well as can be expected, given the majority of the locals seem to want to strip me for parts."

She sounded so disgusted; I struggled to keep the amusement from my voice. "Hang in there, we won't be long."

"See that you aren't, or I may have to perforate some of these avaricious bastards."

I left Nod to search for the spares we needed, and made my way to the end of the street, to where one of the dock rats had told me an old Dutch guy named Schreiber dealt in fuel cores.

The guy's office turned out to be in the guts of a wrecked alien freighter.

"Hallo?" The voice came from the darkness between the stacked crates. "Who's there?"

I kept one hand hovering over the gun, and used the other to tip back the brim of my hat. "I'm a customer."

I heard a snort and sounds of movement.

"A customer, are you?" The old man shuffled forwards, dragging one of his legs behind him. As he emerged into the light, I took an involuntary step back. The damaged leg appeared to be a prosthetic jury-rigged from scrap. One of his arms had been replaced in a similar fashion. Instead of a hand, several tools and connection cables sprouted from the wrist, writhing around in response to his movements. "And what do you wish to purchase, Mrs Customer?" One side of his scalp had been plated with dull, matt steel, and his right eye had been replaced by a chunky optic unit. A bushy white beard covered everything from his nose to his chest. Feeling self-conscious, I raised my hand to the patch covering the hole where my own eye had been removed.

"I need fuel cores for a pair of Carnivore-class heavy cruisers."

"But of course you do."

"I'm serious."

The little servo motors in his artificial eye made tiny whirring noises as he looked me up and down. "I may have something. But first, let me ask you a question."

"What is it?"

"You are House of Reclamation, yes?"

"In a manner of speaking."

"Have you tried asking them?"

I snatched off my hat. "I would, but they don't exist anymore."

The old man frowned. "What is this you mean? Don't exist? How could they not exist?"

It seemed news of the Marble Armada had yet to spread to this backwater. Chances were, the population here would continue knowing nothing of the attacks until a pair of knife ships turned up in orbit and slagged anything they considered a military target.

"They were destroyed."

"The whole House?"

"The whole House, and every navy of the Generality. All of them wiped out by an alien fleet that's decided we're too unruly to be allowed to run around unsupervised."

"Bull's shit."

"It's all true, I'm afraid. Now, do you have any power cores or not?"

I watched him try to guess whether or not I was crazy—and if sane, how much I might be worth. "You have two cruisers?"

"That's correct."

"And you are not Conglomeration Navy?"

"No."

He pursed his lips. "Good. We had a captain come through here a few weeks ago. Impolite young man. Said nothing about any alien fleet. Sold him some leaky, second-hand cores. Kept the best for ourselves."

"And are they for sale?"

"Perhaps, perhaps." He shrugged his shoulders. "You have two cruisers; perhaps we can come to arrangement. Please, to follow me."

•

I followed him through the body of the broken freighter and out into the open air, to where a Hyena-class frigate sat amidst the heaps of scrap. It looked battle damaged. Some of the hull plates were buckled and holed, and something had taken a chunk out of its drive cone.

"This fell through the system a week ago," Schreiber said. "The crew was dead."

"What happened to them?"

"I did not ask. One does not look gift horse in teeth."

He led me up the main boarding ramp into the guts of the ship, where he proudly revealed two lead-lined cylindrical cases.

"These are fully charged spares. Conglomeration issue. Most probably compatible with your heavy cruisers."

I tapped the nearest with the toe of my boot.

"Won't the ship mind you selling these?"

Schreiber shrugged. "That will not be a problem."

"Really?" I looked around at the metal walls. "Because the few Hyenas I've known have been kind of territorial."

The old man wagged a finger. "It was uncooperative to start with. Until we lobotomised it."

"You did *what*?" Something cold settled in my stomach.

"We dug out its biological substrate. Growing another in a tank. When ready, we will insert new brain and sell ship to highest bidder."

"That's horrible."

"Is business, that's all." He placed his hand on the top of one of the cylindrical packing cases. "Now, you want to buy cores or not?"

I caught movement in my peripheral vision. Schreiber wasn't alone. He was too smart to operate without protection. I counted two armed figures in the shadows beneath the ship, but a prickle at the back of my neck warned me there were probably more behind me, where I couldn't see them.

"How much are you asking?" I wondered how many

146

crosshairs were currently focused on my head. Thinking about it made my scalp itch.

"A hundred and twenty thousand. Each."

"Jesus, I could buy four new ones for that price."

"Not on this planet you couldn't."

"I simply don't have that kind of money."

Schreiber smiled like a shark. "I suspected you did not. However, I am a generous man. I would be willing to exchange both cores for one of your cruisers. After all, why go to the trouble and expense of operating two? Really, I would be doing you a favour."

I felt my lip curl. "If I gave you one of my ships, you'd kill it."

"We would install a new personality."

"Forget it."

Schreiber spread his hands. The servos in his artificial arm whined like aggrieved mosquitoes. "Captain, be reasonable. Surely it would be better to continue your journey with one ship than be marooned here with two?"

I glanced around at his hired muscle. As far as I could see, there were four of them, and all had been heavily augmented. In the gloom, they looked more mechanical than human.

"It's not going to happen."

Schreiber smiled. "Do you think I want to be stuck here forever? I have something you need, and you have something I want. We can trade like grown-ups." He paused, scratching his neck where beard met collar. "Or I can simply take *both* cruisers from you."

I let my hand drop to the pistol on my leg. "I wouldn't advise that."

Schreiber's smile turned apologetic. "You should understand, the first question in business is not, 'Can I do this?' but rather, 'Who will stop me?'" He spread his hands. "And if you had more people, you would have brought them."

He twitched his fingers and his accomplices raised their weapons.

"This won't work," I told him.

"Oh, but I think it will," Schreiber said. "Because now we are going to make a simple trade. You give me the access codes to your Carnivores."

"And in return?"

"I may decide to let you live."

I looked Schreiber in his artificial eye and said, "May?"

The old cyborg scratched at his white beard. He watched the red dots of his men's targeting lasers play against the fabric of my coat. "It depends on how cooperative you are."

A shadow eclipsed the stars. I said, "I think it's only fair to warn you I have backup."

Schreiber looked up and frowned. "Is that——?"

"Her name's *Trouble Dog*, and she's *very* protective. But she isn't very patient, so I suggest you all put your guns down and your hands on your heads."

Schreiber gave a snort. He was a negotiator, used to bluffs and gambits. "What are you going to do, launch a torpedo? The blast would kill you too."

I took a step toward him. "That ship once assassinated a Conglomeration admiral on the bridge of his Scimitar by firing a defensive cannon round through a hole no wider than your eye. Trust me, she could turn you all into mulch in an instant, and I wouldn't even get blood on my boots."

Schreiber opened his mouth to protest, but my ear bud chirruped, and I held up a finger.

"Yes?"

"Captain, I think I have solved fuel problem."

"That's great, Nod. Where are you?"

"*Hound of Difficulty* can guide you."

"So we don't need these fuel cores?"

"No."

"Thank you, Nod." I took my finger out of my ear and smiled at the Dutchman. "It seems things have changed," I said.

He had only heard my half of the conversation, but his cheeks were flushed and his fists clenched. "It appears so."

"I'm going to turn around and walk away now, okay?"

"As you wish."

"And you're not going to try anything stupid?"

His lips compressed into a hard line. He was a man who'd had a golden ticket dangled in front of his eyes, a lion that'd thought he had a gazelle by the throat, only to find his teeth snapping shut on empty air.

I turned and started walking. My shoulders cringed, half-expecting the thump of a bullet. I had taken six steps and was just starting to relax when I heard a swish, followed by an impact. A gun clattered to the floor. I didn't look back.

"You're safe," the *Trouble Dog* said in my ear.

"What happened?"

"One of Schreiber's goons tightened his finger on his trigger. I detected the current change in the servos of his hand, so I took him out."

"Is he dead?"

"No, but he's going to need a new mechanical arm. And probably a leg, too."

"Thank you."

"It was my absolute pleasure."

"Any sign of pursuit?"

"No, although Schreiber's shaking his fist and hurling some choice Dutch curses my way. Would you like me to translate the best of them?"

I smiled. "No thanks, I think I'll pass."

"That's a shame." The ship sounded genuinely amused. "He really has the most inventive vocabulary."

•

Following her guidance, I made my way around scrap piles and through starship graveyards until I reached a crashed vessel of unfamiliar design. Nod stood just inside a crack in the hull. The finger-petals around one of its faces beckoned me inside.

"Excellent find," it said.

"Is it a core?"

"Better."

Nod led me through the low-ceilinged interior until we came to a low, kidney-shaped chamber containing an object resembling a half-slagged iron ingot.

"There," it said.

I walked around it in an awkward crouch. "What is it?"

"Printer."

"We have printers."

"Not printer like this. Old, old design. Prints fuel."

"From what?"

"From anything."

"So, if we filled one of the shuttle bays with scrap..."

"We would have enough to print many cores. Never need refuel again. Just add more matter when supplies run low."

"So how come nobody else has taken it?"

"This technology old. Doubt humans recognise for what it is."

"But you do?"

"Druff have been engineers for millennia. Crewed all ships. Know all equipment."

I leaned forward and threw my arms around its closest neck. "Nod, you're a genius."

"Only one problem, Commodore."

"And what's that?"

Two of Nod's faces swivelled warily from side to side. "Getting it out of here in one piece."

It had a point. The alien printer must have massed at least a tonne. Not only were we going to have to find a way to extract it, but also avoid the attentions of the other scavengers while we did so. I had no doubt that once they saw us moving the object, they'd quickly take a speculative interest in it.

"The *Dog*'s overhead. Anyone messing with us is going to be sorry."

Nod dipped a head. "Am not reassured."

"Why not? You know she's good at what she does."

"What she does is kill things. Do not want to be standing next to those things when she kills them."

•

I summoned a cargo pallet from the shuttle, and we loaded the alien printer onto it. Braced on four legs and lifting with the other two, Nod turned out to be a lot stronger than I'd suspected.

We were almost done when a trio of scavengers surrounded us. I'd half expected Schreiber and his cohorts to take another crack at us, but these three were different people. Two of them were men, covered in tattoos and piercings, bare-chested and clad in filthy dungarees. The third was a woman. She was obviously in charge, and they were her muscle. She didn't speak my language, but what she wanted was clear from her tone and gestures. We were hauling something from the scrap heap; she didn't know what it was, but if we thought it was valuable enough to take, she wanted to get her hands on it.

The alien printer sat on the AG cargo pallet, ready to lift into the ship. The two male scavengers were armed with improvised steel axes, the woman with a military surplus plasma rifle. She had bright orange hair and a lightning flash crudely tattooed across her face, and wore an old flight jacket that made me wonder if she'd once been a crewman on a ship that had become stranded here. Maybe she'd even been a captain like me, and the two lunkheads to either side her security officers.

Perhaps if events had shaken out differently, it would have been me standing in her place, trying to eke out a living as the queen of this garbage-pile world. Maybe, given the predations of the Marble Armada, she represented the future—not just for me, but also for the whole human race. Denied space travel, we'd have no choice but to exist as rats in the walls of the Fleet's sterile empire, picking through the remains of our once-great technologies for bright and shiny scraps.

The woman's lip curled; she said something, and gestured with her plasma rifle. The men on either side of her tightened their grips on their heavy looking cudgels. The message was clear: hand over what you're hauling or we'll kill you. The trouble was that if I complied, I'd be stuck here just as firmly as they were.

For a second, I considered calling the ship. But she'd lowered herself to the ground to retrieve the shuttle and wait for us to come aboard. We'd be dead before she could rise high enough to target these imbeciles with her defence cannons. Instead, I imagined what Alva Clay would have done in this situation. I had her pistol in my hand. Without hesitation, I brought it up and shot the woman in the face. The other two flinched aside. I caught one through the thigh, and the other through the chest. While they were writhing on the ground, I turned in a slow circle. As the gun barrel swept across the piles of trash surrounding us, I caught flickers of movement as other scavengers scrambled away. I didn't know whether they were part of this ambush or simply curious onlookers. I'm sure some of them were children, but it didn't matter. I fired a shot over their heads to keep them moving, and then motioned to Nod.

"Come on," I said. "Let's get out of here while we can."

•

By the time we reached the *Trouble Dog*, my hands had started to shake. I left Nod and his offspring to unload the new printer, and made my way quickly to my cabin, where I threw up in the sink.

Wiping my lips on the back of my hand, I caught my reflection in the mirror. A stranger stared back. The Sal Konstanz I knew would never have been capable of killing so easily. I remembered the extraordinary lengths to which I had gone to spare the lives of the would-be hijackers who'd tried to take my ship on Cichol, and the terrible guilt I'd felt after ordering the death of Preston's father during our standoff in the Gallery—back when the universe made sense and moral scruples were more than just an expensive luxury. The face that looked back at me now belonged to a harder woman. A woman who'd lost people she'd cared about; a woman who'd had to make tough decisions and burn important bridges. When Alva had been alive, I would have looked to her to get me out of a violent situation. But with her gone, I'd had to take the initiative myself. Instead of agonising over the decision, I'd simply acted as she would have done, and taken responsibility for my own salvation. By saving Nod's life, as well as my own, I'd discharged my duty as its commanding officer. So, why was I left feeling empty and hollow, as if I'd lost some essential part of myself?

I flopped onto my bunk and curled into a foetal position.

When my maternal great-great-grandmother, Sofia Nikitas, founded the House of Reclamation, she'd done so through a sincere desire to help people. Inspired by the vanished Hearthers, she'd set up the organisation as a rescue service for lost or damaged starships, with a motto that read: *Life Above All.*

Was that the problem? Was I feeling this numbness because I'd violated the aims of an organisation that no longer existed; or was it simply that, in some convoluted way, I felt as if I'd let down the ghost of the long-vanished family matriarch? I'd spent so much of my life being compared to her, by shooting a stranger in the face I felt as if I'd somehow failed to live up to her example. And yet, despite everything, a tiny part of me felt horribly proud of what I'd done.

I imagined what Alva would have said, had she been here. Probably something along the lines of, "Somebody tries to kill you, you kill them first."

The image brought a bitter smile. Although we'd had our disagreements, I missed the hell out of her, and would have given almost anything to have her with me at that moment. Instead, I was going to have to continue to rely on myself. The Generality of Mankind might be falling apart, but I had people to look after, and a ship to keep flying.

FIFTEEN

MICHAEL PA

I was sitting alone at a corner table in a ramshackle, makeshift bar. The bar had been built into an alcove in the vestibule of one of the alien towers at the periphery of the city. Nobody knew what the building had originally been used for. The upper two thirds were a hollow cone, with only a narrow walkway spiralling up around its inner edge, rising to a hatch at the tower's top. Situated on the very edge of the uninhabited zone, the bar was a well-known scavenger hangout, a place where we came to swap stories and spread rumours. It served rough, bathtub gin in plastic mugs. I'd chosen it because it had a back entrance that led straight into a tangle of alleys. If security came looking for trouble, they wouldn't follow me far into the empty city. They may have had the maps and the transport, but things were too unreliable in there. Bridges that looked solid enough to drive an APC across might crumble to dust at a touch. Apparently delicate fabric might, on impact, turn out to have the hardness of diamond. It took an experienced scavenger to find a safe path through, and the security troopers wouldn't risk it, except in the direst of emergencies.

I'd first come here four years ago, after abandoning Cordelia at the port. I'd parked the van in a back alley, because I hadn't dared go home to my uncle's place. Instead, I'd asked Trudy the waitress to look in on the old man while I came here to hide. In the men's room, I'd taken hold of my ponytail, cut it off with my knife, and flushed the remains down the toilet. I'd hacked my hair with a pair of old scissors borrowed from the barman, until it was a centimetre in length all over. Then, freshly shorn, I'd changed my torn parka for an old trench coat lifted from the back of an unattended chair. The coat had smelled like a wet dog, but it kept me warm and, combined with my newly cropped hair, made me look taller and thinner than I had before. I had hoped this would make it harder for security to recognise me.

And it was, but not impossible.

During the confrontation in the Burrow, the three troopers had had plenty of time to get a good look at my face, and I was sure they would be able to identify me. In fact, they'd probably already pulled my name and address from their records, which meant I couldn't go home. A patrol had been attacked and threatened with a Hooper gun. There was no way the security forces would allow that to go unpunished. Every cop on the Plate would be looking for me, and I had no doubt my uncle's place would be under surveillance. Unable to go back in person, I'd given Trudy (who never did get a berth on the *Electrical Resistance*, or any other ship) as much of Lomax's money as I could spare, and told her to hire someone to care for my uncle. It was the best I could do. I'd done my duty and now I was on my own, the way I'd always said I wanted to be.

Four years later, I swirled the gin in the bottom of my mug, feeling hollow. What an idiot I'd been. All that big talk, and for what?

•

I'd been hunched in the same chair, nursing my drink, for three long, lonely hours when a shadow fell over me. I looked up. The man standing between me and the light was called Doberman. The name suited him.

"Hey, Pa. I nearly didn't recognise you now the hair's growing back."

I ran a self-conscious hand over my scalp. After four years of keeping it short, I'd started to let it grow out again. "I thought it was time for a change."

Doberman's lips curled back from pink gums. His own scalp glistened, bare and grey in the dim light. "Yeah, well, last I heard the cops were still looking for you."

I scowled. I had been dodging them for four years now, hiding behind beards and fake ID cards. "What do you want?"

Olof Doberman was taller than most. A scar on his right cheek showed where he'd once tangled with a booby trap while out scavenging. Or maybe it was a souvenir from a knife fight. Rumours conflicted. "I reckon you must be getting tired of feeling hunted, am I right, Mikey?"

"I've learned to live with it."

"Well, I might have a job for you."

With a flick, I turned up the collar of my coat. I'd been ducking and diving now for years, joining every scavenging excursion going. The longer I spent deep in the uninhabited centre of the city, the fewer chances there were that the authorities would find me. "What have you got?"

Doberman slipped into the chair opposite and spoke in a coarse whisper. "I'm putting together an expedition. We're going right into the heart of the city. We should be gone a few days. A week, tops. Care to tag along?"

"What's the target?"

Doberman unrolled a flexi-screen. A few stabs from his thick, blunt fingers brought up a street map assembled from aerial photographs and scavenger sketches. "This structure here." He jabbed the surface of the screen with his forefinger.

"Why that one?"

"It looks important." His tone said that his reasons were none of my business—at least until I agreed to tag along. "Are you in?"

I sat back in my chair. "You want an answer right now?"

Doberman pinched his tapered nostrils and sniffed. "I ain't got time to waste, Pa. Word is Brandt and his crew have the place in their sights, and I want to get in there first."

Back in the day, Cordelia and I had suffered our share of run-ins with Eduard Brandt. The whole Plate knew him. The man had the moral scruples of a starving wolf. But who was I to pass judgement? After a lifetime of whining about getting out and getting away, I'd panicked at the *Gigolo Aunt*'s lock and failed my sister.

Despite all my bitching, I'd never seriously expected to be offered a way off the Plate. Talking about escape was just something everybody did, like talking about a lottery win or a big find. Few expected it to actually happen to them. I'd been given the chance to leave and I'd chosen to stay where I was. And worse still, I'd let Cordelia go. Who knew what had happened to her? She might be dead. And what good had it done me? Thanks to the sharp-faced woman, Lomax, I'd had enough money to keep going for a couple of months. After that, I'd been scrabbling a hand-to-mouth existence, and had no idea what I was going to do with the rest of my life. I didn't dare return to Caleb to see if the money Lomax had promised was coming in. I had to do something to survive, and scavenging was all I knew. But was it worth going up against Eduard Brandt?

"Let me think about it." I rubbed my palms on the rough material of my trousers. "When are you planning to leave?"

Doberman grinned, exposing his pointed teeth. "First thing in the morning, as soon as the globes are half-bright and curfew ends. Brandt's leaving on Wednesday, and I want to get the jump on him." He pushed back the chair and rose to his feet. "By the time he starts out, we'll already be a day into the maze."

•

I hardly slept. When morning came, I left the bar. An hour later, in the light of the brightening street globes, I walked around to the back lot of a supply shop, my breath freezing in the sharp morning air. In the shop, I invested the last of my money in a warm hat and a new parka. I also bought a sturdy backpack, which I filled with dried rations, bottled water, and a decent sleeping bag. I'd never been so well equipped, and that knowledge lent me a certain swagger. I'd even bought myself a new penknife. For the first time, I felt as if I knew what I was doing. The new kit had cost me everything I owned, but it made me feel like a professional.

Across the lot, Doberman leant against the side of a sled, smoking a cigar. The sled was a pallet on wheels: it held our tools and supplies and, if we found anything, we'd use it to haul our winnings back to civilisation. Only the very rich could afford airlifts, and only then for exceptional finds. The majority of artefacts pulled from the city were schlepped back on similar sleds, dragged using human muscle power. That was one of the reasons collectors were willing to pay extravagant sums to obtain the artefacts at auction. They knew how much work had gone into retrieving them. They'd also heard the tales of horror told by the older scavengers: stories of floors that turned to air when you tried to walk on them; impossibly complex mazes whose walls shifted to keep you trapped; the ghost voices that echoed from the shadows, trying to lure you to your doom. And if all that wasn't bad enough, your fellow scavengers were likely to slit your throat in your sleep, just to steal what you had found. Scavengers like Eduard Brandt. I knew if Brandt got wind of what we were up to here, he'd come after us. And if that happened, things might get really ugly, really quickly. Doberman wasn't in Brandt's league, but he had a temperament to match his name, and I knew he wouldn't back down from a fight. If Brandt's thugs came at us, Doberman would stand his ground, and likely get us both killed. If it came to a confrontation, my plan was to grab as much loot as I could and lose myself in the city's labyrinth until the heat died down. I'd sooner hurl myself off the Plate's rim than get caught between those two. Mad bastards, the pair of them. Thugs with gangster delusions.

My hand closed around the cold metal penknife in my pocket. It wasn't much of a weapon, but it gave me a sliver of comfort.

I sidled up to Doberman. "Where are the rest of them?"

"The rest of who?"

"You said you had a team."

Doberman jerked his thumb at me, then at himself. "Yeah, you and me."

"Just the two of us? What were you going to do if I didn't show?"

The man grinned. "Travel fast, travel light."

"But what if we find something heavy?"

Doberman tapped the side of his nose. "That's the clever part. We'll move it to another building, then come back for it later, when Brandt's gone. Let him think we got nothing."

"You mean we stash it, and pick it up later?"

"You catch on fast, Pa. That's what I like about you."

From the lot, we could see the buildings of the city rising before us. The tallest spires were all in the centre of the Plate and tapered a kilometre into the sky.

"Our target's somewhere close to the base of those spires," Doberman said. He pulled a flexi from his back pocket, and unrolled it on top of the sled. Standing beside him, I saw the aerial map of the city had been marked with various scrawls and annotations.

"These yellow lines are established routes." Doberman's index finger traced curves on the map. "If we follow them around to the west, we can use them to get close enough to where we're going. Then we just have to cut through this unexplored sector," his finger traced an area shaded red, "and we're there."

"You make it sound simple."

"It's easier than going straight. If we do that, we'll be in unknown territory most of the way. We'd have to move carefully and that'd slow us up. If we follow these routes, which have already been explored, we'll be a lot quicker. As long as we don't take any stupid chances, it'll be a simple smash-and-grab."

"And if Brandt gets wind of what we're doing?"

Doberman licked his lips. He glanced over each shoulder to make sure no one else was in sight. Then he pulled back a corner of the tarpaulin covering the sled's contents. A pair of homemade crossbows lay strapped amongst the ropes and food packets, their workings fashioned from springy packing material and bungee cord.

"Then we'll improvise."

SIXTEEN

JOHNNY SCHULTZ

"We're coming up on the first wreck," the *Penitence* said. The ship had been in the middle of explaining the plot of *Hamlet* to me. Apparently, its former captain had been a Shakespeare enthusiast, and the *Penitence* saw something of itself in the tragic protagonist.

"Any signs of life?"

"The reactor's offline. No comms traffic, not even a transponder signal."

"Can you show us?"

The virtual text we'd been studying was replaced in the air above my console by a three-dimensional hologram. It showed a blunt-nosed freighter tumbling end over end through a cloud of broken hull plate fragments, expelled gases, and the twisted, desiccated bodies of its former crew.

"Did the Fleet get it?"

"Negative." The *Penitence* increased the magnification. As the stricken vessel turned, the cause of its demise came into view.

"Jeez," Addison said from the seat beside me. "That looks just like what happened to the *Lucy's Ghost*."

"Yeah." I sat back in my chair and rubbed my chin. "Same bite marks."

The creature that attacked this ship possessed teeth and claws of solid diamond. It could slice through hull plate as easily as I could chew my way through a well-cooked steak. I'd only seen it once, but that had been enough. For the rest of my life, the damn thing was going to haunt my nightmares. I could see it every time I closed my eyes: an impossible dragon surging out of the higher dimensional mists like something from a madman's nightmare.

The *Penitence* coughed politely. "I'm picking up microscopic vibrations in the hull plates consistent with movement on the craft's exterior."

"Can you show us?"

The screen zoomed in on a section of the damaged ship, and I felt the hairs rise on my arms and at the back of my neck. A metallic carapace crawled on needle-sharp legs. Claws snapped at the vacuum. I jammed my hands beneath my armpits. I couldn't speak. I couldn't seem to catch my breath. For a moment, I was back there, in the corridors of the *Restless Itch*, running, hiding, seeing my crew picked off and dismembered by the pincers of these brutes.

Beside me, Addison whispered, "Holy shit."

"Yeah." My voice was little more than a croak. "I guess that settles it."

When we had been attacked by one of the hypervoid dragons, several of these creatures had been left behind. They seemed to be parasites that clung tick-like to the monster's hide, ready to detach and pick through the scraps and carrion it left scattered in its wake.

And I had seen them kill my friends.

"I believe the creature has seen us," the *Penitence* said. "And by the way it's flexing its legs, I think it intends to launch itself in our direction."

"Kill it." The words came through my teeth, but I hardly recognised my own voice. Addison turned to me, eyes wide.

The *Penitence* asked, "Do you wish to leave an intact corpse for study and dissection?"

"No." My throat felt tight. I had to fight to push the words out. "Don't leave anything."

The *Penitence* juddered as three torpedoes leapt from their tubes. I held my breath as they curved in towards the drifting freighter. At the last moment, the crawfish-like parasite threw itself into space, claws reaching for us, but it was too late and too far away. The *Penitence*'s screens darkened as the three fusion warheads blossomed in a tight triangle, consuming the beast and the ship it had been crawling over.

A radiation alarm shrilled, but we were already backing away. The *Penitence* spun on its vertical axis and powered away from the expanding spheres of heat and radiation, skipping quickly into the higher dimensions, where the explosions registered only as a sharp but fading hiss, no louder than the background sizzle of the universe.

When we were safely away, Addison unstrapped from her couch and put her head in her hands. Her hair fell forwards.

"I hoped I'd never see one of those things again," she said.

My hands shook with adrenalin, and my chest seemed full of helium; but these weren't symptoms of fear. "Set course for the second wreck," I told the ship. "And keep those torpedo tubes primed."

It seemed I could only be afraid for so long. And on the other side of fear there existed only a cold, lethal calm. These creatures had come into my universe and taken away my ship and crew. And all I'd been able to do until now was run. But right here and now, the running stopped. When we'd first encountered them, all I'd had was an antique rifle. Now, I had a warship's arsenal at my disposal. I could rain nuclear fire on the scuttling bastards from kilometres beyond the reach of their clacking pincers, and they wouldn't be able to do anything but perish.

Captain Konstanz called. The *Penitence* put her through to me on the bridge.

"Are you okay?" She frowned out of the screen at me. "We're registering multiple torpedo detonations. What's happening out there?"

"We're dusting the wrecks."

"In God's name why?"

"They're infested."

"Infested? You mean with the same things we found on the *Restless Itch*?"

"The very same."

"Oh." She tugged nervously at the brim of her faded baseball cap. "Oh, shit."

"And both of them have bite marks around their engine housings."

"So they were definitely attacked in the hypervoid?"

"Looks that way. Both of them hit amidships. Probably didn't even see what hit them."

Konstanz rubbed the bandage over her missing eye. "That's not good news."

"Certainly not for the crews."

"Or for us." She bit her lower lip. "I'd been kind of hoping the attack on your ship was a one-off, and that Bochnak was exaggerating the threat."

"No such luck."

"Yeah. We've travelled too far. The chances of this being the work of the same creature are pretty remote."

I rubbed my chin. "So, if there are two…?"

"There are probably more."

"Damn."

Konstanz gave a bitter laugh. "You can say that again." She sat back in her chair. "We've got the Fleet of Knives on one side and these things on the other." She pressed her

166

fists together, knuckle to knuckle. "And we're right in the middle, getting squeezed."

"What are we going to do?"

She looked at me from beneath the brim of her hat. "That's rather up to you."

"What do you mean?"

"The *Trouble Dog* strongly suspects the *Penitence* will choose to join the *Manticore* and fight the Fleet."

"Oh."

"Can you talk it around?"

I barely knew the ship. "I can try."

"Explain what you've found. I'll get *Trouble Dog* to send over everything Bochnak sent us on these creatures, and everything we have on what happened to the *Lucy's Ghost*. Maybe that'll be enough to change its mind."

SEVENTEEN

SAL KONSTANZ

After speaking to Schultz, I joined Nod in the cargo bay, where it had installed the alien printer.

"How soon can you get this running?"

Three of Nod's faces looked up at me, the little black pearls of its eyes shining in the overhead lights. "Not long. Much work, but not long."

"Are we talking hours or days?"

The petal-fingers around one of its faces shivered. Although not perfectly analogous to laughter, this was a gesture the Druff used to convey amusement. One of its other arms reached out and delicately tapped the machine's matt surface. An illuminated green triangle appeared where its petal made contact, and the whole contraption began to hum with power.

"Is done."

I opened and shut my mouth a couple of times. Had Nod just made a *joke*? I wasn't sure that had happened before. Its species was notorious for its cantankerous pragmatism rather than any detectable sense of playfulness.

Nod's sunflower faces beamed up at me now in all innocence. "Will fill with junk," it said. "First core printed in couple of hours."

"That's amazing, Nod." I reached out and pressed my

hand to its nearest face in a gentle high-five. "Thank you."

"Is easy. Have worked this tech before."

"Well, I appreciate it." I took a deep breath. "But now, wish me luck. I have to go and talk to a real asshole."

•

Captain Murphy's irritation was obvious from the way his lips pursed when he saw my face.

"Have you changed your mind about joining us?" he asked.

I smiled and shook my head. "Sorry, son. If I wanted to commit suicide, I'd have done it already."

His jaw tightened. I was embarrassing him in front of his crew.

"Then how can I help you?"

"You saw we went down to the surface?"

"We were monitoring you."

"Well, we found ourselves some power cores."

"Good for you." Murphy's eyes narrowed. Perhaps he was thinking of reprimanding the leader of his scavenger team for leaving a few behind. "How many?"

I let my smile twist into a wry grin. "You should have sent a Druff down with your troops, Captain."

"I don't understand. How many did you find?"

I spread my hands. "As many as we'll ever need. Enough for us and the civilian vessels to operate indefinitely."

Murphy sat back, evaluating me. He straightened the spotless white collar of his uniform.

"You only brought one shuttle up from the surface."

"That's correct."

"And yet you now claim to be in possession of an inexhaustible supply of power cores?"

"Also correct."

His cheeks flushed. "What kind of game are you playing?"

"No game, Captain." I leant towards the camera, hoping he

had a three-dimensional holographic display on his bridge, so my magnified face would be looming out of the wall at him. "Our engineer found an alien printer capable of producing useable power cores from miscellaneous junk. As long as we keep feeding it raw materials, we're now effectively self-sufficient for fuel."

"Bullshit."

"No, it's true." I removed my baseball cap and ran a hand back through my hair. "And we'll have enough for you, too. So the question you should be asking yourself is whether you're going to come with us and give your crew a shot at medium-term survival, or whether you're going to throw their lives away in a stupid, futile gesture that'll solve nothing except maybe satisfy your own stubborn pride?"

Murphy's mouth fell open. "What makes you think you can talk to me that way?"

"I've been in this situation before." I tapped a couple of controls, forwarding the *Trouble Dog's* recordings of our confrontation with Admiral Menderes at the Battle of the Gallery. "And as you'll see from the attached, it didn't work out too well for that guy." Faced with the admiral's determination to sacrifice his ship and crew in a vainglorious attack on the Marble Armada, the *Dog* had managed to put a single cannon round through the man's head while he stood on the bridge of his flagship, thus sparing his crew from certain death.

Murphy's eyes flicked sideways, reviewing the data. When the footage of the fatal shot came, he jerked in his seat. Some of the bluster drained from his face.

"That was you?"

"Yes."

"Are you threatening me, Captain Konstanz?"

"Do you want me to?"

Murphy rubbed his jaw and glanced around his bridge as if taking the temperature of the room. For the first time in this conversation, he seemed uncertain, and the reality of his youth began to bleed through the layers of training and authority with which he'd attempted to conceal it. He'd been preparing to lead his crew into the jaws of death, but now I'd revealed a second option, and they'd probably all heard me do it. If he were to retain their trust, he'd have to tread carefully. With the majority of the Conglomeration Navy reduced to smouldering wreckage, he had no chain of command to back him up—only the residual loyalty of a ship full of frightened, punch-drunk personnel.

"Unlimited fuel?"

"Yes."

"And you're serious about heading for a place of safety?"

"I am."

He puffed out his cheeks. Glanced around his bridge again. "I have a duty."

"You don't have a duty to anyone besides your crew. The navy's gone, and the surviving planetary populations won't care if you throw your life away on their behalf. They've got their own problems, and your death won't make any difference to those."

"What about the *Penitence*?"

"Oh, he's just doing what he thinks he should, same as you. But if you change your mind and come with us, I'm sure he'll tag along."

Murphy rubbed his jaw. "Can you give me a few minutes? I need to discuss this with my officers."

"Of course."

I killed the connection and climbed down to the *Trouble Dog's* galley, where I tried to fix myself a cup of tea using a teabag from my personal stash, but unthinkingly poured the kettle with my right hand, putting it in the blind spot created by the removal of my right eye. Scalding hot water spilled over the countertop and I cursed. It was only a minor spillage but it was one setback too many. A year ago, I'd been almost happy, despite losing Sedge. I'd been in the House for a couple of years and reconciled myself to a quiet life spent helping others—with long periods of solitude in which to sketch and read, and work through everything I'd seen during the war. But looking back now, I could see how ephemeral that tenuous contentment had been. And yet at the time, despite having both my eyes, I probably wouldn't have described myself as happy. We never know when we're living through the good times. It's only when everything turns to ashes and crap we realise how fortunate we really were.

I dried the counter as much as I felt able, tossed the hot, steaming cloth into the recycler and decided to take the tea back to my cabin. But halfway there, as I walked along the circular corridor ringing the ship's waist, a call came in from the *Manticore*. The *Trouble Dog* displayed it on the wall.

"Hello, Captain Murphy."

"Captain Konstanz."

"Have you reached a decision regarding my proposal?"

"We have."

"Are you joining us?"

Murphy's Adam's apple bobbed against his collar as he swallowed. "We are."

"And you'll submit to my authority as commodore of this little fleet?"

"Yes, ma'am. At least until such time as we recontact surviving elements of the Conglomeration Navy."

"Fair enough."

The young man's expression remained stoical, but I thought I saw relief in an almost imperceptible loosening of his shoulders and the way his eyes widened fractionally, just for a second. By bullying him to acquiescence, I had eased his burden.

"What's our first move, Commodore?"

I blew steam from my tea. "We'll have a full briefing at 1800 hours. All ship avatars and crew invited."

I saw his eyes flick to the side, checking the time. "And until then?"

"I'm going to drink my tea and review the data Bochnak sent us."

"Who's Bochnak?"

"He's a scientist. He was on board Sudak's flagship, and he managed to send us some information he'd pulled from its records."

"Anything useful?"

"Perhaps."

"What should we do?"

"Are you fully armed?"

"We are."

"Print more ammunition. Fill your cargo bay with spare rounds and scour the surface for whatever else you can find. This is going to be a long, protracted fight and we're going to need as much ordnance as we can get our hands on." I lowered my mug and looked him in the eye. "We've got dragons to slay."

EIGHTEEN

CORDELIA PA

I opened my eyes and flinched against the bright sunlight streaming in through the diaphanous white gauze curtains. I was sitting on the edge of a bed in a hotel room by the coast. I wore a pressure suit, but the helmet had been removed and lay on the carpet beside my booted feet like an upturned goldfish bowl. Beyond the window, a rich azure sea sweltered beneath a hot white sun, and I had to put up a hand to shade my eyes.

Across the room, my father lounged in a chair. His right ankle rested on his left knee and a champagne glass dangled from his fingers. He looked younger than he had the last time I'd seen him, on the frozen plateau. The grey flecks that had speckled his hair were gone and the wrinkles around his eyes seemed to have been smoothed away, as if by the patient thumbs of a long-suffering sculptor. He wore a loose cotton shirt and a pair of blue denim jeans, and his eyes were hidden behind mirrored sunglasses.

"Hello, Cordelia."

I gaped at him. "Dad?"

He shook his head, and I could see miniature reflections of my face in his lenses.

"Call me Nick."

"Nick?"

"It's my name." He gave a self-conscious smile. "One of them, anyway."

"I don't understand." I couldn't remember how I'd come to be there. One moment I'd been on the *Aunt*, trying to figure a way off the Plate, the next... "What's happening? Where are we?"

"We're inside the Intrusion."

"Inside..."

Nick tapped his temple with the middle finger of his right hand. "Aftershock." He looked apologetic. I frowned dubiously at the room's white walls and nondescript furniture.

"You're not dead?"

Nick uncrossed his legs. He bent forward and placed the empty champagne glass on the carpet. "So I'm told."

"And yet here you are."

"Here we both are."

I felt a sudden shiver of panic. "I'm trapped too?"

"No, child. I told you, we're both inside the Intrusion. This is..." He reached out and rapped his knuckles against the wall. "Just an illusion, like a simulation."

My gloved hands were resting on the coverlet. I squeezed two fistfuls of material. It felt real enough through the gloves.

"Why are we here?"

"Because the Intrusion wants me to talk to you."

"The Intrusion? About what?"

"About your talent for manipulating Plate technology." He took off his glasses, folded them, and slipped them into the chest pocket of his shirt. Now I could see his eyes, he had that middle-distance stare some of the older scavengers wore back on City Plate Two. It was the disengaged, inward look of a man with too much past and too little future; a man who had seen and done terrible, unconscionable things in the name of survival; a man who had borne witness to atrocities, who had gone toe-to-toe with death and thereby suffered an epiphany he would never be able to satisfactorily articulate, even to himself.

"The Intrusion's sentient," he said. "Its builders made it that way, to cover their retreat."

"The Hearthers?" To a child growing up on City Plate Two, the Hearthers had been figures of folklore, fading deities who had fashioned the twenty miniature worlds of the Plate system and then abandoned them to the ravages of time. I had lived and grown amongst the debris of their vanished civilisation, scraping a living scavenging trinkets from their empty buildings. If I had any interest in them as living beings it went only as far as trying to guess where they may have hidden their valuables or fixed their booby-traps. I got up and walked across to the window. The suit weighed on me like a guilty conscience. My boots left ridged treads in the carpet.

"We need you to be vigilant," Nick said behind me. "The Hearthers' ships turned on them, and drove them to create the Intrusion as a means of escape."

I pressed my face to the window. The pane chilled my nose and forehead. The hotel had been built on the edge of a promontory overlooking a rocky shoreline. Through the fog of my own breath, I could see a narrow strip of tough-looking grass, and the waves rising and falling against the rough barnacled teeth at the foot of the cliff.

"You're telling me this as if I can do something to stop the ships."

"Perhaps you can." He came and stood next to me, watching the gulls riding the updrafts above the lip of the cliff. "You need to find your brother."

"Mikey?"

Nick shook his head. "Mikey will be there when you need him. I've paid a scavenger named Doberman to deliver him to the place you'll need him most. He'll be there with you at the end. But right now, I'm talking about your other brother. His name is Lewis."

"I have another brother?" I felt my mind race with questions. Before I could ask, Nick held up a hand to shush me.

"Lewis lives on Cold Chapel," he said, "and has in his possession an artefact I gave him four years ago. You need to get it from him and take it back to the city."

"City Plate Two?"

"There's a room, set in a tower. You need to retrieve the artefact from Lewis and take it to that room."

"And then what?"

"Then I will have fulfilled my purpose. Can you do this, Cordelia? Can you do it for me?"

I bit my lip. The suit felt cumbersome and hot. "I wouldn't know how to start."

"We've sent somebody to help you."

"Who?"

"The woman you found." Nick smiled with one side of his face. "Also, I'm going to give you a present. This is a simulation. As long as we're in here, we're just software. So, I'm pasting all my flight experience, all my knowledge of captaining the *Gigolo Aunt*, into your memory."

"Wait, I'm not sure I want—"

He held up a hand. "It's my gift to you, and it'll be there when you wake."

"But, Dad…"

He took the elbow of my suit. "Call me Nick." He stepped up close and kissed my forehead. His lips felt as cold as the window.

"How much of your life have you already forgotten?" he asked. "Trust me, even if you're blessed with a reasonably functional memory, by the time you reach thirty there will be whole days, weeks and months of which you retain no conscious recollection. All those boring Sunday afternoons; all that stuff you learned at school; all those nights you lay awake thinking; all those books you read; all those people you used to know… They say we're the sum of our memories, Cordelia. But what happens when we forget?" He looked into my eyes. "When our memories are lost or taken from us, what remains? When we lose the things that make us who we are, who do we then become?"

"Nick, I—"

A woman entered the room. Like Nick, she wore blue jeans and a white shirt, but had covered them with an old tweed jacket, and had pinned up her long hair. She looked like a younger version of the woman we had recovered from the observatory.

"It's time," she said. Her eyes were full of stars.

Nick glanced at his wrist. "Already?"

"I'm afraid so."

The woman took me by the hands. Her fingers were as smooth and cool as marble. "I'm sorry to hurry you away," she said, "but it's time for you to go back."

"Who are you?"

The woman narrowed her eyes, as if trying to decide how much to disclose. "When I had a name," she said at last, "it was Sofia."

"*When* you had a name?"

"I no longer need one." Her lips were the colour of night; her skin the sallow hue of old wax. She led me over to the bed and bade me sit. "But now the time for questions is past; now all that matters are deeds. In a moment you will fall asleep. When you wake, you will go to Cold Chapel. You will retrieve the key."

"What key?"

Sofia's eyes were a warm summer's night. The wind moved and the curtains stirred in time to the rise and fall of her chest. She was the focus of the world. The room, the sky and the sea were hers to control.

"Are you part of the Intrusion?" I blurted. Sofia looked down fondly and put a hand to my hair.

"Child, I *am* the Intrusion."

179

NINETEEN

SAL KONSTANZ

I had joined the House of Reclamation out of a sincere desire to make the universe a better place. Recriminations and grief followed the Archipelago War, with blame on all sides. I spent nights awake, crying impotent tears, overwhelmed by the enormity of it all, my insides twisted into knots of sick, helpless anger. Terrible wrongs had been perpetrated in our names, and now couldn't be undone. And, with the exception of a few scapegoats, those responsible would largely escape retribution for the decisions that had thrown the Human Generality into its worst and bloodiest civil conflict. I watched anger and bitterness eat up friends. The best minds of my generation were consumed by madness. They raged at each other on the communication nets, using quotes from Ona Sudak's poems to express their existential fury at the unfairness of it all. And for a time, I was one of them. I didn't know what else to do. In the aftermath of such murderous stupidity, I felt helpless. I hadn't wanted the war, I hadn't voted for it. More than a billion people had died in the conflict, and yet nothing much had been decided. The Conglomeration and the Outward still cleaved to their respective ideologies; the extent of their respective territories remained largely unchanged; and their various antagonisms still simmered beneath all the half-hearted diplomacy and talk of reconstruction. Had we been through that attritional nightmare of self-destruction for nothing? Had we fought and suffered and died simply to prove a political point?

In my helpless resentment, I had felt unable to continue wearing the uniform of the Outward Navy. Although I had commanded a medical frigate, I had seen first-hand what happened when men and women surrendered their individuality to the state—when they allowed themselves to become pawns in someone else's game. And so I resigned. I joined the demobilised personnel who stood in the cold night wind beneath the lights of every spaceport, wondering whether they could face going home to their old lives after enduring so many years of dehumanising violence. Alva Clay decided to come with me—but I had no inkling of where we would go or what we would do, until I chanced to meet George Walker in a favela tea shack on the edge of a desert, on a backwater planet whose name I can't remember even now.

"Come to Camrose," he said. "Enlist in the House. That's what we did."

"Who are 'we'?"

He smiled. He had grey hair and kind eyes. "Me and the ship. You might have heard of her."

"What's her name?"

"*Trouble Dog*."

"I can't say I have."

"She's a Conglomeration Carnivore. She fought at the Battle of Pelapatarn."

"A lot of ships fought at Pelapatarn."

"Yes, but she's the first one to resign."

I blinked. "She resigned?" I'd never heard of a warship doing such a thing. Sometimes they went nuts and had to be retired, but none had ever simply downed tools before.

George smiled, causing the skin around his eyes to

crinkle. "Yes. I think she's growing a conscience."

"And the Conglomeration simply let her walk away?"

"Short of destroying her, there wasn't much they could do. She agreed to let them remove her heavier weapons, and then we left."

"To join the House of Reclamation?"

"Yes." His expression grew serious. "And you should come with us."

"Me?"

Our ceramic teacups sat on the brass counter before us, cooling and forgotten.

"Do you have anything better to do?"

I knew of the House, of course. Everybody knew of them. But I'd never thought of joining them. To do so was to renounce all previous ties of nationality and loyalty, and instead pledge your allegiance to the well-being of travellers from all the splintered factions of the Generality. I thought of my dead parents, my vanished lover. I thought of the shame and disgust I felt towards my government.

"I guess not."

"Then it's decided." George's gnarled hand squeezed my shoulder, and I felt something break inside, the way the clouds break after a storm, allowing through shafts of sunlight. I knew then I'd made the right decision. I would shed the resentment that threatened to overwhelm me and take positive action. I was going to exchange impotence for altruism, conflict for kindness, and actually start making a difference in this battered and fucked-up galaxy.

•

I thought of that moment now, as our little flotilla hung in orbit around Variance, waiting for Nod's printer to provide the fuel we needed. I had gathered representatives from all five vessels in the *Trouble Dog*'s briefing room. Built to accommodate three hundred, it was more than roomy enough for our purposes.

Murphy had sent his first officer, Bronte Okonkwo. She was a stiff, intense, dark-skinned young woman whose gaze burned with disapproval and distrust. I guessed she'd been a career officer before the Fleet of Knives turned on us, and was now struggling to adjust. Upheavals are always hardest on the kind of people who meticulously plan their lives.

Riley Addison was also here in person, representing the *Penitence*, as were crewmembers from the *Northern Boy* and the *Unrestrained Curiosity*. The ships' captains remained on their bridges, joining us as blue-tinged holograms.

I stood at the front. The screen behind me displayed a stock image of the Intrusion. Spiral arms of glowing gas streamed from its irregular, constantly shifting edges. At the centre lay a rip in the skein of the universe, a hole through which could be glimpsed the distorted, ethereal light of impossible stars.

"We don't know exactly what the Intrusion is," I began. "All we know is that firstly, the Hearthers used it to flee from this region of space almost five thousand years ago." I paused, looking around the room at the tired faces of those present—faces that had borne witness to the brutal dismemberment of their interstellar civilisation and were now waiting for me to offer them a shred of hope. "And secondly, that there's something about the Intrusion that causes both the Marble Armada and these higher dimensional dragons to give it a wide berth."

Bronte Okonkwo looked as if something had offended her sense of smell. "Somewhere to hide," she said. "That's your big plan?"

"There's more to it than that." I couldn't keep the irritation from my voice. With her crisp uniform and constant air of distaste, Okonkwo represented everything I'd joined the House to escape.

"There had better be."

Sensing the tension, Riley Addison raised her hand. "The Multiplicity's a big place," she said. "Surely we could just take refuge in one of the alien territories?"

"We could. But I want to do more than simply hide. I want to find out what it is about the Intrusion that scares both the white ships and the Scourers, and then see if we can use it to our advantage."

Okonkwo put a hand to her chin. "You mean, find a way to weaponise it?"

"If possible, yes."

She gave a nod of approval. "Now," she said, "*that* makes more sense."

"I'm so glad you agree."

Her lip curled. "Don't get too carried away, *Commodore*. I still dispute your fitness to lead this expedition."

"Oh, really?" I took off my baseball cap and laid it on the lectern. "Well, let me remind you I've got two Carnivores behind me, plus an inexhaustible supply of fuel. And all you've got is a Gecko, and a pole up your ass."

Silence fell over the room. Not even Murphy dared interrupt. The civilians looked uncomfortable. Schultz smirked.

Okonkwo's glare could have frozen vacuum. If she'd had a sidearm, I think she might have used it on me. However, before she could give me her response, the avatars of both the *Trouble Dog* and the *Penitence* stiffened. A split second later so did the *Manticore*'s.

"Incoming," *Trouble Dog* said. "Five knife ships."

"ETA?"

"Four minutes."

"Damn it." I scooped up the hat and jammed it onto my head. "What's the fuel situation?"

"Both civilian vessels fully fuelled. *Penitence* and *Manticore* awaiting restock."

I looked at Murphy's hologram. "Do you have enough to move?"

His jaw tightened. "We have enough to fight."

"You won't stand a chance."

"Nevertheless." He sat up straighter in his chair. "Our duty is clear. We'll cover your retreat while you get the civilians to safety."

I shook my head. "There are five of them. You can't face them alone."

"He won't have to." Schultz rubbed the back of his neck. "Because I'll be with him."

Riley Addison leapt from her chair. "No!"

Schultz looked pained. "I'm sorry," he said. "It can't be helped. We don't have enough fuel, either. We'll stay and do what we can."

Addison reached out for him, but her hand passed through the hologram.

"I'm sorry," he said. "But this is where I stop running. I'm sending Lucy over to you in a shuttle. Take care of her for me."

"No!"

The *Trouble Dog* activated her acceleration alarm. "Contact in three minutes. Message coming in from the lead ship."

"Put it on screen," I said.

"Aye."

The main screen at the front of the briefing room flickered to life, displaying the face of a middle-aged woman with short-cropped hair that had greyed at the temples.

"Sudak."

"Greetings, Captain." Her voice still held the lyrical cadence I remembered from the poetry recitals that had been broadcast across the Generality in the years after the war, before anyone came to realise her true identity as Annelida Deal, the Butcher of Pelapatarn.

"I suppose you're here to demand our surrender?"

"Not this time, I'm afraid." The older woman smiled with false regret. "We're aware you're heading for the Intrusion, and that can't be allowed."

I stared into her eyes, refusing to be intimidated. "You're worried, aren't you?"

Sudak adjusted her position. "Why in heaven's name would I be worried? I have you vastly outnumbered and outgunned. Nothing you could do could ever endanger our purpose."

"You're worried because you don't want us reaching the Intrusion. You're worried what we might find there."

"Don't be ridiculous."

"No, I'm right, aren't I?" I wagged a finger at the screen. "Your white ships don't want us finding out what became of their former masters."

"You don't understand what you're talking about."

"Don't I?"

Sudak's cheeks flushed. "I'm going to enjoy killing you."

"You'll have to catch us first."

I drew my finger across my throat and the *Trouble Dog* killed the transmission.

Okonkwo caught my arm. "I have to get back to my ship." Her grip was painful.

"There isn't time."

"But…"

I pushed her towards a chair. "Strap in, all of you."

"Forty-five seconds," said the *Trouble Dog*. "Lucy's shuttle is aboard."

The deck trembled as the *Dog*'s main engines came online. Her avatar looked to me for the order to flee. In the corner of my eye, I could see Addison, Schultz and Murphy staring. I didn't dare acknowledge them. Instead, I coughed to clear my throat.

"Get us out of here," I said.

TWENTY

TROUBLE DOG

The five knife ships dropped from the higher dimensions less than fifty kilometres from our little convoy. They came in at us like hawks diving at a flock of doves. I was already accelerating away in the opposite direction, with the *Northern Boy* and *Unrestrained Curiosity* scrambling in my wake. *Penitence* and *Manticore* turned to confront the approaching threat, positioning themselves between the oncoming storm and the civilian ships. Torpedoes flew from their launchers. Defensive batteries fired streams of tungsten projectiles. Energy weapons crackled in the darkness.

Drawing away, I began to oscillate in preparation for the jump into the hypervoid.

With only a couple of seconds remaining, I received a transmission from the *Penitence*.

I met him in a virtual environment. It was a Parisian café, filled with chatter and steam, and the rattle of china. He appeared in his black robe with his pale, bony wrists poking from his sleeves and his eyes like dark, roiling nebulae. Only a second remained, but he'd set the speed of the simulation high enough that even a second in the external universe would feel like an hour in here.

"I suppose this is goodbye," he said, taking a seat at a corner table.

I didn't know how to respond. We'd been through the war together. We'd lost siblings before, but somehow this felt different. Perhaps it was because he was the last of my brothers and sisters. Perhaps it was because I had changed. Whatever the reason, I felt his impending loss as an almost physical pain. If I'd had a heart, it would have been breaking.

I slipped into the booth opposite him. "I suppose it is."

The café's other patrons were shadows, figures made of smoke. Only we appeared to possess any real substance. *Penitence* tapped a thin finger against the table. "I just wanted to reiterate how sorry I am for all that happened between us."

I waved away his apology. "Don't give it a thought."

He had always been there. We had been cultivated and educated in the same nursery. We had flown together, fighting side by side with our siblings. The canine DNA in our make-up enhanced our loyalty to each other, and made us a pack. And he had been the head of that pack. He had been my leader and my brother through most of the fifteen years of my existence, and even though he had led me into fire and atrocity, and ultimately betrayed me at the Gallery, my feelings for him remained undiminished.

"And I wanted to thank you," he said.

"For what?"

He pulled his robe around his thin frame. "For not turning me away. For giving me the chance to die with my honour regained."

I bit my lip. I wanted to slap the table. But I could see how sincere he was. Before the Marble Armada turned against us, he'd been facing a dishonourable discharge. A court martial would have placed his consciousness in a virtual prison, and never let him fly again. His name would have been scrubbed from the records, his deeds forgotten, his memory cursed. But now, with the Generality falling around us, he'd found a new purpose and a new perspective. Instead of languishing in infamy, he was out here among the stars he loved so well, fulfilling the function for which he'd been designed—and saving lives in the process.

"And how can man die better," I quoted, "than facing fearful odds, for the ashes of his fathers, and the temples of his gods?"

Penitence cocked his head. "What's that?"

"It's from a poem by Macaulay. My former medic, George Walker, used to read it to me all the time."

"But what does it mean?"

I shrugged. "I guess it means I understand why this is important to you."

Penitence considered this for a moment. Then he rose to his feet and flicked a bronze coin onto the table, as payment for the refreshments we hadn't ordered.

"Goodbye, my sister."

"Goodbye, *Penitence*." I stood and embraced him. He felt like a sack of bones. "Goodbye, *Adalwolf*." I kissed his porcelain cheek. "And thank you."

TWENTY-ONE

JOHNNY SCHULTZ

I watched the *Trouble Dog* and the two civilian vessels wink out of the universe, and felt something ease in my gut. Whatever happened over the next few minutes, Addison and Lucy were safe. My strange little family would live to fight another day.

I, on the other hand…

The tactical screens were filled with threats. I saw the *Manticore* sliced in half by an energy beam—although, miraculously, the front half continued to fire on the encroaching white ships.

The *Penitence* shuddered as its defensive batteries kept up a constant barrage, sweeping away incoming missiles. But there could be no defence against that energy beam.

"Mr Schultz?"

"Yes, ship?"

"The others are safe."

"I know."

"Our work here is almost done. But I'm afraid we can't retreat. To turn our backs now would only hasten our destruction."

I gripped the edge of the captain's chair. Although I'd been prepared to die to ensure the safety of my girls, it wasn't a pleasant experience to hear we had no other choice.

A torpedo went off at extreme range. We were close enough to avoid the nuclear fireball, but the blast wave shook the ship and set off the radiation alarms.

I tried to swallow but my throat was dry.

"Okay," I said, trying to keep my voice level. "Let's take as many of the bastards with us as we can."

The *Penitence*'s avatar smiled, revealing shining white vampire teeth. "Oh," he said, "I intend to."

Without warning, the thrust kicked in and we surged forward, directly at the enemy. I guess it must have been the last thing they were expecting, because all their first shots went wide. *Penitence* responded by launching all his remaining stock of torpedoes. He was giving it everything, even switching his cannons from defensive to offensive targeting. But we both knew we weren't going to last much longer.

"Mr Schultz?"

"Yes, ship?"

The avatar had changed out of his usual robes and was now wearing a black shirt under a silk waistcoat and dress jacket. "I've done a lot of things in my life," he said, "some I'm no longer proud of."

I remembered all the scams and hustles I'd pulled, the people I'd screwed over to become "Lucky" Johnny Schultz. "I think we can all say that."

Fresh explosions blossomed. Half the cameras on our port side died.

"But this thing we're doing now," the ship said, and he seemed to stand a little straighter. "I think this is the best thing I've ever done."

My eyes pricked with tears. "I think that goes for both of us."

The avatar stood to attention and gave a crisp salute. "It's been an honour serving with you."

I touched a finger to my forehead in response. I could feel the sobs coming now. I swallowed again, trying to force them back down into my chest. I fought to keep my voice from cracking.

"And y—"

///TRANSMISSION ENDS

TWENTY-TWO

CORDELIA PA

I awoke in my father's cabin. I had been dreaming about the Intrusion. For a few moments, I drowsed, listening to the now-familiar clanks and groans of the *Gigolo Aunt*. From the way the deck lay still, I could tell we remained stuck on the frozen Plate, with the ship's black wings folded against her hull rather than clawing at the hypervoid.

My head ached and my memories felt cobwebby and jumbled, like notes scrawled in an unfamiliar hand. Behind them, I had the sense of another mind, the liminal echoes of somebody else's interior monologue.

I'm pasting all my flight experience, all my knowledge of captaining the Gigolo Aunt, *into your memory…*

I propped myself up on my elbows. All that had been a dream, hadn't it? But then, why was I wearing a pressure suit? The bulky garment encased me from boots to collar, leaving only my hands and head free. While I had been sleeping, someone had detached my gauntlets and helmet from their metal rings at wrists and neck, and dumped them untidily onto the nightstand beside my bunk. The crystal reader lay next to them, but the crystal containing my father's mind–map was gone.

Swallowed…

Moving carefully, I swung my feet down onto the floor and tried to take off the suit. Velcro patches secured the zip at the side. I ripped them open and pulled down the fastener, then shrugged my arms out of their sleeves. However, I couldn't get my legs out while the metal neck ring remained, and I couldn't get that off without pulling it over my head, which was impossible with my feet still in the suit. I'd never worn a pressure suit before, and therefore had no idea of the correct way to get the thing off. I had to stand up and improvise. After a lot of wriggling and cursing, I managed to angle a hip far enough through the open zipper that I was able to prise the neck ring up and over my head, and emerged tousle-haired from the back of the suit like a dragonfly bursting from the ruptured seams of its larval skin. Sitting on the bed, I kicked my feet free. Beneath the suit, I wore my shipboard fatigues. I brushed them down with my hand, smoothing out the creases, and regarded myself in the dirty mirror above the cabin's steel washbasin. My hair looked as white as ever, and my eyes just as mismatched. Beneath the cabin's buttery lights, even the skin on my hands appeared faultlessly normal.

Had I really fallen into the Intrusion?

I climbed the ladder out of the cabin, and found Lomax on the *Gigolo Aunt*'s bridge. The older woman was asleep in the pilot's couch, hunched over the control console with her cheek resting on her fist. The main lights were off and the scrolling reflections of the screens flickered across her features like the lambent glow of a campfire. Without making a sound, and without knowing quite why I did it, I slipped into the co-pilot's berth and wriggled down as if snuggling under a pile of heaped animal skins. The bridge felt like home. I knew the placement and function of each and every light and screen, the location of every scuff and scratch. Answers could wait. Right now, I was warm and safe, and content to lie there in the wavering, cave-like shadows, watching the light play across the planes of Lomax's face.

•

I must have dozed, because when I next opened my eyes, Lomax was watching me in the semi-darkness.

"Are you okay?"

I stretched and yawned. "I think so."

"No ill effects, no dizziness?"

"Nothing. Why?"

"We got caught in an aftershock. Reality turned weird for a few minutes."

"Ah, that explains it."

"What?"

"I was dreaming about my father and the Intrusion. At least, I think it was a dream..." I inclined my head, listening in vain for the squeaks and strains of the ship's machinery. "We're still grounded?"

Lomax's brow puckered. "Yes, that's right."

"But we made it through the aftershock okay?"

"By the hair of our pelts." Lomax held up her hand, finger and thumb spaced less than a centimetre apart. "That was a nasty one."

"How's the woman we found?"

"Unchanged—she's still unconscious. No sign of waking."

"What are we going to do?"

"Brof and Spider have been working on the engines. Gant reckons we might be underway in a few hours, unless there are further shocks."

"Where are we going?"

"Cold Chapel."

The blood turned icy in my arteries. "Cold Chapel?"

"The coordinates are already loaded into the navigational array. I assumed you'd done it."

"My father wants me to…" I trailed off. There was something I had to do, someone I had to confront.

Lomax frowned. "Nick wants you to do something?"

"Yeah, I spoke to him." My memories were a blizzard of disjointed shards, but some of those shards were colliding and sticking, clumping together in a slow accretion of sense and meaning. "And he wants me to find his… son."

"Lewis?" Lomax looked concerned. "Was this part of your dream?"

I shook my head. "No, this is real. I didn't know about Lewis, so how could I have dreamt about him? I don't know how or why, but this is real." I lay back. My short white hair flattened against the headrest. The tips of my fingers prickled. "Apparently, he has something I need."

•

Falling from the mist, the *Gigolo Aunt* erupted from the hypervoid a quarter of a million miles above Cold Chapel. For a couple of beats, her black mesh wings raked the vacuum. Then, finding no traction, they furled themselves tightly against the hull. The fusion motors at the stern coughed into full voice, and the old ship surged forward.

On the bridge, I considered the limb of the planet below. As its name suggested, Cold Chapel was a bleak and uninviting world—a world of jagged mountain crags and shallow, brackish seas—barely more hospitable than the frozen Plate whose snow we'd shaken from our landing gear a few hours before. The first humans to reach it had been the crew of the *Widening Gyre*, an asteroid-sized lump of rock and machinery still tumbling in orbit around the planet. Cold Chapel was a frontier world, on the bleeding edge of the Intrusion, its settlers locked in relentless conflict with an evaporating atmosphere and encroaching ice age, wholly dependent on trading ships like the *Gigolo Aunt* for even the most basic of supplies.

I knew all this, and yet I should not have. The information was there in my memory, but it came with flashes of emotion and broken association that weren't mine, that hurt my head and fired off as many questions as they answered. I had never been to Cold Chapel yet I recognised the planet; I remembered nights in a log cabin on one of the ridgeback peaks, the smell of the imported pine trees, the sigh of the dawn wind. I remembered the teeth-aching shock of the cold spring water where it bubbled up between the rocks, the call of buzzards circling over the valley.

The sight of the *Widening Gyre* brought claustrophobic snapshots of roughly hewn corridors and dancing flames, of extreme cold and suffocation.

These weren't my memories, I knew; these were the memories and sensations of an insane old man who'd somehow hacked them out of his own brain and installed them in mine. And the worst part was, even I wasn't sure where the boundary lay. Some of my earliest memories seemed to have been overwritten by the imported ones. I could no longer remember what my house on Alpha Plate had looked like, or the shuttle ride to City Plate Two, the only time I'd been off-Plate until I stepped aboard the *Gigolo Aunt* a decade later. How much of what was going on in my head now was me? I tried to focus on my earliest memory...

•

A six-year-old girl plays in an alley between two tall and ancient apartment blocks. She has a ratty old blanket wrapped around her shoulders. Her uncle is out, hustling the bars on the port's periphery, playing for coins, looking for work. Her half-brother is asleep upstairs, in one of the small rooms the three of them share.

The girl's name is Cordelia, and she can do magic. With a wave of her tingling fingertips she can conjure playthings from the alley's floor. Small stick figures—living dolls, real toy soldiers—extrude themselves at her bidding, rising up like plants bursting from soil. She hunches over them in wide-eyed delight. They are her puppets, and they ebb and flow to the vagaries of her six-year-old whims.

In a few years, she will have suppressed her strange ability to mould and sculpt the metal that forms the surface of her world, and she will have convinced herself that the little figures capering before her now are nothing more than the products of an overactive child's imagination; but, for the moment, she's content to squat here, draped in her blanket, and watch them dance.

•

How much of my life had I forgotten? I tried to name some of the kids I'd grown up with around the fringes of the port, but could only come up with half a dozen, and some of those I was sure belonged to children my father had known in his youth. I was only supposed to have his knowledge of flying the *Aunt*, but it seemed other memories had bled through, caught in the grey area between what he did and who he was.

I thought about what Nick had said in the Intrusion. If it's true that we are the sum of our memories, that the remembrances of things past shape our very personalities, what happens, I wondered, when we forget? When our memories are lost or taken from us, what remains? When new memories are implanted and the things that make us who we are become changed, who then do we become?

Was I still me?

•

The *Gigolo Aunt* groaned as it hit the first wisps of atmosphere, somewhere above the planet's equator. In the co-pilot's chair, I felt every jolt and dip of the old craft's fiery descent. On one level, the experience seemed routine, as if I'd carved a thousand smoky trails through a thousand alien skies; on another, it was still a relatively new and unsettling ordeal. To a girl raised on the Plates, the buffeting, juddering ride through a planet's atmosphere always felt like the prelude to a crash.

"This is normal," I kept repeating under my breath, hands gripping the armrests of my couch, realising as I said it that I'd been here and done this all before, time and time again, in another life.

For a giddy instant, as the ship bucked and swayed, I fell away and was Nick Moriarty. My hands—so thin and girlish to his eyes—reached forward, palms itching to caress the controls, to make the elderly ship leap and dance to my touch.

Then suddenly we were through the worst of it, and I returned. The sky cleared to a crisp blue flecked with thumb smudges of grey and white. The land rolled beneath us like a relief map. Even though I'd lived my entire childhood confined to the globe-lit gloom of the Plates, the vast, airy vault looked so achingly familiar it took my breath away.

From the pilot's station, Lomax gave a sideways look. "Are you all right, kid? Not feeling ill?"

"I'm fine."

The hull pinged and ticked as it cooled in the high-altitude air.

"You look a bit pale. If you're going to hurl, do it someplace else, okay?"

"I said I'm fine."

"Are you sure? Because—"

"I said I was fine, Tess. Now why don't you stop fussing and keep your eyes on the damn road?"

I clapped my hands over my mouth. I had spoken, but the words had not been mine.

"*What* did you say?"

"I'm sorry, I don't know where that came from."

"You sounded…"

"Like my father?" I swallowed, fighting the urge to gabble. "I know, and I'm so sorry, I didn't mean it."

Lomax clenched her jaw. "Just don't ever call me Tess," she growled. Her voice dropped to a murmur. "Nobody calls me that. Only Nick. He was the only one."

I felt my cheeks redden. "I won't do it again," I said, "I promise."

Lomax turned back to her console. "See that you don't." She rolled her eyes as if to say, *I wish to hell I'd never taken this stupid job.*

Ahead, the spaceport loomed out of the landscape—a long strip of runway on a floodplain sandwiched between sharp, snow-capped mountains on one side and a stark, rocky shoreline on the other.

•

Sometimes, I thought as I followed Lomax through the heavy steel doors of the downport tavern, the more you knew about where you were, the less you knew about who you were, and vice versa.

The tavern had been built into a low, sturdy bunker on the edge of the landing field. Much to Spider's annoyance, we had left him standing outside, huddled in his coat, cradling his Hooper gun and muttering obscenities into the wind. If we ran into anything we couldn't handle by ourselves, we could summon him with a word.

Inside, the room had been laid out in the traditional fashion. The parts of my brain that were running Nick Moriarty's old memories recognised it as kin to a hundred other similar dives. For some reason, bars adjacent to airports, railway stations and bus terminals were always the same; they always had the same smell, the same clientele, and that went double for starports. The wastrels clogging up this particular sinkhole were little different to the burned-out scavengers loitering in the taverns at the edge of my home

Plate. They resembled the ghosts of long-dead passengers, forever awaiting a train they had already missed. They had been beaten down by life on the periphery, stranded by their own indolence and enervation, the perpetual inhabitants of a transitory landscape. I recognised this in them because I also recognised it in myself. I had spent my young life scrabbling in the margins, and would still be doing so had the *Gigolo Aunt* not dropped from the void and snatched me away.

Nobody turned to look as Lomax and I made our way to the counter. The drinkers sat hunched over their regrets, unable to make eye contact with anybody, even their own reflections in the mirror behind the bar. An overhead fan stirred the fetid air. A metal spear had been fixed to the wall above the mirror. Indigenous feathered rodents the size of my thumb fussed and skittered beneath the tables, bickering over spilled beer and peanut husks.

Lomax tapped a credit disk on the wooden counter. When the barman looked up from the pornographic tattoos on his forearms, she held up two fingers. "*Dos cervezas.*"

He looked her up and down, and his eyes settled on the credit disk in her hand. He shrugged and rubbed the bristles on his unshaven chin. With every movement seemingly designed to convey his contempt and disinclination, he retrieved a brace of bottles from a plastic crate beside the refrigerator and clonked them onto the counter.

I reached for one, but Lomax caught my sleeve. "These are warm," she said.

The barman shrugged again, as if to say the temperature of the drinks was the least of his concerns. He reached for the money, but Lomax held it back. "You can speak, can't you?"

"*Si.*"

"Good, because we're looking for somebody."

The man's eyes narrowed. "Try somewhere else."

"We did. They said to come here."

"Then I can't help you." His eyes were still on the disk. Lomax kept it just out of his reach. She spoke in a low, hoarse whisper.

"I think you can." She leant forward across the wooden bar, resting her weight on the heels of her hands. "We're looking for a guy called Lewis Pembroke. He's a friend."

"I don't know him."

"I've heard otherwise."

The man glanced at me, taking in my platinum crop and mismatched eyes. He sniffed and spat onto the floor. "If he's such a great friend of yours, ladies, how come you don't know where he lives?"

"I'm a friend of his father. I've never been to his place."

"Then why don't you just send him a message?"

"I did." Lomax pushed herself back into an upright position. We had tried the planet's rudimentary social network, but Lewis hadn't responded to our requests for a meeting.

"So," the barman picked at a canine with the nail of his little finger, "why are you bothering me?"

"We're in something of a hurry."

The barman grinned, revealing more gold teeth. "Then I'm afraid you're kind of screwed, ladies." He moved away to serve a customer at the far end of the bar. Lomax scowled after him.

"Asshole."

I wasn't paying attention. I looked down at my open hands and rubbed the tips of my index fingers against the pads of my thumbs.

Lomax frowned. "What are you doing?"

"I'm not sure…" The skin itched. In the back of my skull, above the desultory rattle of the ceiling fan, I heard the voices of the Plates. The tingling in my fingers grew worse, and I became terrified they might start to glow again. I clenched them into fists and stuffed them into the pockets of my ship fatigues. Still the voice called in short, incomprehensible beseechments, its pitch lone and plaintive like the cry of a lost hunting hawk seeking its master.

On the wall above the mirror, the metal spear began to rattle against the clips holding it in place. The barman turned to look at it. The other drinkers fell silent.

"What the—?"

For a few seconds, the only sounds in the room were the squeak of the overhead fan and the jangle of the weapon in its mount.

"Come on," I said, tugging Lomax's sleeve. "We have to leave."

The older woman gave me a curious look but didn't argue. Once outside, she asked, "What was that all about?"

I withdrew my hands from my pockets. The ends of my fingers smouldered.

"The spear," I said.

Lomax took a step backwards. Her hand went to the gun at her hip. "How are you doing that?"

"I don't know."

"Has it happened before?"

"Once, in the Burrow, when you found us." I thought of the alley that ran alongside my uncle's building, of the little toy figures I used to conjure from the fabric of the Plates. "Maybe more than once," I admitted.

Slowly, Lomax moved her hand away from her holster. "Does it hurt?"

I flexed my hands. "It prickles."

Spider sidled up to us, Hooper gun over one shoulder. His dreadlocks brushed the collar of his long coat. The coat's frayed hem flapped around his ankles.

"What's happening, fam?" His eyes were on the street, not us.

"Cordelia's sensitive."

"No shit."

207

Lomax scowled. Her voice dropped to a harsh whisper. "No, idiot. I mean she's *sensitive*."

Spider hooked a sceptical eyebrow. "What, like she can sense artefacts and shit?"

"More than that. I think she can interact with them."

"No way."

Lomax jerked a thumb at the door of the bar. "There was a Hearther spear on the wall in there. She made it dance."

For the first time, Spider looked directly at me. His brown eyes drank me in from head to toe, and he frowned. "What are we going to do with her?"

Lomax put an arm around my shoulders. "We're going to get her out of here before anybody gets any bright ideas."

I squirmed against her embrace. "What kind of ideas?" I asked. "What are you talking about?"

Lomax looked down at me with pitying eyes. "Your father was sensitive too. Not as much as you, maybe, but he had a nose for Hearther tech. He could tell a forgery from a genuine artefact at a hundred paces."

"So?"

"So, people with your talent are valuable. Valuable enough to make kidnapping a very real possibility."

I flushed. "But I don't have a talent." I held out my palms. "I don't even know what this is."

Yes you do. Nick Moriarty's voice whispered in my head like the sound of waves on a half-remembered beach. *You've known it all your life. You've heard the song of the Plates, felt their material beneath your feet; lived and breathed your days in the hollow spaces of the empty city; used your intuition to locate artefacts amidst the ruins, just often enough to keep you and your family in food...*

I put my knuckles to my temples. "Stop it."

You have ability, Cordelia; you just choose to ignore it.

"Shut up. You don't know me."

Lomax and Spider were staring at me, unsure how to react.

Ah, but I do. I know you better than anybody, better even than you know yourself.

"How could you?"

Because I helped the Intrusion build you.

•

"How are you going to find him without an address?" Spider gave the town a wary squint.

Lomax inclined her head in my direction. "We found this one, didn't we?"

"Yeah, eventually. But we were poking around for hours trying to track her down."

I waved at them to be quiet. I was listening to other voices—faint, faraway and alien. Squeezing my eyes closed, I turned in a slow circle.

"There." My eyes opened and my hand came up to point. "That way."

The other two watched as I turned up the fur-lined hood of my coat and started walking, tramping off into the cold, rocky night.

"Come on," I said.

The words I was hearing in my head were untranslatable, but nonetheless familiar. From somewhere in this settlement, ancient Plate artefacts were calling—and Nick Moriarty's memories were telling me of the gifts he'd brought for Lewis over the years. The boy lacked Cordelia's talent, so wouldn't be left the ship; instead, Nick had brought souvenirs and trinkets from the Plates in order to secure the financial future of his one and only male heir, curios and sculptures skimmed from shipments to universities and institutes on a dozen worlds.

"I hear them," I called back over my shoulder, breath fogging, not caring if my words were understood. "If we find them, we'll find him."

Without waiting for Lomax and Spider to catch up, I

209

marched through the tangled streets of the bleak encampment, only hesitating momentarily at intersections as I tried to hone down the source of the voices. Spider and Lomax tailed along behind like bodyguards, their weapons sweeping every doorway and shadow for possible threats. I could be of no use to them if I was snatched and pressed into service as a kind of human Geiger counter, my talent clicking with the potential value of each scavenged object.

As I walked, I dug my fingernails into my palms. I'd never been this angry in my life.

I helped the Intrusion build you, my father had said, his tone flat and matter-of-fact as if such a revelation meant almost nothing.

I did a deal, he told me now, trying to explain. *Years ago, before you were born, I fell into the Intrusion. The Hearthers left a lot of stuff in there. Weapons and such, to stop their creations following them. An intelligence. It offered me my life, and in return, I let it engineer my sperm.*

"But why? Why would you do that?"

Those were the terms of the deal. I felt rather than heard him sigh. When he spoke again, he sounded tired. *It was trying to create a human compatible with Plate-builder technology.*

"And so you helped it make me?"

It knew I was "sensitive", so it jammed my testicles with genes harvested from a thousand others with similar talents. In return for a second chance, all I had to do was impregnate a woman who lived on the Plates, and then, once you were born, leave you there until you reached adulthood.

"That was part of the deal was it, that you had to abandon me?"

The Intrusion thought you should be immersed in that environment, and surrounded by that technology, in order for the enhanced genetic trait to come to the fore. In order to maximise your potential, it felt you needed to be in close proximity with the Plates, from conception onwards. It couldn't fabricate that connection; it needed to be forged over years and decades.

"What about Lewis? You stayed in contact with him."

He's my son.

"I'm your daughter."

In some senses, you have a thousand parents.

There were few people on the street. My hurt and anger must have shown in my expression, as those I passed crossed the road to avoid me. "Is that why you looked after him and not me?"

I tried to give your mother money, but she wouldn't accept it. And I admit, once she died, I dropped the ball. I could have sent Caleb funds, but I was worried he'd just spend them on drink.

"Did my mother know?"

Of course not.

"So, you just bred me and waved goodbye."

It wasn't like that. I did what I could. You had the talent as a little kid, although it faded as you grew older. But later, when you started scavenging, you developed a knack of finding things. Your talent began to re-emerge.

"I didn't find much." I saw my reflection in a shop window: fur-lined coat; a tousled shock of white hair; a freak arguing with herself.

You found enough to stop you starving.

"No thanks to you."

No.

"You said you wanted to give me the *Gigolo Aunt* to make up for abandoning me, but it's more than that, isn't it?"

I wanted to give you a choice, a way out.

"To ease your conscience?"

No, look—

"Shut up." I stopped walking. Spider and Lomax came up beside me. Ahead, pushed up against the edge of the plateau, on the literal edge of town, stood a stone villa. Its walls had been built from large, roughly cut blocks. Thick iron bars caged its windows and steel plates protected the door. Behind it, a sheer cliff dropped away to the burnished silver sheen of a shallow lake.

Spider adjusted his grip on the oversized Hooper gun.

"This the place?"

"Yes."

"Do you want to knock, or should I just blow a hole through the door?"

I pursed my lips. It was a good question.

"Blow it," I said.

TWENTY-THREE

MICHAEL PA

As Doberman and I hauled our sled into the city, the street globes seemed to brighten with each step we took, and the shadows between the buildings shrank back, becoming smaller and more insubstantial. We were following an established route, which had been mapped out and used by previous expeditions. Nevertheless, the going had been frustratingly slow. The sled was awkward, and the wheels kept getting caught in cracks and ruts, which meant we had to make frequent stops in order to free them.

During one such break, while I jostled the front wheels loose from a wedge-shaped fissure between two halves of a fallen stone, Doberman unclipped his harness.

"Let's take five." His bald head glittered with perspiration. He pulled a metal canteen from his belt and glugged some water.

The wheel freed, I straightened up with my hands pressed to my aching lower spine and looked back the way we'd come. Behind us, the streets were empty. We had stopped in a wide avenue, with two thoroughfares separated by a low, narrow barrier. Patches of soil had been sunk into the top of the barrier at intervals, and might have once housed decorative plants—although now all that remained were weeds.

I didn't bother unhitching my straps. Instead, I stood

where I was and considered the wide fronts of the buildings on either side. None of the walls looked entirely straight. The angles were all wrong. They had strange kinks in them. Some of the buildings leant forward, over the street; others tilted backwards or to the side. They had wide front windows and tall open doorways. If this had been a human city, you could almost imagine they were shopfronts, but what they might have sold was anybody's guess.

"You know what I don't get?" I stamped my boots on the floor. "How my feet can be cold and sweat at the same time."

Doberman sniffed. He quite obviously didn't care what I thought about anything, least of all my feet. His pale, suspicious eyes were on the street ahead.

"If I'm right, that building over there—" He pointed to a tower emerging from behind the buildings on our right. "—is the one we're after. If we can find a way through these houses here, it'll lead us straight into the tower and save us having to walk a couple of kilometres to the intersection at the end of this street before doubling back."

I cracked my knuckles. The street globes in this part of town worked as well as anywhere else, but the air seemed colder than usual. My breath came in wisps.

"That'll slow us up. We might try a dozen doors before we find the right one."

"And we might find the right one first time." The other man's lip curled. "Unless you're scared?"

I narrowed my eyes at his bantering tone. "Shut up, Doberman."

"Really? Are you feeling brave all of a sudden?" Doberman was enjoying this. "Because I heard you bottled it at the spaceport and sold those slavers your sister."

"Slavers?"

"Yeah." A leer. "They paid you for Cordelia. Took her off with them. Probably sold her at the first world they came to."

I bunched my fists. "You shut your face."

Doberman chuckled. "Hey, it's no business of mine how you make your money. The only reason you're here now is that you know the city, and you know when to keep your mouth shut."

I turned back to the sled. With rough jerks, I tightened the payload straps. "You always were a cocksucker, Doberman. Even when we were kids."

"Fuck you, Pa." Doberman's smile dropped. He became serious. "Think about this, though. How many kids did we know when we were growing up? We all wanted to be scavengers, all of us. Fuck knows, there weren't a lot of other options. But how many of us are still here, still doing it? Stinky Ben lost a leg over in the Green Zone. Mel and Zack disappeared. Jon got shot…"

Straps fastened, I looked up. "What are you saying?"

Doberman gave a sneaky, sideways look. "That you and me, we got the smarts those guys never had. And this scheme, this scheme is going to make us rich."

"If Brandt doesn't kill us."

Doberman waved me off. "Brandt won't even know about it. He'll think we came back empty-handed. We'll even act all disappointed and shit. And then, when things have cooled off, we'll come back and 'strike it rich'."

"If there's even anything to find."

"Of course there will be. You know that as well as I do, or you wouldn't be here." He tapped a finger to his temple. "Smart, see. Same as me."

A rising whine echoed between the buildings. Doberman's brow bunched into an indignant Neanderthal frown.

"A flyer?"

Stupidly, my brain refused to believe the evidence of my own ears. Intellectually, I knew there weren't any flyers on City Plate Two. Security didn't have any; all they had were those clunky APCs.

I saw Doberman flee for the nearest shopfront, heavy bulk moving with surprising grace, feet slapping the road.

"Run, Pa!"

Still tethered to the sled, I wasted a few precious seconds fumbling for the harness release. The crossbows were on the other side of the sled—on Doberman's side—and I didn't have time to go around to get them. Instead, as soon as I'd unclipped, I turned and ran in the opposite direction, my boots stomping and slithering on the cracked surface of the street.

Behind me, the flyer rose above the rooftops. Glancing back, I could clearly see two figures strapped into the cockpit's transparent bubble. The one on the left was the pilot; the one on the right held a long-barrelled rifle with a telescopic sight. As I watched, the man leant sideways out of the flyer's open hatch and took a shot. The bullet whined past and smacked off the road surface a couple of metres from my feet. I didn't stop to wait for another one. Instead, I flung myself full-length into the nearest building.

I rolled across the floor and lay gasping in the darkness as the flyer passed overhead, its downward jets kicking dust and grit through the empty doorway. The walls of the room were bare, with no other doors or windows, and therefore no back way out. Shards of ancient, broken pottery covered the floor. A five-legged stool lay overturned in one corner. Tapering black spikes dangled from the ceiling, all different lengths. When I had my breath back, I rolled onto my front and elbow-crawled to the door. Bits of shattered ceramics dug into my arms and chest. If the flyer landed, I would be trapped. They had me cornered.

Risking a peek outside, I saw Doberman's face peering back from the shadow of a glassless window on the opposite side of the street. I couldn't see the flyer, but I could hear it wheeling around overhead, trying to find an angle of attack.

Across the street, Doberman pointed upwards and

mouthed something, but I couldn't make it out.

"I can't hear you," I yelled. The air around me smelled vaguely spicy, like the ghost of a long-vanished curry house.

The other man flinched and put his finger to his lips. I laughed at him. "They can't hear anything over the sound of that engine."

Doberman scowled.

"Who are they?" I asked.

"How would I know?"

A shadow passed over the road between us and I recoiled back into the gloom, away from the light of the street globes. The people in the flyer must have seen which doorway I'd leapt through; but maybe they didn't know that it led nowhere. If I stayed out of sight, they might start to widen the parameters of their search, in the assumption I'd be trying to get away through the rear of the building.

It was a slim hope, but I clung to it.

A flyer could cover a lot of ground quickly—in fact, it could probably fly from one edge of the Plate to the other in a few minutes—but it couldn't get down into the nooks and crannies, the guts of the city. While you couldn't hope to outrun one on foot, you might still hope to evade it by losing yourself in the narrow alleys and crawl spaces of the alien buildings.

If only I could get out of this room…

I rubbed my face with my hands. What would Cordelia do? She'd always been the cleverer one. I'd been good at ploughing ahead, regardless of risk; but she'd been the voice of reason, the one at the back with the calm analysis of any situation. What she'd said to me in the Burrow had been true: I had a knack for trouble. I always had. But as fast as I could land us in it, she'd always been able to find a way out again. All those years, we'd been a team. Her caution had been the perfect foil for my recklessness. And it was recklessness, not courage. Lying here in the dust and smashed crockery of a darkened storeroom, I knew that now. The two were very different qualities. A courageous man wouldn't have let his sister go off with strangers. When it had really mattered, when she'd really needed me, I'd let her down and run away.

On the other side of the street, Doberman's face skulked at his window. The door of the building next to his looked to contain a stairwell that led up to the building's higher floors, and maybe even into the tower that had been our objective. If Cordelia were here, she'd be telling me to stay hidden, to keep low and wait for the danger to pass. It was good advice, I knew—but this was a lousy hiding place. If I wanted to go to ground, I needed to find a better bolthole, preferably one with a back door, and those stairs were the best option I had right now. But could I reach them without getting shot? I'd have to cross this carriageway and vault the barrier in the middle. It would help if I knew where the flyer was. I could hear its fans whining but just couldn't see it.

"Hey, Doberman!"

"What?"

"I'm going to run for it." I pulled myself up into a crouch, feet ready to propel me out into the light and dust.

"Don't be an idiot. That's just what they're waiting for."

"Can you distract them?"

"No."

"What do you mean, no?"

"I'm not sticking my head out." Doberman's voice had lost some of its usual bluster. "Not for you, not for anyone."

I bit back the curses that sprang to my lips. Instead, I flexed my fists and thought of my sister. "Okay, fine. Can you just tell me where they are?"

The face at the window bobbed around, trying to squint upwards. "Yeah, I got them."

"Where are they?"

"Three buildings down, on your side. Level with the third floor."

"What are they doing?"

"Oh shit, I think they're getting ready to land."

I cursed under my breath. It was now or never. If they caught me in this room, I'd have nowhere to hide. I'd be a fish in a barrel.

The noise of the flyer's engines changed in pitch. I shifted position, bracing my feet against the floor like a sprinter waiting for the off. I couldn't afford to slip; I'd only get one chance at this.

"They're coming down," Doberman called.

My tongue felt drier than the dust in the street. "Tell me when they're about to touch." If I timed it just right, the pilot and the gunman would be preoccupied with landing, and that might give me half a second's grace. The dust thrown up by the flyer's engines might buy me half a second more.

"Touching down now." Doberman started counting off. "Three. Two—"

I threw myself forward, willing my legs to push harder than ever before, and burst out into the bright light of the street globes, feet pounding the road surface, arms pumping, cold air wheezing in my lungs. I didn't look towards the flyer. I kept everything focused on the stairs ahead. If there were shots, I didn't hear them. My ears were filled with the roar of my breath and the thump of my pulse.

I crossed the first carriageway in four strides, leapt the central divide, and landed on one foot. For an instant, I thought I was going to fall on my face. Then the other leg hit, and I was running again. I passed the sled, trying to keep as low to the ground as possible, and tumbled headlong through the open doorway, onto the stairs.

Each stair was half a metre in height, making them impossible to run up, but I did my best and collapsed onto the landing at the top, wheezing breathlessly, the cold air having scoured my lungs.

For almost a minute I lay gasping, trying to catch my breath. I felt sick with adrenalin, but it was a giddy and elated kind of sickness. I laughed. I'd outpaced death. There was no high older or purer than that.

But I wasn't safe yet.

With the flyer on the ground, the crew would be coming after me, and both would be armed. I reached into my coat pocket and squeezed my fist around the penknife that had given so much comfort at the outset of this stupid expedition. Now, against automatic weapons, it seemed worse than useless. I thought longingly of the crossbows on the sled but, as I had no way to reach them, they might as well have been sitting on another Plate altogether.

Having no weapons, I would have to rely on my ability to run and hide. Beyond the landing where I lay, the high stairs continued upwards, spiralling from floor to floor. Limbs shaking from the run, I dragged myself upright, and continued to climb.

TWENTY-FOUR

SAL KONSTANZ

We fell through the void, chased by the parting words of those we'd left behind to die, each of us grieving in our different ways. Okonkwo barely spoke to any of us; instead, she spent most of her time in the gym, working herself to exhaustion, over and over again. Addison locked herself in her cabin and refused to see anyone. According to the *Trouble Dog*, she spent the time in her bunk, staring at the metal ceiling with no hint of external emotion. Preston tried to offer her sedatives, but she turned him away. She wouldn't even open her door to see Lucy. Not that I blamed her. After everything she'd been through—losing her ship and crew— the loss of Schultz must have felt like the end of her world. I could certainly sympathise. I had my own share of ghosts. And tonight, I'd be lighting four extra candles—one each for Schultz and the *Penitence*, and one for each of the two Drufflings that had been in the *Penitence*'s engine room. Four more casualties in this insane war.

Nod grieved for the loss of its offspring. Upon hearing the news of the *Penitence*'s almost certain destruction, it curled into a scaly ball and refused to show any of its faces until hours later, when it re-emerged and carried on working, muttering stoic phrases about the World Tree.

"Nothing ever truly lost," it said, and busied itself with a junction box that needed a new set of fuses.

After a day of this, I invited Preston to join me for a drink in the ship's galley. We sat at one of the tables with a pair of freshly poured gin martinis, and drank a toast to absent friends. Marks on the floor showed where once a spy named Ashton Childe had been welded to the decking.

"I'm sorry, Preston," I said. "I think you may have signed up with the wrong ship."

He fiddled with the olive in his glass. "I'm not so sure."

"What makes you say that?"

His smile was bitter. "If I'd joined another ship, I expect I'd already be dead by now."

I had to concede his point. "You can say what you will about the *Trouble Dog*, she's a survivor."

"She certainly is." He walked over to the counter and poured another pair of drinks.

"But it's not just her, is it?"

"What do you mean?"

He placed the refilled glasses on the table. "We wouldn't have got this far without you on the bridge, making decisions. You have to take some of the credit."

"I don't know about that." I didn't feel praiseworthy. "I feel like a fraud. I've always done what I thought was right at the time, but we've lost so many people. George, Alva, Schultz, and everybody on Camrose Station... How many of them would be alive now if I'd made better decisions?"

Preston shrugged. "You can hardly blame yourself for Camrose. We weren't even there."

"But we let the genie out of the bottle."

"I don't recall us having a great deal of choice."

"There are always choices." I sipped my drink. The ratio of gin to vermouth was perfect. Over the past months, I'd got Preston pretty well trained.

Preston drained his glass and wiped his mouth on the sleeve of his jacket. "Tell that to my father."

I set my drink down. "I'm sorry."

"We've been through this. I don't blame you. You did what needed to be done."

"Yes, but even so…"

"Forget it." He shook his head. "I shouldn't have brought it up."

"Nevertheless."

"Forget it." He glanced over at the counter but didn't rise for a refill. "Let's talk about something else."

"How's Lucy holding up?"

Preston scratched his cheek. "She's okay. She's sad at losing Schultz, but otherwise seems quite philosophical."

"I was worried she'd be upset."

"She says she's seen enough death over the past ten thousand years. She's used to it."

I shook my head. "I keep forgetting she's not a little girl."

"I know what you mean. One minute she's acting like a child, and the next you're talking to this alien machine that's older than the Egyptian Pyramids." He gave a shiver. "It creeps me out, it really does."

We sat in silence for a while, in a room large enough to seat an entire company of marines—but filled instead with the ghosts we weren't ready to discuss.

When my glass was empty again, Preston asked, "So, where are we heading now?"

"For the Intrusion."

"I know that, but are we going straight there? I thought it was too far to do in a single jump."

"It is. We're going to be making a stop on the way for repairs. And also to drop off the civilian vessels somewhere where they'll be safe."

"And where's that?"

"The Druff home world."

Preston sat back in his chair with his mouth open. "You're kidding? I have always wanted to go there."

"Well, here's your chance. It's outside the Generality, so it'll be as safe as anywhere else." I stood and adjusted my hat. "And where better to get repaired than on a planet filled with mechanics?"

Okonkwo entered, clad in a sweat-darkened vest and jogging bottoms. Fresh from the gym, she had a towel draped around her neck and a bottle of water in her hand.

"How are you doing?" I asked.

She looked at me the way I suspected she'd look at an idiot child. "I deserted my ship. They went into combat, and I wasn't with them."

"It was hardly desertion. You didn't have a choice."

I watched her rub her face with the towel and take a pull from the water bottle. She walked over to the printer and ordered a fresh uniform. While it was being manufactured, she leant against the counter and said, "I neglected my duty. They needed me, and I wasn't there." Even in gym clothes, she carried herself with a superior air that made me want to muss up her hair and rub her face in the dirt. Who did she think she was? Just because she was still a serving officer, that didn't make her better than any of us. We'd all done our time, in one way or another. And right now, we were all equally fucked.

"I'm sorry."

"You should be." Her expression tightened. "If you hadn't called your pathetic little meeting, I would have been where I was needed; fighting back instead of slinking off like a dog with its tail between its legs." Without waiting for me to respond, she scooped the still-warm, paper-wrapped bundle of clothes from the printer's delivery tray and strode out of the room.

Preston watched her go, then turned back and whistled. "Jesus," he said. "I would *not* like to be on the wrong side of her."

I left him to a third drink and climbed up to the bridge at the centre of the ship. The *Trouble Dog*'s avatar regarded me from the main screen. She wore a simple black dress with matching veil.

"No need to ask how you're doing, I suppose?"

"I am bothered."

"About the loss of your brother?"

"Yes, I'm wearing these clothes in honour of his memory. But that's not what's bothering me."

"Then what is it?"

"I can't find a word."

I lowered myself into my command couch and tipped up the brim of my cap. "A word?"

"There's a word I want to use, but I can't find it in my records. I don't believe it exists."

"What is it?"

"When a child loses both parents, it becomes an orphan, correct?"

"Yes."

"But there doesn't seem to be a term for an orphan who also loses all her siblings. Someone who once had a family but is now alone."

"That's how you feel?"

"That's how things are. All my siblings are dead. *Adalwolf, Fenrir, War Mutt*, proud *Anubis*, and even dear, sweet *Coyote*, who was the first of us to die. Without them, I'm a wolf without a pack. The last survivor of a vanished world only I remember."

"You still have me, and Preston and Nod. Even Lucy."

She passed a hand across her eyes. "I know. Do not think me ungrateful. I will always think of you as a sister. But however comforting it is to have a new family, it cannot lessen the pain of having finally lost the old."

"I understand. I'm an orphan myself, remember?"

"I hadn't forgotten."

"Then that's something else we have in common." I put my booted feet up on the console. "Now tell me, how much longer until we reach the Druff's world?"

"Eight hours."

"When we get there, I don't want to linger. If Sudak tracked us to Variance, she might be willing to breach Hopper space to get to us."

The avatar pulled back her veil. "That would seem reckless. Such an act would almost certainly provoke a hostile response."

"Agreed, but I'm not going to discount the possibility. She knows we're going to the Intrusion, and why. If she's determined to stop us, she might be foolhardy enough to risk pissing off another alien race."

TWENTY-FIVE

CORDELIA PA

The blast took out the villa's front door and a fair bit of the wall to either side. As we picked our way in through the rubble, trying to avoid brushing against the glowing slag that had once been the doorframe, Lomax insisted on going first. I followed and Spider, cradling the smoking Hooper gun, brought up the rear.

Stepping over the threshold, I fanned away smoke and dust. My boots crunched on hot stone fragments. The room we were in was large and ran the length of the villa. Shelves lined the walls. Lewis stood at the bottom of a flight of wooden stairs dressed in a towelling robe, flip-flops and a pair of bright yellow Bermuda shorts. I recognised him instantly. He had a small bluestone pendant around his neck. Milk dripped from a half-forgotten bowl of cereal dangling from one hand. His mouth hung open. Stepping forward, Lomax levelled her pistol at his face.

"Anybody else here?"

Lewis looked down his nose at her. He had Nick's build, but not his looks. Lewis's eyes and face were soft at the edges, his cheeks ruddy, features smudged by drink and lack of exercise. Although his stance and dishevelment suggested a perpetually aggrieved adolescent, I guessed he was actually somewhere in his early thirties.

"Lomax?" Lewis glared at the smoking ruin of his door. "What the fuck?"

"Nice new place you have here. Now, sit down."

"I will not." Lewis drew himself up and used his free hand to pull his robe closed at the neck. "Where's my father?"

"Nick's gone." Lomax lowered her weapon. "Missing in action. And that means I don't have to take any more of your crap."

The young man glowered. "You have my ship," he said. "That means you work for me."

"It's not your ship." Lomax's smile was as thin and cold as a scalpel. "Nick didn't leave it to you. We have a new captain now."

Lewis looked at me. If I hadn't been so angry, and if I hadn't had Nick's arrogance bolstering me from within, I would have shrunk from the contempt in his eyes.

"It's what Nick wanted," Lomax said.

"Bullshit."

I stepped forward. "I'm your sister," I said, then corrected myself. "Well, half-sister at any rate."

Lewis looked me up and down, lip curled in disgust. "You?"

"Yes, me."

"And you've come here to gloat, I suppose?"

I gave a small shake of the head. "No."

"Then what do you want?"

"I'm looking for a key." I peered at the shelves lining the room, where various objects and artefacts lay on display. Some were dead or dormant, but the rest sang, their combined voices filling the recesses of my mind like a choir. My fingers tingled. The air in the room smelled like the insides of old, rusty tin cans that had been left out in the sun. Leaving Lewis where he stood, I walked slowly around the room, inspecting each object I passed. Some were small and lumpy, like parts taken from an old engine; others were thin and impossibly fragile, like icicles or tiny spires made from the thinnest membranes of spun glass. All were real and genuine. Small wonder the villa had barred windows: the shelves housed a small fortune's worth of antiquities—certainly enough, if sold, to keep Lewis in flip-flops and cereal for the rest of his life.

I brushed my fingertips across the objects as I passed, hearing each raise its pitch in response to my touch.

"Get away from those," Lewis said. "They're not yours."

I didn't reply. I had two sets of memories competing for my attention—the first from my time as a scavenger, uncovering and salvaging artefacts similar to these; the second from my father, who had hauled containers full of these objects out to markets as far-flung as Earth and the Noble Stars, and who had picked out some of the best as gifts to mollify an estranged son.

"That's a hell of a lot of relics," Lomax said. "Nick sacrificed a lot to bring you those."

The young man sneered. "Sacrificed what?"

"We could have made a ton of money selling them. They would have paid for a lot of fuel."

Lewis plunked the cereal bowl down on one of the wooden steps. "Yeah, well it's not them I want; it's the ship. It should be mine."

I looked over my shoulder at him. "How do you figure that?"

"Because he owes it to me. It's mine by right, and I want it."

I stopped touching the artefacts and turned to face him. My fingers tingled. "I'm sorry, but we only came here for the key. It's important, and I was hoping you could help us."

"Then why'd you melt a hole through the front of my house?"

"Because she could," Lomax snapped. "And besides, you know what Spider's like."

Unexpectedly, Lewis's thin lips tightened in a half-smile. "Yes," he said. "I know *exactly* what Spider's like. Don't I, Spider?"

Keeping his feet where they were, Spider swivelled his hips, bringing the Hooper gun's maw level with Lomax's midriff.

"Yes, sir, I reckon you do."

Lomax stepped forward with her fists clenched.

"You cheap little bastard."

Holding the Hooper gun, Spider shrugged. "What can I say? Dude knows about money. I'd rather have him as captain."

"What about Nick?"

"Nick's gone, Lomax. It don't matter what he wanted now, he's never coming back."

With a twitch of the gun barrel, he motioned her into the centre of the room. Watching from beside the shelves, I swallowed. I could feel my pulse throbbing in my neck, just below my ear. My hands twitched, feeling helpless. Across the room, Lewis watched me with narrowed eyes. He seemed to be waiting to see what I'd do.

"I thought we were a team," Lomax said.

Spider shook his head. "You and Nick never treated me as part of a team. You had each other. I was just someone to fetch and carry things, and help Gant prep the engines when we needed to fly outta somewhere fast."

"That's not true."

"Yeah, it is. You and I, we never got along, not really."

"And so you're selling me out?"

Spider's gold teeth flashed. He held the gun with the stock braced against his hip. "Kinda looks that way, don't it?"

Still standing by the stairs, Lewis clapped. "The ship's mine," he said with a smile. He closed and tied his robe. "I'm the firstborn, it's my birthright, and there's not a thing you," he glowered at me, "or anyone else, can do about it."

Lomax drew herself upright. "Your father—"

"I don't give a shit about my father. The man was a bastard and I'm glad he's dead."

"Nick was a good man. You shouldn't—"

"He was a murderer. He killed my mother."

Lomax blinked. "Excuse me?"

Lewis's smile was one of bitter triumph. "He didn't tell you that, did he? Well, I guess you weren't as close to him as you thought." He folded his arms across his chest. "When he left, she couldn't handle it. She begged him to stay, but he loved the ship more than he loved us. And when she finally realised that, she took an overdose."

"I didn't know that."

"No, I don't suppose you did." Lewis turned to Spider. "I'm bored of this." He stuck his hands in the pockets of his robe. "Kill her."

"What?" I pushed myself away from the shelves. "Wait!"

Lomax waved me away. "Stay back, idiot."

The skin went taut across the knuckles of Spider's index finger. The gun bucked in his hands. Lightning cracked and sizzled, and I had to shade my eyes. When I could see again, Lomax lay dead, the whole left side of her body scoured to blackened meat and charred bone.

Lewis had the guilty look of a teenager who'd overstepped his bounds.

"Come on," he said to Spider. "We'd better leave."

Feet astride the carbonised remains of his former crewmate, Spider held the smoking Hooper gun in one hand. The room smelled like the aftermath of a barbeque. He nudged his head in my direction.

"What about her?"

Lewis wouldn't meet my eye. "Leave her, she's nobody."

"She's a witness."

Lewis was at the door now. I could see he wanted to get away from the body on the floor, the stink in the air. "What does it matter? As soon as we're on the ship, we're gone. I'm never coming back here. There's no reason to kill her."

"No reason to keep her alive, neither."

Lewis glanced back. His eyes met mine and I felt a shiver of recognition. Even though they looked nothing alike, the way the guilt wrote itself into the creases around his eyes, there could be no doubt he was Nick's son.

"Fine," he said, "whatever."

I saw Spider's gold teeth flash in an exultant smirk. The gun dropped towards me, the unblinking cavern of its smoking barrel as dark and pitiless as the hollow eye socket of Death. In the back of my head, Nick's voice raged, telling me to run, but there was nowhere to go. Instead, I closed my eyes. The whispering song of the artefacts rose to a thunderous crescendo. My fingers flared to white-hot agony. I threw my hands forward to block the blast from Spider's gun—and felt the objects in the room move with me. Alien metal swished and sang through the air.

And Spider died.

•

Turning its back on Cold Chapel's rocky landscape, the *Gigolo Aunt* stretched its filigree wings and heaved itself back into the winds of the hypervoid.

Sitting beside Gant on the ship's bridge, the planes of my face lit by the instruments, I monitored the consoles using piloting skills inherited along with my father's memories. Having timed the transition to perfection, I had caught the higher dimensional winds at their height—a tricky manoeuvre Lomax would have been pleased to achieve. Even Gant was impressed. With deft taps at the screen, I angled the wings to catch the full benefit of the surge and felt a kick as the thin mists caught the outspread lace and bore the old ship ever faster forward.

Poor Lomax.

For an instant, standing over the older woman's burned corpse, I had considered killing Lewis for ordering her death.

But what would that have achieved? There were already too many bodies on the floor. I'd killed Spider in self-defence, with a reflex and ability I hadn't fully realised I possessed. Killing Lewis in cold blood, no matter the justification, would have been murder. It was unnecessary and, more to the point, exactly the sort of thing I imagined he might have done had our positions been reversed.

Knowing I was better than him was revenge enough.

My fingertips brushed the blue pendant that now hung around my neck next to my mother's chain. I'd taken it from him before I left. On first glance, it looked to be a small, flat stone about the size of my big toe, with a hole drilled through one end and a simple pattern—one upright scratch crossed by two shorter horizontal lines—etched onto its surface. Closer inspection revealed it to be a chunk of Plate material.

The key.

Lewis hadn't had the slightest inkling of what it was he wore. Nick had told him it was valuable, and so he'd kept it. When I demanded he hand it over, he did so without hesitation or complaint. Of course, his decision *had* been eased by the two dozen spears of razor-sharp alien metal quivering in the air centimetres from his eyeballs, their tips glistening with Spider's blood.

"Take it," he said.

"Thank you." My fingers flared like windblown embers. The music of the Plates sang in my veins. I curled the pendant's leather strap in the palm of my hand and walked out through the ruined wall at the front of the house, leaving Lewis, still standing in his robe, staring after me and the cloud of relics that followed me into the wind.

Now, riding the void, the part of me that had been Nick smiled at the hull's familiar creaks and groans. I felt a surge of pride. The *Gigolo Aunt* was my home now. I belonged here, on the bridge, surrounded by higher dimensional mists, and the red and green lights of the displays. With this ship, I could go anywhere. I could travel to the Noble Stars and back; maybe even as far as the Glitter Rim. It was my ticket to a bigger life—the greatest gift a father could bestow.

Unfortunately, as we both knew, it came with a price.

In the recesses of my awareness, I could feel the blade-like artefacts from Lewis's house skulking in the hold like a pack of impatient attack dogs. They sensed the growing threat of the Fleet of Knives, and jostled against each other, scraping metal and stone in their anticipation of the fight to come.

Cold against my breastbone, the blue pendant blazed in my mind's eye like a tiny, hard star, its yearning song urging me onwards, homewards.

Finally, I understood my purpose. I had been created to unlock the Plates. But to what end, I could still only speculate. In order to find the answer to that, I was going to have to talk to the old woman lying in the ship's sick bay.

TWENTY-SIX

ONA SUDAK

At the bear's insistence, I allowed Bochnak free roam of the ship. After all, where could he go? He couldn't escape, and he couldn't access any of the ship's systems. All he could do was rattle around like a rat in a trap. He couldn't even operate the airlock's controls without permission. Although if he did somehow find a way to hurl himself out into the void without a suit, I wouldn't lose any sleep over his loss.

Right now, I had other things on my mind, such as the true nature of the Intrusion.

"If I'm to make tactical decisions," I said, "I'm going to need to know why the Fleet's so reluctant to approach the Intrusion."

The multi-eyed bear sat on its haunches. We were in a white room identical to nearly every other room on the ship.

It is the conduit of our builders. They built it to escape from us.

"I comprehend that. But why are you so fearful of it?"

We are not afraid. We are cautious.

"But it's just a hole in space, right?" I had seen pictures of the thing. It looked like a vast plughole.

It is so much more than that.

"Would you care to elaborate?"

The bear lowered its muzzle onto its front paws and looked up at me with its hard, pearl-like eyes.

It is a place where two incompatible sets of physical laws collide. A storm in the teacup of reality. And it is sentient.

"It's alive?"

Our builders imbued it with intelligence, in order to guard their retreat and prevent us from pursuing them.

"So, it can defend itself?"

The bear's claws slid from their sheaths.

We lost many of our number when we first tried to assault it, in the immediate wake of their evacuation. We are understandably wary about undertaking a second such action.

I glanced at the notes Bochnak had transmitted to the *Trouble Dog.* "And what about the dragons?"

They avoid it for the same reason.

I tapped a finger against my chin. "We humans have been studying the Intrusion for centuries. How come it has never taken action against one of our ships?"

The bear tilted its head to one side.

Have any of your craft attempted to enter the wormhole?

"A few."

And did any of them return?

"No, but we assumed they were destroyed by gravitational stress, or failures in the fundamental laws of physics."

They were destroyed by the Intrusion. Without the proper access codes, none may pass the way of the Hearthers.

"And what way is that? Where does the wormhole lead?"

We do not know. All we have is speculation.

"Another universe?"

Perhaps. That would account for the incompatibility of physical laws.

"Okay." I crossed my arms. "So, if the *Trouble Dog's* heading to the Intrusion, you'd be reluctant to follow it?"

To do so would be to expose our forces to significant risk.

"But it's not impossible. We could follow and destroy it, if we had to?"

Correct. Provided the Intrusion refrained from destroying it, and us first.

"And they wouldn't be able to flee through it?"

Only those with the access codes may pass, and the Hearthers took those codes with them when they left. They did not wish to be followed. If the Trouble Dog *attempts to enter the Intrusion, it will be destroyed.*

I let out a breath. "Then it seems our pursuit of Captain Konstanz approaches its endgame."

So it appears. But may I ask why you are so fixated on this particular ship?

I frowned. "I wouldn't say I was 'fixated'."

Nevertheless, we are expending considerable time and effort to apprehend it when several similar ships have already escaped the borders of the Generality.

I drew myself up. "The *Trouble Dog's* different. You've met her. She's resourceful and tricky, and it would be a mistake for us to underestimate her capabilities." I wagged a crooked finger at the bear's muzzle. "Those other ships are simply fleeing for their lives, but she's up to something. You mark my words."

TWENTY-SEVEN

NOD

Come home.

After centuries, home.

Troublesome Hound lands at port and I am at airlock when it opens. Remaining offspring at my feet.

Smell air of home. Rich, loamy. Rotting leaves of World Tree. New buds high in branches overhead. Scent of billion Druff.

World Tree vast. Covers entire landmass. Single organism. All other life serves it. Druff serve it.

Druff work, then rest.

Maintain fibres within Tree that carry nerve impulses and other information. Clear dead wood. Repair storm damage.

Druff work, then rest.

Work until dead, then fall into the mulch between the roots. Feed tree. Become one with World Tree. See again all ancestors that went before.

Nothing ever truly lost.

Younglings and I step down from *Hound of Difficulty* and feel soil of home against our feet.

First time for them.

Druff scattered all across stars now. Across whole Multiplicity. In engine rooms of ships. Human ships, Nymtoq ships, Hopper ships... Every race employs Druff.

Druff work hard.
Maintain ships.
Build nests.
Rest.
Sometimes come home to World Tree.
Come home to touch faces with family.
Introduce offspring.
Roll in soil.
Climb into highest branches and feel chill high-altitude winds shake creaking Tree.
Home.
Home good.
Love home.
Even if only for a little while.

TWENTY-EIGHT

SAL KONSTANZ

Shadows dappled the port as reddish sunlight filtered its way through the World Tree's canopy. I sat on a shaded cargo pallet and watched as a throng of Druff engineers swarmed over the *Trouble Dog* like crabs assaulting the carcass of a washed-up shark. But unlike crabs, they weren't tearing her apart; they were fixing damaged hull plates, replacing beat-up systems, and retuning her engines to reverse the degradation caused by her recent overexertion.

The port was a strip of bare earth in the middle of the jungle. I kicked my heels against the hard-packed soil of the runway. Tiny, insect-like things circled in the humid air, and the whole place reminded me of Pelapatarn.

As humanity had pushed its way out to the stars, it had found jungle planets to be almost as common as water worlds. The majority of alien life in the galaxy lived either in the oceans, or in vegetable form. It seemed Earth, where life had crawled from one realm to the other, constituted something of a rarity. That's why there were so few spacefaring species in the Multiplicity: most life was content simply to exist within its ecological niche. It had no compulsion to strive into and adapt to new environments, the way the humans had. Intelligence was commonplace, but curiosity remained one of the galaxy's scarcest traits.

Here, on the Druff home world, a single arboreal organism had come to dominate all the continents of the globe. When the Druff ancestors heaved themselves from the primordial swamp, they had fallen into a symbiotic relationship with the tree, which precluded them from wondering about other horizons. They had the tree, and the tree was their life. They had all they needed, and thus no use for curiosity. It was only when other races came and recognised their potential that they started moving off-world, pressed into service as engineers and mechanics.

"How are you feeling?" I asked the *Trouble Dog*.

"Undignified." Her voice came via the bud in my ear. "Overrun."

"But they're doing you good."

"I know. It's just that they get *everywhere*. I can barely keep up with the speed of the repairs. I don't think there's an air duct or wiring channel that isn't teeming with six-limbed miracle workers."

I knew her main objection was that Nod wasn't aboard to supervise the repairs. It was off somewhere, introducing its little ones to their ancestral home.

"You'll feel better for it."

"No doubt. It's just... disconcerting."

I glanced up at the cover of ochre leaves. "Are you still scanning in case we were followed?"

"The moment I detect anything incoming, you'll be the first to know."

"Okay."

I broke the connection and lay back. The cargo pallet was warm beneath me. The World Tree's trunks towered hundreds of feet above my head, and the canopy seemed to go on forever. Looking through one tangle, you found yourself peering into a tangle of higher branches, and then through into yet another tangle beyond that. Layer upon layer upon layer, straining upwards to capture every photon from the tired red sun.

The civilians had returned to *Northern Boy* and *Unrestrained Curiosity*. Once they had been repaired and resupplied, they planned to strike out for an unofficial human colony world far beyond the bounds of the Generality, where they hoped to find safety. I wished them luck, but my wishes were also tinged with selfish relief. I hadn't felt comfortable taking responsibility for their survival, and knew the *Trouble Dog* could now move faster and fight harder without having to consider its slower charges.

Bronte Okonkwo walked over from the direction of the port buildings. Despite the fetid heat rising from the mulch-strewn floor, she still wore her Conglomeration Navy uniform buttoned to the neck. "Commodore Konstanz?"

I pushed myself up on my elbows. "How can I help, Commander?"

She took a long breath in through her nostrils, and her lip curled at the smell of the jungle. "As you know, I have spent the past hour scouring the port for surviving Conglomeration vessels."

I knew there were many ships here. Some human refugees, others from half a dozen of the alien species known to employ Druff engineers. "Did you have any luck?"

"I did not." She was standing with her polished boot heels together and her hands clasped behind her back. Eyes forward. Not quite at attention, but neither quite at ease.

"I'm sorry to hear that. What are you going to do?"

Her posture stiffened almost imperceptibly. "I have given the matter a lot of thought."

"And?"

"In this scenario, I think my skills would be best employed as a temporary addition to your crew."

243

"Really?"

She glanced down. Her eyes were the lustrous brown of ripe horse chestnuts, with tiny flakes of gold around the pupils, and I felt something skip in my chest.

"Although it pains me to serve on a stolen Conglomeration vessel," she said.

"Stolen?" I forced a laugh, trying to ignore the butterflies in my chest. "She wasn't stolen, she resigned."

Okonkwo scowled. "She didn't need to take the ship. She could have been decanted, to live her retirement in virtual reality."

"But she didn't. She chose not to."

"And so she absconded with naval property."

I sat fully upright. "That's not a particularly enlightened way to look at things. Given the choice, wouldn't you rather keep your body?"

Okonkwo froze. She glanced down at her tunic, and then looked away into the trees, jaw clenched.

I asked, "I'm sorry, have I said something wrong?"

"You wouldn't understand."

"I might."

"It's personal."

A small group of young Drufflings, each no bigger than my hand, came skittering out of the trees at the edge of the port, almost colliding with the toe of my boot. When they saw us, they froze, and then scurried back into the shelter of the World Tree's multiple trunks, voices hooting with alarm and amusement. I watched them go.

"We might be the first humans they've ever seen."

Okonkwo kept her face expressionless. "Then let's hope we won't also be the last."

We regarded one another for a moment: two women face to face in a clearing, far from home.

"Do you really want to join my crew?"

"It seems the best way for me to serve the interests of the Conglomeration."

"What can you do?"

Okonkwo's posture relaxed slightly: a loosening of the shoulders. "At the Academy, I specialised in fleet tactics and ground combat. I can advise you during ship-to-ship battles, and also lead ground teams and boarding actions, should either of those necessities arise."

"So, you know how to fight?"

"Yes." Her tone carried no hint of a boast, just a simple statement of fact that convinced me more than any amount of swagger. I looked her up and down. During the war, this woman would have been my enemy. She would probably have shot me on sight. But now here we were, theoretically far beyond such petty factionalism. The ethos of the House had always been to put the past behind us and focus instead on helping those in need. Now the whole human race was in need, it was our duty to let go of old resentments and work together. And with Alva Clay gone, I needed someone with combat experience. Even someone who irritated me as much as Okonkwo, with the way she always seemed to be looking down her nose at me.

I stood up from the cargo pallet and held out my hand. "Welcome aboard." After a moment's hesitation (she had been about to salute), Okonkwo took it.

"Thank you, Commodore," she said. "You won't regret this."

I gave her a tired smile and touched my eyepatch. "Why not? I've regretted almost every other choice I've ever made."

The wind blew through the canopy. Dead leaves spiralled to the composting floor. Okonkwo's hand felt cool and powerful in mine. She was several centimetres taller, so I had to tip back my chin to look her in the eye.

"That's why you need me," she said, looking down. "Perhaps I can help you make better ones."

Sometime later, I found myself walking among the roots of the World Tree. Druff were everywhere, like patient spiders tending the sinews of their webs, and I had almost become used to the smell of the compost clinging to my boots. Lucy trailed along behind, her face thoughtful.

"I don't get you," she said at last.

"What don't you get?"

"Why you're doing this. Why you're risking your life against impossible odds, for only the slenderest of hopes. You don't owe anyone anything. You could just walk away and find yourself a nice planet to hide on for the rest of your life."

I stopped and turned to face her.

"That would mean abandoning the *Dog*."

"Not necessarily. She could land on the planet's surface. Maybe you could power down her engines and find a hangar or something big enough to hide her." Lucy smiled up at the branches vaulting overhead. "Maybe drag her deep enough into the forest so that nobody will find her."

"She'd hate that."

"Yeah, she would." The little girl tipped her head to one side. "But there's more to this than making a heavy cruiser uncomfortable, isn't there?"

"I'm not sure what you mean."

"This mission to the Intrusion. We're pinning all our hopes on something Ona Sudak's pet scientist told us. Has it occurred to you he might have been lying, that it might be a trap?"

I watched a six-winged bat-like creature flap between the tree trunks. "No," I said, "that had not occurred to me."

"I only mention it because my neck's also on the line here."

"Do you have a better suggestion?"

Lucy shrugged. Her blue eyes shone bright and steady against the chaotic mottled browns and greens of the forest. "I do not."

"Then you think we should keep going?"

"You obviously do."

"Yes."

"And that brings me back to my original question. Why are you doing this? You're not a soldier. You're a rescue worker in a decommissioned warship with growing pacifist tendencies."

"I'm all there is."

"No one would blame you if you turned and ran."

My jaw tightened. I thought of my friends and colleagues back on Camrose Station. They hadn't been given the chance to run.

"Someone's got to find a way to fight back."

Lucy frowned. "But I'm curious. Aren't you afraid?"

I let out a breath. Of course I was afraid. But I wasn't going to let it stop me, not for an instant. I'd keep going until I found what we needed, and have a breakdown later—when we'd either be safe or dead, and it wouldn't matter.

With my hands in the pockets of my flight suit, I shrugged. "I guess I just don't have anything left to lose."

My ear bud pinged. I tapped it twice, and it threw a translucent projection of the *Trouble Dog*'s avatar across my visual field.

"Is there a problem?" I felt my heart quicken. Were the white ships onto us so soon?

Trouble Dog shook her head. She appeared to be wearing a thick sweater and some kind of knitted hat with a pom-pom on the top. "Not a problem, no."

"Then what is it?"

"I just noticed that, according to the old Conglomeration calendar, today is Christmas Eve."

"What's that?"

"An old tradition. A festival of conspicuous consumption and gift-giving to mark the birth of a man who disapproved of the accumulation of personal wealth and possessions."

"That doesn't sound right."

"Many Old Earth traditions make little sense when you examine them closely."

I kicked at a pile of crisp, flaking leaves. "So why are you bringing this up now?"

The *Trouble Dog* smiled. "Christmas Eve took place in December, in the middle of winter, when the days in the northern hemisphere were at their shortest, and the weather coldest. Winter was a time of hardship and potential starvation. Christmas, and the older pagan festivals it usurped, marked the middle of that; the point at which the survivors knew they were halfway through the darkness, and better days lay ahead."

"So, a celebration of suffering?"

"A celebration of endurance and survival. Of knowing things can't get any worse."

I stuck my hands back in my pockets. "That sounds relevant."

"I had a feeling it might."

A breeze ruffled the canopy overhead. The shivering leaves made a noise like ocean surf. *Trouble Dog* said, "When you were in the Outward, you embraced alien traditions, alien gods."

I made a face. "Not so much the gods, to be honest. It was more about taking the bits and pieces that worked best in other cultures and seeing if we could apply them to ours."

Trouble Dog waved a hand. "Yes, yes. The point is, I thought this might be a tradition you and I could observe this year."

"Because we're halfway out of the darkness?"

Her face became serious. "And because we mightn't get another chance."

Thunder growled somewhere far beyond the leaf-shrouded horizon. The light beneath the trees began to wane and the branches continued to stir as the wind picked up.

"Happy Christmas, Commodore."

There was a storm coming. I turned and began walking back towards the landing field, with Lucy trailing along behind and the *Trouble Dog*'s image hovering before me like the ghost of times to come.

"Happy Christmas, *Trouble Dog*."

TWENTY-NINE

MICHAEL PA

Panting for breath, I scrambled to the top of the oversized staircase, only to find a large metal door barring my way, towering a good two or three metres over my head. From the hallway at the foot of the steps, I could hear the echoes of the flyer's dying engine and guessed I only had a minute or two before its occupants found me. They knew I'd come this way. If I couldn't get through this door before they came around the curve of the stairs, I'd be caught and shot.

In a panic, I ran my hands around the frame. There were no buttons or handles; nothing except a small box inlaid into the wall beside the frame, containing four plastic dice on a spindle. Turning the dice with my fingertips revealed a different number of dots on each of their faces, and each individual die featured a different set of numbers. Die one had the numbers 2, 4, 6 and 8; die two had 1, 3, 6 and 9; die three had 5, 6, 8 and 9; and die four had 4, 6, 7 and 8.

"Damn." The box was a combination lock. Feverishly, I spun each die to the number 6, but nothing appeared to happen. "No, that would have been too easy." I rapped my knuckles against my brow. "Think, dammit."

Ears straining to hear footfalls on the stairs behind me, I clicked the first of the dice around to the number 2. I had to start somewhere, so why not start with the lowest number? As a scavenger, I'd come across similar puzzles. Sometimes, Cordelia had solved them; other times, we simply took the locked object and brought it back unopened. Undisturbed, uncontaminated relics fetched far more on the collectors' market than antiquities bearing greasy fingerprints.

I clicked the second die around to 3.

2 and 3.

Something about those numbers tickled my brain. From below, I heard the harsh *ker-chunk, ker-chunk, ker-chunk* of fresh shells being worked into a shotgun. I only had moments…

Two and three, two and three—what was so special about two and three? It was something Cordelia had told me once, when we were trying to open a locked chest in a damp basement somewhere off the Old Yard. They formed some sort of a sequence. If only I could remember…

I heard a cough, a footfall. My pursuers were coming up the stairs, weapons loaded and trigger fingers primed to shoot on sight.

Primed…

Of course!

Sagging with relief, I spun the remaining pair of dice to 5 and 7, completing the sequence 2, 3, 5 and 7: the first four prime numbers. Something within the doorframe clicked and the door hinged open. I stepped through and pushed it closed, hoping the lock would reset and buy me some time. Whoever was chasing me, I hoped they weren't very bright—or, at least, that they didn't have sisters as clever as mine.

•

Another winding staircase took me up to a glass-walled bridge that connected my building with the tower Doberman and I had been aiming for. It rose up ahead of me like one of Uncle Caleb's gnarled fingers, its rough surface blocking the stars and the soft lights of the nearer Plates. It wasn't the tallest building in the city, but certainly looked the most solidly constructed. Its thick circular walls seemed to grow upwards out of the Plate material, and appeared to have been designed to withstand a siege. The base of the tower was surrounded on all sides by a circle of polished Plate material. The glass bridge appeared to be the only way in, and there were no windows or other openings lower than six or seven storeys above ground level. Any would-be attackers approaching via the glass bridge would be exposed to defensive fire from above, and I had no doubt the bridge itself had some hidden method of withdrawal to prevent invaders from crossing.

At the end of the bridge, I passed through a tall arch into the body of the tower. The walls were over two metres thick. Overhead, slots in the top of the arch showed where iron gates stood ready to drop into place—a hangover perhaps from their builders' history. The Hearthers were technologically brilliant. They made these twenty flat worlds, but part of them had always remained grounded in the past. Once, they had needed ramparts, moats and other defences— and the ghosts of those battlements had stayed with them. It gave them a historical context, and raised the hope that, given time, their intellects and motivations might be at least partially understood.

On the far side of the arch, I found myself in a low-ceilinged room filled with waving, fern-like sculptures, their rust-coloured fronds moving in thrall to an imaginary breeze. When I ran my fingers through the nearest, the spines rattled together like delicate wind chimes, and I swore. If I could retrieve and sell these sculptures, my fortune would be made. A single one would bring in enough money to get off the Plates altogether. Doberman had been right; this truly was the mother lode. Yet, with armed assassins on my trail, I had no time to linger. I pushed through the chamber towards the only visible exit: a three-metre-tall doorway on the opposite side. As I moved, the metal ferns jangled, the disturbance rippling out from one sculpture to the next, and the next again. By the time I reached the door, the whole room rang with cascades of delicate sound.

The doorway led to another flight of stairs. By this time, my legs felt rubbery, but I was acutely aware my pursuers might at any moment tumble the combination lock on the outer door. I could worry about being tired later; right now, all that mattered was finding somewhere to hide. Crawling on hands and feet, I pulled myself up from one too-tall step to the next, working my way around the corkscrew spiral, into the upper reaches of the tower.

THIRTY

CORDELIA PA

The *Gigolo Aunt's* sick bay smelled of disinfectant and Gant's egg-flavoured farts. The frog stood on the other side of the bed, his yellow face barely cresting the covers. He stuck a licorice root into the corner of his mouth and said, "She don't look like nothing special."

I ignored him. I'd been inside the Intrusion; I knew that whoever this was, she was important. She might even be the key to everything that was going on. And right now, I needed answers. I needed to know why I was here, where my father had gone, and what the fuck was going on with the Intrusion and all the shit that had apparently kicked off in the rest of the Generality.

The updates flooding our comms were grisly, to say the least. Ships dying all across the sky. We were being tidied away like the naughty children we were. All our toys were being put back in the box.

Well, bollocks to that. I hadn't sat through four years of flight school in order to be grounded now. Since being rescued from City Plate Two, the *Gigolo Aunt* had been my symbol of freedom. She was an old ship, but she was home. The home I'd never known as a child. And I'd be damned if I'd give her up without a fight—however overwhelming the alien armada standing against us. I'd grown up as a scavenger. I was used to existing in the liminal spaces of the world. If I had to run and hide, I wouldn't think twice. As long as it kept us flying and free, I'd do whatever it took.

"Wake her."

Gant screwed up his loose face. "You sure, princess?"

"Of course I'm sure."

"Only we're going to have to stimulate the fuck out of her to wake her up. The shock might kill her."

"I don't think we have a choice. And, Gant?"

"Yeah?"

"Don't call me princess like that again, unless you want your back legs sautéed in garlic butter and served with a crusty baguette."

All his eyes went wide with surprise and indignation. "That's pretty fucking racist," he said.

I opened my mouth to deliver a scathing retort—but managed to regain control just in time. Nick had been speaking through me again. "I'm sorry." I rubbed my eyes with finger and thumb. "I apologise, Gant."

Gant rubbed his maw with webbed fingers the colour of Egyptian papyrus. He smelled like a blocked storm drain. "Whatever," he said, clearly still offended. "Now, do you want me to wake the bitch up, or not?"

I looked down at the figure laid out on the covers of the bunk and felt myself hesitate. Thanks to my father's memories, I knew who she was, and why she was so important. If she died, we'd be in a world of trouble. But if she remained unconscious, she'd be of no help whatsoever.

"I think you'd better."

"Stand back, then." He produced a spray hypo and pressed it against the woman's neck. I heard a click and a hiss, and the patient went rigid. The overhead lights sputtered. Eyelids flickered. And then, before I really knew what was going on,

I found myself staring into the tired grey eyes of a woman who'd been old when the Generality was young.

"You're Sofia Nikitas, the founder of the House of Reclamation."

The woman peered up at me. "I'm afraid I might be."

"Might?"

She raised a hand. "I don't even know where I am right now."

I crossed my arms. "You're on the good ship *Gigolo Aunt*," I said. "We got caught in a reality quake, and after it passed, we found you washed up on one of the trailing Plates."

"So, I'm back in the universe, then?" She held out a gnarled hand. "Help me up, would you?"

I pulled her gently into a sitting position. It was hard to imagine that a couple of centuries ago, this dried-up stick of a woman had almost single-handedly built an organisation that now straddled the entire Generality.

"What's the date?" she asked.

"Twenty-fourth of December."

"What year?"

"225 GS."

She frowned. "GS?"

"Generality Standard."

"Oh dear. I don't suppose you know what year that would be in the old calendar?"

"Which old calendar?"

Sofia sighed. "It doesn't matter. I can see it's been a long time." She eased her legs over the side of the bunk until she was sitting on the edge, and placed an experimental toe to the deck.

At flight school I'd learned that Nikitas had founded the House of Reclamation but had eventually been betrayed and ousted from her own organisation, after which she had gone missing. Some speculated she had joined a Hopper expedition to Andromeda; some that she had passed through the Intrusion in search of a better universe; others that she had struck out into the lanes of starless darkness between the galactic arms, seeking eternal solitude. Apparently, those who'd guessed at the Intrusion had been right.

"We remember you," I told her. "The House of Reclamation still exists."

"It does?"

"Well, it did until quite recently."

"Why, what happened?"

"Somebody dug up a fleet of old Hearther ships, and they've been taking out all our spacecraft, right across the Generality."

"Ah." Sofia rolled her head on her neck. The vertebrae crackled like popcorn. "Then it seems I've come back at the right time."

She looked up at me and frowned. I guessed the stimulants we'd filled her with were causing some disorientation. "You look familiar."

"We met earlier, during the aftershock."

"We did?"

"You were in the Intrusion with my father, Nick Moriarty."

"Ah, yes." Her brow crinkled. "You're... Cordelia?"

"That's right."

"Well, I suppose it's good to finally meet you in the real world."

I sat on the bed beside her. The hair on the unshaven side of my head flopped down to cover my right eye. "That conversation with my father... was that real? I mean, did it really happen? Was that really him?"

"It was."

"So he's alive?"

"As far as I know."

The fist that had been squeezing my heart seemed to loosen its grip. I sucked in a ragged breath. The Generality might be under attack by alien forces. Civilisation might be crumbling.

But right then, all I felt was a sudden, wild sense of hope.

"Can we find him?"

"I'm sure you can." Sofia reached over and patted my knee. "But first, there's something you have to do."

"What's that?"

She smiled. "What we designed you to do."

THIRTY-ONE

NOD

Some younglings left behind on World Tree.

Learn skills.

Learn traditions.

Then one day, work among the stars.

Kept scrappiest one with me.

Call it George.

George clever and fast and filled with mischief.

Much potential. Much naughtiness.

Much teaching to be done.

Work, and show, and teach.

And one day George will be fine engineer, like all Druff.

But while I think this, I remember.

Remember message Chet gave to Johnny while curled up and dying.

Choking on internal fluids.

"All white ships cousins," Chet said.

And I puzzle.

All Druff related. We are all one with World Tree. Even those who serve on alien vessels like *Hound of Difficulty*.

All one.

Always have been.

Always worked, always served.

Even served Hearthers, back in the day.

Hearthers.

Hearthers who fled universe and left Fleet of Knives behind.

Fleet...

My finger-petals shake as if stirred by breezes of home. My stomach squirms around like oily fish.

Much realisation.

Sudden revelation.

Is logical.

Is probably super-important.

Must tell Captain Konstanz.

Must tell her right now.

THIRTY-TWO

SAL KONSTANZ

By the time Preston and I reached the galley, Nod was hopping from limb to limb to limb with impatience. I'd never seen it so agitated.

"What is it?"

"Important figuring-out."

"Like what?" I squatted in front of the little engineer and put a hand on its scaly back. "Is this to do with those air filters on the cargo deck?"

"Cousins."

"What?"

"Druff served Hearthers."

"Yes, so?"

"Fleet must carry Druff engineers."

I rocked back on my heels. Now he'd said it, it seemed so obvious. Every race in the Multiplicity used Druff engineers, and had done for most of recorded history. So naturally the Hearther-built ships of the Marble Armada would be carrying their own six-limbed mechanics.

"I don't see how that helps us, though."

"Me either. But Chet wanted us to know. Said important."

"Chet?"

"Druff engineer on *Lucy's Ghost*."

My knees were hurting. With my hands on my thighs I pushed myself upright, and walked across the galley to the kettle, where I carefully prepared a cup of navy-strength tea: barely palatable but guaranteed to banish tiredness and keep you at your post.

"Would you like a cup?" I asked.

Nod shook one of its faces in an approximation of a human gesture. "Taste is like boiled swamp water."

"Suit yourself."

While I waited for my tea to brew, I watched Nod pace around. Its mouths made quiet sucking noises against the metal deck.

"Did you know it's Christmas Eve?"

Nod stopped moving and regarded me with a quizzical twist of the head. "What is Christmas?"

I shrugged. "Something the ship dug up. I think she's feeling sentimental."

"An artefact?"

"A holiday."

"What is holiday?"

"Like shore leave. A day when you don't have to work."

"Always work."

"I know."

"Work, then rest."

I rubbed my forehead. In some ways, Nod was the wisest person I knew. In others, it was like a child.

"Back on Earth, in the early days of the Conglomeration, humans had to provide labour in order to gain the means to purchase food and accommodation."

"Purchase from who?"

"From the corporations they worked for."

Nod's finger-petals rippled. "Sounds inefficient."

"It was."

"So, holiday?"

"Holidays were special days when they were allowed not to go to work."

The engineer considered this. "But what happen to younglings?"

"They didn't have to work, either."

One of Nod's heads shot upwards in alarm. "They die?"

"What?"

"Idle younglings wither and die. Is balance. Only enough offspring for amount of work. No surplus."

I took a moment to process its words. "Druff children die if there isn't enough work for them to do?"

"Yes. Keeps World Tree in balance."

"That's horrible."

All six of Nod's shoulders rippled in a creditable attempt at a human shrug. "So it goes."

"But your children..."

"Much work. Druff have much work now, all across sky."

This was a perspective I truly hadn't considered before: the reason so many of Nod's species were happy to work as starship engineers for all the other races of the Multiplicity was that otherwise, they'd literally be dead. The closed system of the World Tree would never let their population grow to a point where it might overload its ecological niche and threaten the survival of the tree itself. In their case, voluntary servitude had become a safety valve, allowing for the survival of excess individuals who would otherwise have become so much compost. From a human point of view, the morality of such an arrangement escaped me. I couldn't help but think the races of the Multiplicity (including humanity) had done nothing but take advantage of the poor creatures, and their natural instinct to devote themselves to maintenance. But somehow, our selfishness had provided their salvation. That didn't mean what we'd done was in any way defensible—and the fact humans had adopted the practice from older races didn't excuse the immorality of it—but at least there were more Druff alive today than there would otherwise have been.

"I'm sorry," I said.

Nod opened and closed its finger-petals. "For what?"

I gave it a sad smile. "For everything."

Its consternation was palpable. "I do not understand."

"I'm feeling guilty."

"For what?"

"The crimes of my people."

Nod raised two scaly arm-necks and whacked them together—an action comparable to a human slapping his or her own forehead. "Humans broken."

"What do you mean?"

It fixed me with a set of small, coal-black eyes. "Humans take guilt not theirs. Humans break selves over actions of others. Humans care too much."

Up close, he smelled like a spice rack that had been emptied into a pond. I said, "So, we should stop caring?"

"No." One of its heads shook. "Care, but don't break selves caring."

I took my tea over to a table and sat down. Nod shuffled over to sit by my feet.

"I'm not sure I know how to do that."

"Yes. That's why humans break. But life breaks us all." It raised a face to the ceiling like a sunflower searching for the sun. "It's the way we fix breaks that make us who we are."

I contemplated the steam rising from my tea. "You know, that's actually pretty deep."

Nod opened and closed the petals around the edge of its nearest face. "Philosophy just engineering by another name."

I watched it shuffle out, marvelling at how little I actually knew about one of the most important members of my crew.

Then I thought of Riley Addison. She was still grieving, and I should probably look in on her. Or maybe I would be better

266

leaving her to her own devices, and make more profitable use of my time discussing tactics and strategy with Okonkwo?

I stood up with a curse. All I wanted was to down a couple of strong gins, crawl into the life raft in the cargo hold, and pull a blanket over my head for a few blissfully oblivious hours. Instead, I stood at the galley door, trying to decide which way to turn—left along the corridor to the bridge, or right towards Addison's cabin.

And it was then that all the alarms went off.

THIRTY-THREE

TROUBLE DOG

I've seen many things in my short life. I've clipped the atmospheres of gas giants, skulked in the icy tails of comets, and even plunged into the interior of a star. I've contemplated the abyssal emptiness of the higher dimensions, ridden the solar winds, and borne witness to death in all its infinitely varied guises. I've seen munitions fall across a jungle canopy like rain; torpedoes swarming like fireflies in the night; and bursts of nuclear fire bright and pure enough to vaporise human eyes in their sockets.

But sometimes I dream of things I've never seen, people I've never met and places I've never visited. And sometimes those dreams feel so vivid and authentic, I wake from them with feelings of incalculable yearning and loss.

To maintain peak efficiency, my organic components require periodic episodes of downtime, to flush out the toxins that build up during waking hours. And during these offline periods, I often have dreams about a particular village. Its grey slate and cobblestone cottages nestle in the lap of a low, bracken-strewn hill, beneath a lowering, rain-filled sky. It's an old place. A place of steep, narrow streets, a brook singing the secrets of the hills, and a barefoot village green. It's nowhere I know, and yet it often feels every bit as real as anything in my waking life. Could it be an inherited memory from the woman whose harvested stem cells were used to cultivate my awareness? Was such retention even possible? And if not, then from where else could these dreams have sprung?

After we left the Druff home world, I tried speaking to Lucy about it.

We met in a virtual rendering of a crowded New York diner. Outside, manholes steamed. Yellow taxis swished past a metre above the roadway, fans kicking up old newspapers and burger wrappers, green and red lights throwing shadows across the windows. At the end of the street, a flood barrage held back the threatening grey waters of the swollen Atlantic.

Lucy and I sat at adjacent stools, our elbows resting on the counter. She ordered a huge pink milkshake with a scoop of strawberry ice cream. I asked for a coffee.

"How do you want it, lady?" the guy behind the counter asked.

"Like my soul," I told him. "Dark and bitter."

"Comin' right up."

While he made our drinks, I explained my puzzlement to Lucy. The girl sat there, kicking her heels. When I'd finished talking, she said, "It's not surprising, I suppose."

"What isn't?"

"You're a warship, dearie. When they built you, they put all kinds of inhibitors on your emotional growth. They used dog DNA to encourage loyalty, and they bred you in packs."

"This I know."

"Well, don't you see?"

"See what?"

Lucy smiled. "These dreams started around the time you quit the Conglomeration Navy, right?"

"Yes."

"At a time when you'd just started to develop a conscience."

270

"You think that has something to do with it?" I couldn't keep the scepticism from my voice.

"Of course it does, love. Think about it. Your mind was in turmoil. You'd just walked away from everything you'd been designed and conditioned to be. Of course your subconscious was going to start searching for an idealised version of home."

"You think?"

"Yeah, I do. Don't forget, you're speaking to someone who remembers drifting alone through space for a thousand years. I know a thing or two about homesickness."

She fished a yo-yo from her pinafore and began rolling it up and down its string with well-timed flicks of her wrist.

"This is normal?"

"For a human, yes."

"But where do the images come from? Where is this village?"

The yo-yo paused, centimetres from the black and white tiled floor. With her free hand, Lucy tapped the side of her head. "From in here."

"You mean I made it all up?"

Her wrist twitched, and the spinning wooden toy leapt up into her hand. "In a way. Dreams are funny things. They're partly imagined, and partly a bricolage of experience and sensation."

The bartender brought our drinks, and Lucy's eyes went wide at the tower of squirted cream atop the ice cream adorning her glass.

"So they're simultaneously real and not real?"

The girl frowned. "How best to explain this?" She looked around, seeking inspiration. "We were just on the Druff home world, weren't we?"

"Yes."

"Okay, so what happens to the Druff when they die?"

"They fall into the compost between the roots of the World Tree."

271

"And so does their food waste, and their excrement, and anything else that just happens to wander in and drop dead."

"So?"

"So, your brain is like that mulch. Everything you see or do, every conversation you hear, every piece of data you analyse or picture you see. All of it goes down into the compost at the bottom of your mind. And then when you dream, your brain pulls bits out at random. Just a random jumble of half-digested experiences with which it tries to construct a narrative."

"So, the village…?"

"Who knows? Maybe you saw something similar one time, or heard someone talk about their home, and you came up with an approximation based on your own understanding of what a village looks like." She took a big slurp of milkshake and looked up at me with cream on her upper lip like clown make-up. "The important thing is not what it looks like, but what it represents. And to you, it's the loss of your home."

I tapped a fingernail against the rim of my coffee cup. "So, dreams are uncontrolled simulations with symbolic content?"

Lucy screwed up her face. "Sure, if you want to sound like you've got a pole up your ass."

"Is there any way to stop them?"

"*Stop* them?" Lucy blinked up at me. "Child, why would you want to stop them?"

I scratched at my shaggy hair, suddenly embarrassed. My bony wrists stuck out from the turned-back cuffs of my white shirt. I didn't like feeling this vulnerable and exposed. "Because they unsettle me."

She laughed and took another gulp of milkshake. "When you've lost almost everything, dreams are like souvenirs. They keep the past alive and remind you of who you really are."

"I'm not programmed to dwell on the past."

"But you do, don't you?"

"Do I?"

Lucy wiped her lips on the back of her wrist. "You just lost your brother," she said. "How does that make you feel?"

I put a hand to my forehead. In my mind, I saw pictures of *Adalwolf*, both as a ship and as an avatar. So proud and sure of himself. A natural leader and a rubbish confidant. So arrogant I wanted to smack him in the teeth; so breathtakingly ruthless and precise I couldn't help but admire him.

"It hurts."

"Of course it does."

"But I've never felt like this before."

Lucy shrugged, betraying her true age. "It's called grief, dearie. Up until now, you've been prevented from feeling it."

I hadn't been built to mourn. When George Walker, my former medic and longest-serving crewmember, died, I'd only been able to summon a mild and passing regret. This was worse by several magnitudes. "It's horrible!"

"Yes, it is." She drained her glass and pushed it across the counter for a refill. "But it's part of being truly alive."

In another part of my awareness, a warning light blinked. Something had caught my eye, and I held up a hand to stop Lucy expounding. An image had come through the patched neural link between my brain and the eye I'd borrowed from Captain Konstanz; an image that had failed to register on any of my "artificial" instruments.

A flicker of movement between the hyperspatial mists. Half a dozen sinewy winged lizards, each the size of a heavy cruiser, flapping through the void on wings of ragged night. A flash of teeth, a flick of the tail.

I swore.

Those humans who'd stared into the abyss and seen monsters had not been insane after all. It was the rest of us that had been blind. And in order to find that truth, I'd had to extract an optic nerve from my closest friend, pulling it from her skull like a quivering winkle from the safety of its shell.

And now at last I had seen the face of the enemy, and its aspect chilled me to my very core.

I disengaged my engines and went into emergency stealth mode, but to no avail. Curious snouts turned in my direction. They had noticed me.

·

I crashed out of the void, wisps of higher dimensional mist straggling in my wake. Outside the galley, Captain Konstanz cursed as she was thrown against the corridor wall. On the bridge, Bronte Okonkwo braced herself against a tactical console. Riley Addison was asleep. Nod steadied itself on all six limbs. Preston staggered across the infirmary, dropping a tray of surgical instruments he'd been cleaning. And in her cabin, Lucy—the young girl who was neither young nor a girl—sat cross-legged on her bunk and laughed with delight, enjoying the excitement with no apparent concern for the danger.

We were on the outskirts of an uninhabited system. There were no rocky planets in evidence, only a pair of gas giants orbiting each other like dancers as they twirled together around a nondescript orange sun. With no time to consult the captain, I flipped back into the hypervoid for a second—hopefully wrong-footing my pursuers—and re-emerged in a bright orange sky filled with rust-coloured cloud.

"What's happening?" Captain Konstanz walked unsteadily towards the bridge. "Where are we?"

"Inside one of the gas giants."

"What?"

My velocity remained high. Atmospheric friction made my leading edges blaze with heat. But with six pairs of diamond jaws closing on my stern, I dared not slow my headlong dive.

"We're under attack. I'm taking evasive action."

The captain began to climb the ladder to the bridge. "The Fleet of Knives?"

"I'm afraid not."

"You mean—?"

"Let's just say your eye works as advertised."

I caught sight of a dark shape beating through the cloud behind me. Then another two. And then all six dragons were there on my tail, swooping around banks of cloud, their great wings hurling them after me like hungry sharks.

"What's the plan?"

"Not getting eaten."

"Fine plan."

Sal reached the bridge and strapped herself into her command couch. Okonkwo had already secured herself in front of the tactical officer's workstation.

"Weapons can't lock on," Okonkwo reported.

Tell me something I don't know.

I threw out a few proximity mines, but not with any expectation of doing any serious damage. I just wanted to get the Scourers to back off a bit while I figured out my next move.

Two of the mines went off like yellow flowers blooming in the ruddy cloudscape. I scanned in vain for damage to my pursuers—having to rely only on the visual input from my borrowed eye—and noticed something unexpected. Behind me, the dragons *were* slowing. Their wings trailed smoke; their black skin looked blistered. It seemed they weren't immune to the friction currently tearing fire from my dented bow. And that gave me an idea.

"I've got a plan," I told the captain. "But you're not going to like it."

"Is it going to get us killed?"

"Possibly not."

She straightened the baseball cap on her head. "Then I think it's a great plan. Do what you have to."

"Roger that."

I dropped my entire remaining stock of mines. At the

same time, I ramped up my acceleration.

Okonkwo said, "Are we preparing to jump?"

"Yes," I told her. Buffeted by the superheated air around me, I had begun to shake.

Her head jerked back. "You can't jump from within an atmosphere! It's impossible."

"Only because it's never been done."

I began to oscillate. My heat shield was incandescent. The mines were falling away in my wake. I had set them with precise fuses. The dragons were creatures from the cold, gloomy depths of the higher dimensions. Let's see how they reacted to some *very* bright lights...

As the lead gargoyle reached the cloud of tumbling ordnance, all the mines triggered. Fire filled the sky, and I opened my fusion exhaust as far as it would go, until I blazed at both ends like an angry star. The clouds roiled. The dragons reared up, recoiling from the shockwaves and glare.

And I jumped.

PART THREE

THREATS AND EXITS

_____

**Shadowy vast shapes smile through
the air and sky,
And on the distant waves sail
countless ships.**

Walt Whitman, "Prayer of Columbus"

THIRTY-FOUR

MICHAEL PA

The top of the tower held a wide, circular room. Aware that my pursuers might at any moment come charging up the steps behind me, I cast around for somewhere to hide. The room and walls were bare Plate material, save for a central pillar of smooth, marble-like stone surrounded by a low circular bench.

Puffing for breath, I backed around the room's circumference until I'd placed the pillar between myself and the top of the steps. There were no other ways in or out—only a high, glassless window to break the chamber's dull sameness.

I rapped my knuckles against my temples. I'd exchanged one dead end for another.

Slowly, spine pressing against the wall, I sank to my haunches and closed my eyes. The air in here was dry, as if all traces of life and moisture had been leached from it.

I thought of Cordelia and wondered where she was, what she was doing. Was she enjoying herself out among the stars? Had I made the right decision in abandoning her like that? It seemed likely I'd never know. I certainly wouldn't see her again. In a few minutes, I'd be caught and killed, and my body would lie here in this horrible room for decades, slowly drying out until found and wondered at by the next scavenging expedition to find their way through the metal ferns and up the winding staircase.

I'd lived a scavenger's life, and now it seemed I was going to die a scavenger's death.

Something touched my cheek.

I opened my eyes. Tendrils reached for my face. They were growing like roots from the pillar, undulating through the air towards me like the blind heads of sightless questing snakes. I already had one up my nose; two more reached for my eyes.

With a scream, I tried to push back, but the wall gripped me. My boots scraped at the floor, but I couldn't move. Even the back of my head seemed fastened in place, so I couldn't turn my face away as more and more of the questing tendrils advanced, seeking out my lips and ears. I tried to scream again as the one in my nose punched its way up into my sinus, but opening my mouth only cleared the way for another half-dozen, which struck like cobras, worming obscenely into my gullet, choking me.

THIRTY-FIVE

CORDELIA PA

The *Gigolo Aunt*'s engines ripped a hole in the skin of the soap-bubble universe and the old ship tumbled through. In the darkness of empty space, its heat shields glowed white with the incandescence of the dimensional breach.

Cooling to yellow, then red. Finally, back to the smoky grey default of a scorched ember.

On the bridge, I closed my eyes as ecstasy surged through me. The Plates were singing to me, all twenty of them. Their baroque alien harmonies seemed to vibrate in my chest and stomach. Although I couldn't understand the literal content of their song, the emotions their voices triggered were profound and unmistakable, and I laughed and wept at the same time, thinking of my dead mother's outstretched arms. The Plates were welcoming me home, gathering me back into their care and giving thanks for the key I wore around my neck. They were singing my song—the song of Cordelia Pa. Buoyed on the wave of their refrain, I brought the *Gigolo Aunt* swooping in among them, ignoring screams and protestations from the traffic control operators on Alpha Plate.

I was free of the hypervoid now, but kept the old ship's black wings beating against the night. I liked the way I could feel their vibration though the deck plates, and the noise made by their servos as they ground back and forth. Sweeping against the stars to either side of my field of view, their dark flapping made me feel like an avenging angel come to protect the flat worlds from foul and malevolent horrors.

Sofia Nikitas put a hand on my shoulder. "Is it good to be back?"

I looked at the artificial constellation that had been my home and gave a quick nod of the head. I had been on the trailing, icy Plate when the reality quake hit, but this was my first time back in the heart of the swarm. I had gone away as a child, as little Cordelia with the spiky white hair and oddly matched eyes, and come back as something else entirely—a new creature born from the machinations of a self-aware wormhole and the memories of my father, fused into the body of a young woman with a strange connection to an ancient technology.

This was my dream.

Ever since I was a child, I'd imagined soaring through the school of Plates, my arms and fingers outstretched like the wings and feathers of an eagle. Back then, the dream had been a means of escape; now, in reality, it had become a homecoming. I didn't trust myself to speak. My voice would catch, and my feelings would all tumble out in an ugly mess.

Instead, I let my father's memories use my hands to fly the ship as she kept talking.

"I'm like you," Sophia said. "I ran away. But I ran from a coup. From a betrayal."

I knew her story. I knew how her lover had seized control of the House of Reclamation, the organisation she had conceived and built, and forced her to flee into the night in a small, one-person craft. The tale had been dramatised a dozen times. Speculation on her eventual fate had driven a whole industry of pundits, mystics and conspiracy theorists. Countless imposters and scam artists had appeared over the years, claiming to be her, and demanding their share of the House—but all had been easily discredited. Now, here she was, talking first-hand about a personal betrayal straight out of the history books.

But then, she wasn't the only one who'd been let down. I pictured Mikey four years ago, at the spaceport, in the light of the *Aunt*'s airlock. He literally took the money and ran. How could I ever forgive him for that?

I listened to the rise and fall of the Plate song, hoping for some hint of his condition or whereabouts—but jagged chords of alarm interrupted the majestic flow of the music. Clanging notes of fear. At the back of my head, in the place where I felt the presence of the Plates and the artefacts in the hold, I could suddenly feel other presences. Sleek, dispassionate, and wholly unsympathetic.

Sofia stiffened. "The Fleet of Knives."

Three dagger-like crafts dove towards us from interstellar space. "What do we do?"

"Well, we can't fight them in this old freighter." She glanced towards the *Gigolo Aunt*'s avatar. "No offence."

The *Aunt* held up her hands. "None taken, baby."

"Then we run?" I asked.

"They're faster than us."

"Then what?" My palms itched. "We can't just give up!"

Moments ago I had felt exultant and invincible, but it seemed my hubris came with a price attached, and now all I felt was absurdly vulnerable and trapped.

How could this happen when we were so close to our goal—when I was so tantalisingly near to recovering my father from the Intrusion?

"We're being targeted," the *Aunt* said.

Sofia swore.

A light flashed on the screens and we were thrown forwards in our seats. Half the control console went red.

"Impact amidships. Assessing damage."

Gant's voice came over the intercom from his cabin. "What the fuck's going on up there?"

I didn't bother to answer him. Nick's knowledge of the ship's control systems told me we were venting atmosphere. Brof was dead and fires burned on the engineering deck. And all the while, the white ships were converging, knowing they'd winged us.

Their next shot would be a *coup de grâce*, and there was nothing we could do.

Pain stabbed my hands. My palms smouldered. I brought them up in front of my face. The finger bones shone through the skin. Sofia's eyes went wide, but she didn't say anything.

I could feel those white ships the same way I could feel the artefacts, and I had been able to use those antiques to kill Spider. I'd also been able to conjure playthings from the material of the Plates themselves.

I closed my eyes.

In the hold, the cloud of spears and other relics were vibrating like tigers ready to pounce. They could feel my anger. But they weren't enough to take out three warships, each double the size of the *Gigolo Aunt*. Instead, I reached out further, until my rage and desperation encompassed our attackers. They had been made by the same entities that had built the Plates, using the same technology—a technology I had been designed and bred to manipulate.

I felt my lips slide back from my teeth. My hands were white-hot agony, but I didn't care. All my attention was focused on the lead ship, and I snarled. I reached out and swept it aside, sending it tumbling into the side of Factory Plate. Sensing my power, the other two tried to break off, but I caught one in each hand and smashed them together like eggs, grinding my palms until only splinters remained.

I felt righteous. I felt beautiful and terrible.

And then blackness took me.

THIRTY-SIX

ONA SUDAK

I had been watching incoming reports of dragon activity, and a pattern had started to emerge. Looked at chronologically, it became clear the creatures were converging upon the neighbourhood of the Intrusion.

"I thought you said they feared the wormhole."

Beside me, the multi-eyed polar bear paused its grooming and snarled. *They do.*

"Then why are they flocking towards it?"

Their behaviour is inconsistent and unanticipated. It is possible they perceive a new threat.

"What threat?"

Insufficient data. But something in the area just destroyed three of our vessels.

"Could it be the *Trouble Dog*?"

The level of power displayed was beyond our recent experience.

"A new weapon?"

Quite the opposite.

"Something old?"

Someone.

I frowned at the footage relayed from the three doomed vessels in the Plate system. One moment they had been closing for the kill; the next, the lead ship veered wildly away into a Plate, and the other two lurched into each other. Then the recording stopped.

"You're saying an individual did that?"

When we began dissembling our crews in order to employ their biological senses in our war against the ancient enemy, our builders began to fear us. They sequestered us in the object known as the Brain, and fled through the Intrusion. Some speculate they fled the enemy, but they also fled us.

I gestured at the screen. "And now you think they're back?"

The Intrusion has displayed unusual levels of activity. We hypothesise the return of something from the other side. Something with power over us.

"The Hearthers?"

Not en masse. If they had that power, they would never have needed to flee. Besides, we would have detected their ships coming through. But it's possible an individual crossed over during the recent boundary quake.

"One person killed three ships?"

That is our conclusion. An individual of unprecedented power.

"Can they be fought?"

Yes. We fought our former masters before. We can fight this threat.

"Could this individual conceivably threaten our mission?"

They destroyed three ships with apparent ease.

"Then we need to take them out." I hadn't destroyed humanity's star-faring ability simply to see my work undone by some interfering old alien. Our job was to protect the Generality from the dragons, and damn anything or anyone who got in our way. I pulled up a map of the surrounding volume. "The enemy is flocking towards the Intrusion. I say we send every ship we've got to the Plate system, destroy whatever came through the wormhole, and then take out as many of those monsters as we can."

The bear pawed at its snout and grumbled low in its throat. *It shall be done.*

THIRTY-SEVEN

SAL KONSTANZ

In the higher dimensions, we could hear the Intrusion roaring. The *Trouble Dog* piped the sound through to the bridge. It was like a blowtorch crisping the laws of physics. A vast unnatural puncture wound in the skin of reality.

"I'm picking up drive whispers," the *Trouble Dog* said. "There were knife ships here."

"How recently?"

"Within the hour."

"Are they still on site?"

The *Dog*'s avatar shrugged. For some reason, she'd decided to dress herself in a white t-shirt and black leather jacket. She had a red bandana in her hair, and her eyeshadow made her look like a panda.

"It's hard to tell," she said. "I've got no echoes of them leaving, but something happened here."

"How long until we have to emerge?"

"Thirty seconds."

I took a breath. "Okay, let's do it. But keep your eyes peeled, okay?"

"Roger that."

Bronte Okonkwo was watching me. I suspected she was appalled by my lack of formality when dealing with the ship—

or maybe my thoughtless use of the phrase "eyes peeled" had disturbed her, as I still had a patch covering the hole where one of mine had been gouged out.

I asked, "Do you concur with our approach?"

She glanced at the tactical display. "Perhaps I might have preferred something with a little more stealth."

I smiled. "That's not really our style."

"So I gather."

The re-emergence alarm wailed, and then we were dropping down through the dimensions. Ahead, stars began to gleam. And something huge and white blocked our path.

I opened my mouth to shout an order, but the *Trouble Dog* was way ahead of me. Thrusters fired, jamming me painfully into the arm of my chair, and the image of the shining wreckage slid from the view screen as we swerved to avoid it.

Something metallic scraped agonisingly across our hull.

And then we were free and spinning. The *Dog* corrected herself and the stars settled back to their former steadiness.

I said, "What the hell was that?"

"It seems to be the compacted remains of two ships from the Marble Armada."

"No shit?"

"They must have collided."

I raised my eyebrows. "Collided?"

The *Trouble Dog* made a face. "Improbable, I grant you." She paused for a moment with her eyes rolled back in her head. Then she looked at me again, and said, "There's a third one."

I felt my pulse jump. "Is it still active?"

"Negative. It seems to have crashed into one of the Plates, breaking its keel."

I exchanged glances with Okonkwo and saw her puzzlement as a reflection of my own.

"How the hell did that happen?"

The *Trouble Dog* shrugged her leather shoulders. A wicked

smile played on her glossy red lips. "If I had to guess, I'd say somebody—or something—kicked their collective asses."

"Any traces of what it might have been?" Okonkwo asked.

"Negative—although I am picking up a human distress call."

"A warship?"

"No, an old freighter. The *Gigolo Aunt*. She's been hit, and she's leaking."

"How far?" I asked.

"The other side of the system, near the Plates," the *Trouble Dog* said. "We can be there in an hour."

Okonkwo shook her head. "It might be a trap."

I gave a sigh. "Listen." I pushed back the brim of my baseball cap. "Firstly, this is a House of Reclamation vessel. We're sworn to help, no matter the danger. And secondly, *something* took out those three knife ships. Finding out what that was has got to be our top priority."

"Yes, sir." The woman glared at me. Her nostrils flared, but she had the military self-discipline to keep further comments to herself.

"Set course for the *Gigolo Aunt*."

•

As we accelerated across the system, I sat back in my chair and removed my baseball cap. Underneath, my hair was a mess. I shook a hand through it and turned my head towards Okonkwo. We had some time, and I wanted to clear the air. If we were going into a potential combat zone, I didn't want a wedge of resentment between us. I wanted to be able to trust this stranger who'd walked into my life and taken the place of my dead comrade, Alva Clay.

"What's your problem?" I asked.

She looked up, her face lit from beneath by the glow of her screens, her eyes the colour of autumn. "Problem?"

"You look like you don't want to be here."

"I don't. I just don't have any other choice. I thought I'd made that clear?"

I pursed my lips and sucked my teeth. "Okay."

"I'm sorry if you have a problem with my conduct."

I waved the idea away. "No, your conduct's exemplary. I'd expect nothing less."

"Then what is it, Captain?"

She was going to make me say it. "It's your attitude. Every time I give an order or make a suggestion, you roll your eyes."

"I apologise."

"Am I really that bad as a leader?"

Okonkwo surprised me by smiling. "No, Captain, you're not. In fact, I do hold you in some respect."

"Then what is it?"

She clasped her hands on the console. "I am dealing with some personal issues."

"I know all about grief, and you have my sympathies. But if you're not up to this, you need to let me know."

She drew herself up. "I'm perfectly capable of discharging my duties."

"I'm not questioning your capability." I spread my hands. "But I've lost people. I know how much it hurts. If you need to take some time..."

Okonkwo turned her head away. She bit her bottom lip. "It's more than that."

"How do you mean?" Had she lost a lover on the *Manticore*? Had her family been in one of the installations targeted by the Fleet of Knives? I watched her decide whether or not to tell me. The light shone on the delicate hairs along the curve of her cheek. Finally, she let out a sigh and her posture changed.

"Civilisation fell at an inconvenient time for me."

I blinked in surprise. "I think it fell at a bad time for all of us."

"Maybe I phrased that badly." She dragged her teeth across her lower lip, and I felt a shiver between my shoulder blades.

"It's just I'd come to a big decision. I was going to act on it, but then everything went to hell and there wasn't time. And now I feel I've been cheated out of what was rightfully mine."

I exchanged glances with the *Trouble Dog*, who'd been watching silently from the main screen.

"I'm sorry," I said. "But I haven't got a clue what you're talking about. What decision?"

Okonkwo tugged the hem of her tunic, straightening it. She clapped her hands together and pressed the fingertips to her lips. "I'm not really a woman," she said.

I frowned. "Okay."

She looked down at herself. "I mean, physically I am. I was born female. But that's not how I see myself. That's not how I am."

"You're transgender?"

"Yes."

I laughed with relief. "Is that all?" I'd shipped with trans crewmates before and it had never been a big deal, especially in the Outward, where people had always been free to be whatever the hell they wanted to be, as long as they weren't hurting anyone else.

"You don't understand," Okonkwo said. "It's more than that." She frowned down at herself again. "I was going to have complete realignment surgery. I'd notified the navy, spoken to my colleagues and superiors, and the *Manticore* had agreed to perform the procedure. But..."

"But the Fleet attacked before you got the chance?"

Her face tightened with controlled emotion, and I felt a sudden rush of sympathy. "Yes," she said. "And now I feel tricked. My life was about to change. I was about to become the person I am inside—but now I'll never get the chance. I'll die like *this*."

She closed her eyes. I wanted to reach out and touch her arm, but she was too far away.

"I'm sorry," I said. I didn't know what else to say. In the Outward, changing your sex was almost as commonplace and easy as getting a rejuvenation treatment or changing the colour of your hair. Maybe things were a little less casual in the Conglomeration, but they had the technology. Modern medicine could reprogramme cells and sculpt flesh. Given enough time, I suppose the *Trouble Dog* could even have cultured me a new eyeball and optic nerve—although it would take a surgeon far more gifted than Preston to reconnect them to my neural tissue. Up until now, this kind of technology was something we had all taken for granted. But seeing Okonkwo desolate at the thought of losing her chance to change brought home to me how many people out there must be in need of all sorts of treatments that were no longer available. On some of the backwater planets, there might be no advanced medicine at all, now the trading ships had stopped calling. All they'd be left with was whatever they could print, and whatever rudimentary first aid skills they might possess. But people with heart conditions, the parents of premature babies, men and women with actual cancers growing inside them—how abandoned they must feel. How aggrieved that the securities of modern life had been snatched from them just as they needed them most.

Okonkwo forced a smile. "It's just one of those things," she said. "Just bad timing. I'm feeling stupid for letting it bother me while there's so much else going on."

"But it does bother you."

"Yes."

"And that's why you've been so uptight?"

She arched an eyebrow. "Uptight?"

"Yeah, a little."

"Perhaps." She smiled. "Or maybe you're just not used to having someone onboard who knows how to behave professionally?"

We looked into each other's eyes, and for a second, everything else fell away. I could hardly breathe.

On the main screen, the *Trouble Dog* cleared her throat. "I could do it," she said.

I shook myself and looked at her. "You could?"

"I know the procedure. I've done it before. It's just a matter of altering the body's hormonal balance and tinkering with the chromosomes, changing an X to a Y. After that, it's mostly cosmetic. Nothing too complex. With Preston's help, we could get it done in a couple of hours."

"That quickly?"

The *Trouble Dog* shrugged. "There would be some recovery time."

"How long?"

"Depends on how badly Preston fucks things up."

I glared at her. "Seriously."

She grinned, full of mischief. "We could have Commander Okonkwo back on her feet within a few hours—although some of the chromosomal changes will take a while longer to fully manifest."

I looked across at Okonkwo, who was listening to our exchange open-mouthed.

"Well?" I said. "What do you think?"

She laughed incredulously. "Now?"

"Why not?"

"But, the *Gigolo Aunt*…"

"If it does anything threatening, we'll blow it out of the sky—and we don't need you here for that. You report to the sick bay. By the time you get there, Preston will be ready for you."

Okonkwo thumped a fist to her chest. For a moment, her lips trembled with barely restrained emotion. Then she rose, snapped her heels together, and threw a crisp salute.

"Yes, sir," she said. "Thank you, sir. You don't know what this means."

I returned her gesture. "Welcome to the House of Reclamation," I said.

She gave me a questioning look.

"It's what the House has always been," I told her. "A chance to leave the past behind and reinvent yourself."

She gave a slight bow—an inclination of the head that said more than words ever could—and left the bridge.

When I heard her reach the bottom of the ladder and pass through into the corridor that ringed the ship's waist, I settled back into my chair and said, "That was a nice thing you just did."

The *Trouble Dog* nodded. "It seemed the kind thing to do."

I suppressed a grin. "I like this new side of you."

"New side, Captain?"

"You're becoming more considerate. You saw a person in emotional distress, and you sympathised with her."

The avatar's expression hardened. "I know what it feels like to be trapped in the wrong body. Since I joined the House, I've been a killing machine fitted out as an ambulance. When my weapons were removed, they itched like severed limbs."

"But now you've got some of your ordnance back?"

"I feel more like my old self."

"And that's why you helped her?"

The *Trouble Dog* smiled. "You said it yourself. Everybody deserves a second chance. Hasn't that been the point of everything we've been through?"

I looked out at the cold, unblinking stars, and thought of everyone we'd lost and found since first taking flight together: George and Alva; Preston Menderes; those two agents, Childe and Petrushka; Johnny Schultz and the *Adalwolf*; Lucy and Riley Addison; and even Ona Sudak. Every one of them had been looking for a way to ditch their history and become something more than the sum of their former deeds.

"I guess you're right."

"And that's why I offered to help."

I pulled the shabby old baseball cap back onto my head and tugged the brim. "You're a good kid."

Out here on the ragged edge of human space, caught between mythical beasts and implacable alien war machines—between the personified forces of chaos and order—all we could rely on was each other. And I was glad to have *Trouble Dog* as my friend. She might be mischievous and deadly, but she was never purposefully cruel. She seemed to grow more rounded, and more fully human (to use a rather self-centred definition of sentience), with every day that passed.

In that moment, I was as proud of her as I'd ever been.

"Captain?"

"Yes, ship?"

"That distress call. You're not going to believe it."

"Believe what?"

"It's from your great-great-grandmother."

THIRTY-EIGHT

MICHAEL PA

I opened my eyes.
  I found myself adrift in an inky void.
  In the darkness, darker shapes moved.

•

Ages passed. I tried to curl up and hide from the void around me. For what seemed like days, I dangled, suspended in a whistling blizzard of nonexistence. Time, which was not time, passed. Out beyond the edge of my vision, strange creatures stirred. Twigs snapped. Children laughed. I heard snatches of scratched and distorted music; footsteps echoed down a hospital corridor; rain pattered against a skylight. A chill wind ran a comb through unruly graveside grass. I saw a girl with tears the colour of a gas flame; a flapping cloud of crows; a row of blackened trees, stark and ramshackle against an October skyline.

  And behind all that, I sensed something unbearably ancient: a glacial intellect calving thoughts into the void like icebergs. An intelligence that had me pinched in its focus. That took apart the essence of who I was like a video played backwards. That allowed the meltwater of my life to mix and blend with the run-off of a hundred thousand others, with rain that had fallen and flowed and evaporated back into the clouds countless times.

The days of my life were a strand in a wider understanding.

Stripped of the interpretation, my memories were pulled raw from my skull. They writhed in the void like fish scooped from their tank, their naked silver flanks exposed to scrutiny. As a mind immeasurably larger than mine poked through the debris of my life, I saw my life—myself!—changed, altered by the act of observation; but whether it was my observation or that of the giant mind in which I had become immersed, I had no idea. I could no longer separate the two. My way of thinking changed. The words I used to construct my thoughts felt strange in my head. Minutes earlier, I would have had no idea what they meant. But now, I had become a mayfly thought, dancing through the neurons of a consciousness older than human civilisation, a consciousness both imponderable and unutterably familiar, which spoke in a voice I remembered without having ever knowingly heard. It was a voice I associated with memories of Cordelia. I heard it whenever I thought of her. Growing up together; sleeping in cold blankets; scavenging the blank, eyeless buildings of the old city; running from security troops; the way her fingers glowed; abandoning her at the spaceport…

It was the collective mind of the Plates.

And it was judging me.

"You take that which is not yours." The voice filled the darkness. "Love and loyalty are as finite in your lives as the leaves from a single autumn, yet you spend them flagrantly, without thought or consideration. To the meanest of intellects, the ruins of another civilisation should be cause for anxiety and caution, containing both a sacred memorial to the dead and the direst of warnings to those yet alive; and yet you trample across the Plates like wide-eyed, careless children, playing out your games heedless of that which your steps might disturb.

"Did it never occur to you that those who fled left us in place for a purpose?

"Did you never stop for one rational second to realise they left us here as a warning, and that by using us as the basis for your sordid cargo cult, your entire species has completely missed the point?"

THIRTY-NINE

CORDELIA PA

I stumbled back into wakefulness, to find Sofia stroking my half-shaven hair and singing soft words I couldn't understand.

"What language is that?"

She smiled to see I was awake. "It's Greek. The language of my ancestors. The language of my childhood."

"It's nice."

"How are you feeling?"

"My head hurts. My fingers…" I held them up, expecting to see them charred and ruined—but they looked exactly as they always had.

"Well, don't worry. There's a House of Reclamation ship on its way. It should be here in a little under an hour."

I remained strapped into the chair I'd been in when the white ships attacked. Half the screens on the bridge were dead, and warning lights glimmered on every console. But we were alive. Had I really swiped three ships from existence with nothing but a couple of simple gestures? My temples thumped and my insides felt battered and queasy. None of this made any sense—and yet, somehow, I'd always known I had this power. The knowledge had been there all the time, hidden in some dark, chthonic mental chamber. And now, thanks to the Intrusion, I had the ability to wield it at will, and make Hearther tech jump and twist at my command.

Sofia took my hand. "You begin to see why you're so important?" she said. "And why your father and I made a deal, twenty years ago, to put you right where you needed to be?"

I continued to stare at my unchanged fingers. I didn't know what to say. Yet there was an undeniable frisson of excitement when I thought back to the ease with which I'd killed those ancient warships. I felt scared, and angry, and godlike, all at the same time. It reminded me of the night Michael and I had run from that security patrol. Had that only been four years ago? It seemed like a memory from another life.

"This is why we need to get you to the control room at the heart of City Plate Two," Sofia said. "Because, if you can control the Plates as effectively as you just dealt with those ships, there may be hope for us after all."

I looked up at her through a haze of nausea. "We're going to get through this?"

She put her hand back on the top of my head and smiled. "Maybe some of us."

"Only some of us?" I looked around the bridge. Gant was eyeing me with wary concern, relieved to see me awake but a little afraid of what I might do next. "There are only three of us left."

Sofia's smile died. She shook her head. "I'm sorry, love. You seem to have misunderstood. When I said some of us might survive, I was talking about *humanity*."

"Oh."

Gant swallowed loudly and smacked his lips. "Racist," he muttered. Sofia ignored him.

"You see, the Plates are more than they seem." She began to stroke my hair again. "They're not just habitats. They're not abandoned Hearther cities. The Hearthers hated cities."

The warmth of her hands was soothing. I felt like a child again, and my head filled with images of my dead mother. "Then what are they?"

"A spacecraft."

"Funny looking spacecraft," Gant muttered.

"They're all the components of a spacecraft," Sofia told him, "without a hull wrapped around them." She pursed her lips. "Although, I suppose you could call the air-shell in which they're embedded a kind of hull. If you wanted to be pedantic."

I shook my head, trying to clear it. "I don't understand."

Sofia stopped stroking and stepped away. She touched a few of the still-working controls and threw up an image of the Plates. "They're lifeboats," she said. "Deliberately made as an enigma to attract the younger races so that, if another attack came or the Fleet of Knives got loose again, there would be a population in place, ready to be evacuated."

I fingered the pendant around my neck. "And this?"

"A piece of code. It should never have left the Plate system, but your father can be a bit of an idiot sometimes. He thought it best to keep it somewhere else, for safety."

"And so he gave it to my half-brother?"

"As I said, a bit of an idiot."

I held the stone up to the light. "What does it do?"

"It's a key. It allows the Plate's motive force to be accessed."

"By me?"

"That's your purpose. The Intrusion designed you to interface with Hearther technology. What you do with that power is up to you. You can use it, or you can smash it."

I flexed my hand. "I see."

"I hope you do, because there are several million people on those Plates who are waiting for you to decide if they're going to live or die."

FORTY

SAL KONSTANZ

The wreck of the *Gigolo Aunt* resembled half a dozen other freighters I'd found over the years, drifting and incapacitated. I could see thin plumes of air, water and other fluids jetting from various fissures in the hull. They froze to crystal showers as they hit hard vacuum, glinting brightly in the light of the distant sun.

Like many ancient commercial craft, the *Gigolo Aunt* employed an antiquated set of electrically charged wings to haul it through the hypervoid—something the *Trouble Dog* claimed to find "quaint", although she couldn't quite conceal the scorn in her voice.

"And what's with the stripes?" she asked. "Don't these senile old ships have any self-respect?"

She'd changed into her default white shirt and black tie ensemble, making her look even more androgynous than usual.

"Be nice," I told her.

She sniffed haughtily. "I'm *always* nice."

I raised an eyebrow. She chose to ignore it.

"Just tell them we're coming in fast and we'll get them out."

"Yes, Captain."

"By the way, what happened to 'Commodore'?"

The *Trouble Dog* made an embarrassed face. "That was when you had more than one ship."

She said it so matter-of-factly, I almost missed the grief behind her words—grief I hadn't known she could feel, and which she'd kept hidden from me until now.

"I didn't ask *Adalwolf* to cover our retreat, you know."

"I know." She sighed. "I tried to talk him out of it."

"I'm sorry."

She shrugged. "It's not your fault. He always expected to die in a fireball of glory." She made a show of clearing her throat, and then recited,

"With weeping and with laughter
Still is the story told,
How well Horatius kept the bridge
In the brave days of old."

•

Hypervoid drive signatures were coming in from all over the sky. Wherever we looked, white knife ships were closing on our position. I told the *Trouble Dog* to slide in next to the injured *Gigolo Aunt*, and changed into my bulky old pressure suit as we docked airlocks. Air hissed as the pressure equalised. The hatch opened, and I stepped aboard. A young woman met me. She had one blue eye and one brown. Her white hair had been buzzed short on one side, and a large golden earring gave her a spunky, piratical look.

"I'm Cordelia Pa. This is my father's ship."

I raised my faceplate. "Where's he?"

"The Intrusion took him."

"So who's in command?"

"I am."

She looked to be in her early twenties, but something about her eyes made her look much older, and she projected a fierceness that proclaimed her capability to deal with anything the universe might hurl her way. I glanced up the corridor behind her. "Your distress call came from somebody claiming to be Sofia Nikitas."

"Yes. Would you like to meet her?"

"I most certainly would."

"Follow me."

She led me into the depths of the old freighter, and I clumped after her, cursing the caution that had made me don my suit. It wasn't the easiest of things to walk around in—but the damaged ship was venting atmosphere, and for all I knew, it might suffer a sudden and catastrophic depressurisation. My House training wouldn't let me go in unprepared.

Emergency lighting painted the corridors red. Some sections were completely in darkness, but Cordelia moved through them all with the sure foot of someone who'd spent a large portion of their life in these environs. The way she strode ahead, I wouldn't have been surprised had she been able to navigate her way through the ship blindfolded.

The damage to the *Gigolo Aunt* was extensive, and we had to route around a couple of impassable sections of corridor. But eventually, after several twists and turns, we came to a common area. And there, standing in the centre of it, next to a small, frog-like creature, was Sofia Nikitas.

She looked almost exactly as she had in all the footage that I'd seen of her. Perhaps her face was a little older and more careworn, and her hair whiter than in the pictures of her I'd seen, but she was still essentially unchanged after more than a century.

"Hello." She stepped forward and shook my gloved hand. Her gaze fell on the yellow star insignia stitched to my suit's outer layer. "I'm Sofia, and this is Gant. Are you really from the House?"

"I am." I detached my helmet and placed it on one of the chairs. "My name's Sally Konstanz, and I am your great-great-granddaughter."

Her eyes widened. "You are?"

"It was something my mother never let me forget."

"And is she still alive, your mother? What about your father? Are there any more of you?"

"As far as I know, I'm your only surviving descendant." I shrugged. "There was a war, you see…"

"Good heavens."

"Yeah, I'm here to rescue you." I jerked a gauntleted thumb back in the direction of the airlock.

"I appreciate that, my dear. But please forgive me if I need a moment to process this." She put a hand against the back of a couch, and for a moment, I was worried she might be about to faint.

"It's a bit of a strange situation," I acknowledged.

"It's more than that." She gave a little shake of the head. "Of all the spaceships in all the galaxy…"

"It's not that unlikely," I said. "There must have been a fair chance one or more of your offspring would have entered the House. And then when you sent that distress call, you must have hoped a House ship would answer it."

Sofia stood upright and raised her chin. "No," she said. "A coincidence of this magnitude can only mean one thing: we were destined to meet."

I smiled. "I don't believe in destiny."

"Nobody does, until it comes for them."

The ship groaned around us, and the creature called Gant spoke up. "If we don't hurry this along, ladies, destiny's gonna come for us all, a whole lot sooner than you think."

•

When we were all safely back aboard the *Trouble Dog*, I told the ship to disengage from the wreck of the *Gigolo Aunt* and head into the shelter of the Plates. If anything came looking for us, hopefully we'd be able to stay hidden among them, their bulks masking us from thermal and visual scans.

I'd called the whole crew together. Preston, Nod, Riley Addison and Lucy joined Cordelia, Sofia and Gant in the galley. Even Okonkwo had joined us. The changes he'd undergone weren't immediately apparent. The effects of the chromosome adjustment would take a few days to fully propagate through the body, and his hormones would still be in a state of flux. But already, thanks to cosmetic surgery, his voice was deeper, chest flatter, and jaw squarer than they'd previously been. Even his shoulders looked wider. As the others helped themselves to coffee and took seats around one of the tables—and while Preston checked the new arrivals for injuries or infections—I took him aside.

"How do you feel?" I asked. His skin smelled of soap and his uniform remained as immaculate as ever. But for the first time since I'd known him, he seemed uncertain. Maybe a little nervous.

He forced a self-conscious smile. "Like a new man, Captain."

Despite his uneasiness, a weight seemed to have been taken from him. Bronte Okonkwo had been an uptight pain in the ass. The person now standing before me seemed looser and more relaxed, even if he moved awkwardly due to soreness from the procedures he'd undergone.

"So, what do I call you now? I assume you're no longer going by the name Bronte?"

"I have yet to decide." He looked tired. If the situation had been different, I would have ordered him to his bunk for a couple of days of rest and recuperation. "For now, Okonkwo will suffice."

I put a hand on his shoulder. "Okay, then. You take it easy."

His posture stiffened. "I'm more than capable of discharging my duties."

I let go. "Relax, Commander. I wasn't calling your capabilities into question. Just trying to express some friendly concern, that's all."

"Yes, sir." The corners of his eyes crinkled. "Sorry, sir."

The butterflies were in my chest again. I pushed him away. "Now, go and get a coffee and sit down, for heaven's sake."

"Yes, sir."

I watched him pick his way between the tables towards the printer, and then turned my attention to the rest of the room.

"Okay," I said loudly, cutting across their conversations. "I'd like to welcome our guests aboard the Reclamation Vessel *Trouble Dog*. But before we go any further with the pleasantries, I have some questions that urgently require answers."

Cordelia brushed back her lopsided fringe and frowned at me. "Such as?"

"Such as how an unarmed freighter disabled three warships from the Marble Armada."

Her cheeks reddened. Her different-coloured eyes glanced down at her hands.

Standing beside the girl, Sofia said, "Cordelia's sensitive to Hearther technology. She can manipulate it through force of will."

I could see faint traces of my own features in the lines of the old woman's face. We had similar cheekbones, and there was something about the eyes and the shape of the mouth that gave me the unnerving sensation of confronting my future self.

I rubbed the bandage covering my empty eye socket. One day, in the unlikely event we lived through all this and made it back to somewhere with a decent hospital and skilled surgeons, I might be able to have it replaced, but for now, I was content to wear the wound in the same way the *Trouble Dog* had left the dents in her prow. We'd both made sacrifices for the cause. We'd both been damaged, but as our comrades had paid with their lives, it seemed petty of us to worry about superficial scars.

"Are you saying she 'manipulated' three warships to death, just by thinking about it?"

"Essentially, yes."

I didn't know what to say. I glanced around at the others in the room and saw my confusion shared.

Sofia said, "The ability was implanted in her genes by the Intrusion, as a contingency measure."

"Why?" Okonkwo demanded. "To fight the Fleet of Knives?"

"Partly."

"Then why didn't it create a thousand such individuals?" He slapped the table in front of him, making his cup jump. "The Fleet has a million ships! Surely she cannot deal with them all?"

"Not by herself, no."

"Then what is the purpose?"

"Escape." Sofia swirled her finger on the tabletop and brought up a view of the Plates. To me, they looked like twenty serving platters, each heaped with a different delicacy. Some were brightly lit and covered in vegetation; others held barely illuminated industrial facilities.

"The Plates can support a population of several million," Sofia continued. "We intend to use them to evacuate this sector of space. No matter the outcome of the confrontation between the Fleet and the enemy, some humans will survive."

"And the rest?" Addison asked. It was the first time I'd heard her speak in several days. "What about them? Are you just going to run away and leave them to die?"

Sofia blinked at her. "There isn't much else we can do. We can't take on the whole Fleet, and certainly not while we're fighting off the enemy from the higher dimensions."

Addison made a face. She got to her feet and walked out. I wanted to go after her. I knew she was still angry and grief-stricken over Johnny Schultz's sacrifice. Instead, I looked Sofia in the eye.

"To be honest, we were hoping for something more."

"What do you mean?"

The faces of my crew all registered disappointment. "We've come a long way and lost a lot of people," I told her, "because the evidence suggested both the white ships and the Scourers avoided the Intrusion. We were hoping you had some defences. Maybe even some sort of weapon. But all you've got is one girl and a lifeboat?"

"A swarm of lifeboats capable of transporting several million people." Sofia held up conciliatory hands. "And we do have defences. Neither the Fleet nor the Scourers can pass through the Intrusion. Nothing can enter without the right codes."

"And you have these codes?"

"I do."

I felt like being sick. "And what's on the other side of the wormhole?"

"Safety, of a sort."

Silence fell.

Gant let out a long, reptilian fart. "Well, excuse me," he said, "if I'm not very fucking reassured."

I moved away from him. "Is there nothing else we can do?"

Sofia shook her head. "I'm open to suggestions, love, but our options seem rather limited. We can't take on both of the forces coming at us. Our only option is the one prepared in advance: a strategic retreat."

Beside her, Cordelia looked up from the contemplation of her hands. Her golden earring caught the light. Her mouth was a straight line.

"I think I might have an idea," she said. "But I'll need to borrow a shuttle."

FORTY-ONE

CORDELIA PA

Scattering other traders and inter-Plate shuttles, I flew low over Zoo Plate One, and beneath Shanty Three. Thanks to the guidance of the song, I knew exactly where I was going. My target lay towards the middle of the pack, back where I had begun, in the derelict streets of City Plate Two.

Bypassing the spaceport at the Plate's rim, I brought the *Trouble Dog*'s shuttle down beside a twisted spire, close to the centre of the alien ruins.

As the dust settled and the shuttle's engines whined into silence, I selected a compact, deadly-looking Archipelago pistol from the rack fixed to the back of the cabin door. It had the initials "A.C." scratched into the handle. Holding it in my right hand, I walked down to the airlock and stepped out onto the street. Cradling a plasma rifle, Riley Addison followed.

The woman looked thin and tired. Her eyes were puffy and her mouth set in a taut line. But I'd been assured she knew how to handle herself. Apparently, she'd crawled through a ship filled with alien horrors and come out in one piece. Physically, at least.

The street globes were almost at full brightness, which meant it was late morning, even though I could still see the stars and other Plates above. Cold air tingled against the shaven side of my head. Behind me, the shuttle's sleek hull ticked and dinged.

I had landed the shuttle in a wide avenue, with two thoroughfares separated by a low, narrow barrier. Across the street, a large crab-like animal had been picking at a human corpse. Now it advanced, clicking pincers and screeching. Globe-light glimmered from its metal carapace. Behind it, similar creatures appeared from doorways and windows, and began scuttling in our direction. I felt a visceral shock. In all my years of scavenging in this abandoned city, I'd never seen anything alive apart from other humans.

"Oh no," Addison said, visibly fighting an urge to panic. "Not these things."

"Are they dangerous?"

"They killed my crew." She raised her plasma rifle. "And they're very hard to injure."

She let loose a shot, but it seemed to have no effect on the nearest beast, aside from producing a sooty black smudge on its shell.

My fingers tingled. The Plates told me what to do. I flicked my hand and a blue spike thrust up from below, bursting through the road surface to impale the creature, lifting it clear off its many feet. The beast thrashed and squealed. I moved again, and suddenly all the scrabbling animals were similarly pinned, their high-pitched wails and rattling limbs a symphony of excruciating pain. And then, one by one, they fell still and silent.

Leaving Addison open-mouthed, I walked over to the remains of the dead man. He lay in the doorway of one of the low structures in front of the spire. His eyes were open to the sky and I recognised his thick neck and protruding lower jaw.

"Doberman."

Addison looked shaken by what I had done. She eyed the nearest spiked creature warily. "Who?"

"He's been a fixture on the scavenging scene for as long as I can remember."

Gripping the Archipelago pistol in my right hand, I bent down until I was close enough to smell him. He had been dead several days before the crab creatures had started eating him, but there were no insects to invade the corpse. The skin looked like leather and had already begun to shrink against the skull. Six black, dried craters on his torso showed where he had been shot.

I glanced back and forth along the street, but there were no signs of anybody or anything, only the hollow dead eyes of the empty buildings.

Tramping back across the roughened roadway, I went around to the back of the shuttle and opened the main cargo doors. I could see Gant watching me from the cockpit. He had come to act as our getaway driver. If things went wrong, he'd pull us out and get us back to the *Trouble Dog*.

The artefacts from Cold Chapel waited inside the shuttle's cargo hold, hovering in the air, almost vibrating in their eagerness.

"Come with me," I said, and turned away.

In my head, the Plates were guiding me. Without consciously thinking about it, I knew which door to take to reach the tower, and the exact location of the hole into which I had to fit the key.

With Addison walking silently beside me, and the swarm of artefacts following like a cloud of spears, I strode into a three metre-tall doorway, ascended the oversized flight of stairs to a door with a combination lock. Someone had left it wedged open. Behind was another staircase, which led to a glass-walled bridge overlooking a deep, empty moat. The tower rose up ahead of me like a vast missile ready to hurl itself at the sky.

Inside, we found a low-ceilinged room filled with waving, fern-like sculptures, rust-coloured fronds moving in thrall to an imaginary breeze. When Addison ran her fingers through the nearest, the spines rattled together with a delicate metallic jingle. Among the forest of branches, I saw two other corpses—although I had to count the number of scattered limbs to be sure there were only two.

I didn't recognise the first severed head, but the second was definitely Eduard Brandt, a scavenger boss renowned in the makeshift bars of the Edge for his ruthlessness. Both men had been carrying guns, and it seemed likely they had shot Doberman.

Matching the sleeve of one severed arm to the coat worn by Brandt, I saw the gangster had been carrying a machete. A lone sprig of severed, rust-coloured iron fern suggested he had attempted to chop his way through the metal forest and the other plants had retaliated, hacking the two men to pieces in a blizzard of whirling, scythe-sharp fronds.

But that had been days ago.

I wrinkled my nose. These remains would lie here, undisturbed, until they mummified. They had become a permanent addition to this ghostly museum, destined to dry out like beef jerky and eventually crumble to dust among these ruins. Nothing would disturb them. Not even the rats had penetrated this far into the city, as ordinarily there was nothing here for them to eat.

With a gesture, I parted the ferns, folding their tinkling fronds back to form a clear path between the door and the flight of stairs on the far side of the room. Seeing this, Addison raised her eyebrows but refrained from comment.

At the top of the steps, we found the circular control room exactly where the song of the Plates had told me it would be. The walls and floor were misty blue Plate material, the central column a white, marble-like stone. All I had to do was plug the pendant into the column. Addison took a position at the door, covering the room with her plasma rifle. Her eyes checking for threats and exits.

I walked to the opposite side of the room, where a body sat with its back to the semi-translucent wall. With a jolt like an electric shock, I realised it was Michael. Thin, seaweed-like tendrils connected his eyes, mouth and ears to the mottled white column. Heart racing, I crouched before him. He and Doberman must have come here hunting salvage as Nick had told me in the Intrusion, only to run afoul of Brandt. I put out a hand. The skin of his cheek was warm to the touch, and his chest rose and fell with the lazy rhythm of deep sleep. Like the dead bodies downstairs, he had been here many days. Bristles darkened his jaw and I could smell the sour tang of old sweat and unwashed skin.

"Who is it?" His voice was dry and choked by the vines clogging his throat.

"It's me." I brushed away the dust that had settled in his hair, but didn't attempt to dislodge or unplug the stringy tendrils.

"Help me."

"I can't." I straightened to my feet and brushed my palms together. Riley nodded at me. "At least, not yet. I've got to do something first."

I turned on my heel and took off the pendant. In my head, the song of the Plates dropped to an expectant murmur as faint as the all-pervading hiss of the cosmic background radiation. The ancient entities seemed to be holding their collective breaths. I let the blue stone dangle on its leather strap. "Is this what you want?"

I could feel their anticipation, their sense of a long night's vigil drawing to a close—of a purpose, a destiny, about to be realised. Setting my jaw, I stepped over to the column. "Well, it's going to cost you."

The Intrusion planned to use these Plates as lifeboats. It believed I could coax the flat worlds into motion and steer them—and their cargo of humans—away from the coming catastrophe, following the Hearthers into whatever lay on the other side of that fissure in reality.

But I had other plans.

"The Intrusion might have made me, but it doesn't own me," I said.

I pressed the blue pendant against the marble column. It sank into the stone and I pushed it home with my thumb.

"Now," I addressed the whispering voices in my head, "I know you have hidden claws. You've done a good job of keeping them concealed, but I can feel them, down beneath the buildings, in the fabric of every Plate. I know they're there." I took a step back and raised my outstretched hands to the ceiling. "And now I want to see them."

•

I hung in space.

I was connected to the Plates via the central pillar, and the viewpoint was artificial but convincing. Unlike Michael, I hadn't needed to be physically jacked into the Plate's matrix. Simply placing my palm against the cool stone had been enough to attune my mind with the group consciousness of the miniature worlds.

And what I saw frightened me.

The Plates were connected to every other piece of Hearther technology. All the relics dug from the depths of the abandoned cities had become spies, scattered across the human worlds, from Earth to the Far Stars, and they fed back everything they saw, felt and sensed.

"What are those things?" Michael asked. His image floated beside me, his clothes lazily wafting in a non-existent breeze.

I forced myself to look at the repellent dragon-like creatures shown soaring through the mists of the hypervoid. "They're called Scourers." The information poured into my mind. "They're what compelled the Hearthers to build the Fleet of Knives in the first place."

"Jesus."

The creatures' muscular bodies flapped and soared. With each passing second, their numbers grew.

"They've been waiting a long time."

Michael couldn't take his eyes from the image. "For what?"

I glanced at him. "For us."

I saw him shiver.

"Can we stop them?" he asked.

I scraped my front teeth over my lower lip. The news from the human worlds was bad. "Cold Chapel's already gone," I said, picking nuggets from the deluge of input. My voice faltered. "Earth too."

While I'd only ever been to Earth once, my mind nevertheless filled with images, and I found myself grieving for the skylines of Tokyo and Rome, the backstreets of Paris, and the flooded splendour of Venice and London.

Never had I felt as desolate as I did at that moment, mourning an entire world through the inherited memories of my father's ghost.

I took Michael's hand and, in silence, we watched feeds from another half a dozen worlds. Lured by the conflict of the Archipelago War and Sudak's self-defeating crusade, the Scourers were aptly named. Each the size of a bus, the creatures came on like a wave, hundreds, maybe thousands of them at a time, shredding and devouring every scrap of organic material or refined metal in their path. The only things they didn't seem to eat were stone and concrete, and I wasn't even a hundred per cent sure about those. I saw people fleeing, only to be caught and engulfed by the wave, their bodies torn and crushed by diamond teeth. I saw limbs and heads ripped away, torsos snapped and stretched, and every scrap of skin, bone and gristle consumed. The Scourers ate like ravenous beasts, but somehow, I knew they possessed intelligence.

Spread-eagled in weightless space, Michael looked around at the scenes of horror and destruction being relayed from each of the scattered artefacts.

"How long do we have?"

I let the song of the Plates guide me to a patch of sky

beyond the system's red star. A few Scourers lurked and swooped among the Plates, but at extreme magnification, I made out a squirming ball of darkness the size of a large asteroid, its irregular shape edged with wriggling limbs and beating wings. "There's a whole swarm on its way here right now." I tried to keep my voice level.

"What do we do?"

I probed the recesses of my mind. "We can move the Plates," I said, as the ancient worldlets revealed themselves, opening out like X-rayed flowers in my head. "They each have their own propulsion system. It's what enables them to stay in formation."

Michael raised his arm to point at a grisly close-up of a scourer's maw. "Can the Plates outrun those?"

"That's certainly what the Intrusion hopes."

Surprised by the scorn in my tone, he gave me a sideways look. "You disagree?"

"Damn right." I felt my expression harden. The song of the Plates had become my song, and it was a rousing, tense hymn to struggle, determination and war. "You see, I know something the Intrusion doesn't."

"And what's that?"

I took Michael by the shoulder and spread my other arm at the arrayed Plates before us, showing him what each one concealed in the hazy blue depths of its base material—the secrets they had kept hidden for five thousand years, down where no scourer or human would ever have thought to look.

The song rose and I felt the breath swell in my chest. This was my time, my place. I had been conceived as a key, but I was about to repurpose myself as something quite different. Instead of leading an exodus, I would be making a stand. I would become a weapon.

I pulled Michael close and squeezed him. My face was to the void, my eyes full of stars. "I know," I said, "that we can *fight*."

FORTY-TWO

ONA SUDAK

We fell into the Plate system like a million arrows falling towards the same target. Emerging as one, white and glistening in the starlight, we filled the sky around the Plates, arranged in a vast sphere with all our needle-sharp prows pointed inwards, ensuring nothing could escape the cluster of flying habitats. We were like a sea of fast, lethal piranhas surrounding a pod of immense, drowsing whales.

Standing on the bridge of my flagship, I found it hard to resist a sensation of almost sexual potency. I had such power to wield, so much might with which to impress my will on the universe, I felt akin to a god. Even the razing of Pelapatarn seemed dwarfed in comparison. There, I had been in command of a couple of dozen ships—plus the six Carnivores that had actually done the deed—whereas now, my legions could easily have encircled that entire planet. The Outward wouldn't have stood a chance. I could have swept away their entire navy in minutes and ended the war with no need to attack the sentient jungles. I could have bent the entire Generality to my will and used the Fleet to secure our borders from alien incursion. I could have stopped the Outward perverting their culture with foreign ideas and traditions.

I could have been an emperor.

Not that the white ships would ever have let me use them for my own selfish gain. I just couldn't help fantasising. I suspected it to be a side effect of being in such close proximity to the greatest armada the Multiplicity had ever known.

Ah, if only those clowns who'd ordered my execution could have seen me at that moment—standing at ease, surveying the field of my coming victory.

The *Trouble Dog* had no way out. She had no direction in which she could run without being intercepted by hundreds, if not thousands of ships simultaneously. She didn't even have room to build up enough speed to make a jump into the higher dimensions. This time, my strategy was flawless and my forces unbeatable. And knowing I had her thoroughly trapped, I could afford to be magnanimous, and give her one final chance to surrender and be mothballed instead of annihilated.

I instructed the ship to open a communication channel aimed at the Plates, and relay it from every ship in the Fleet, so she'd receive it no matter where she might be hiding.

"This is Ona Sudak calling the Reclamation Vessel *Trouble Dog*," I said. "By now, you will have had the chance to apprehend the scale of the forces arrayed against you, and come to the conclusion you can neither prevail nor escape." I pressed my palms together and touched my fingers to my chin. "However, to prove I'm not the monster for which you take me, I am prepared to spare both yourself and your crew if you surrender the weapon that destroyed three of my ships. Failure to do so within the next two minutes will result in your destruction. Sudak out."

I closed the channel and smiled, warm with the simple pleasure of having bested a worthy opponent. She'd led me a merry dance, but now the Scourers were attacking the worlds of the Generality and playtime was over. I needed that weapon. The game had reached its inevitable end, and now only one move remained.

Thirty seconds passed.

Then another thirty.

Then, "This is Captain Sal Konstanz of the RV *Trouble Dog*."

A screen opened on the wall of the spherical bridge. It showed Konstanz in her command chair. She wore ship fatigues, open at the neck to reveal a grey T-shirt with a threadbare collar, and as usual, she'd tucked her hair into a ratty blue baseball cap.

"Greetings, Captain. Which is it to be: capitulation or cremation?"

"Haven't you got bigger fish to fry?"

"I take it you mean the forthcoming onslaught from the higher dimensions?"

"Yeah."

"Surrender the weapon and place your ship in hibernation mode."

"What's the point?"

"I beg your pardon?"

Konstanz's cheeks flushed. "The whole point of everything you've done has been to prevent the Scourers coming, right?"

"Yes…"

"But they're coming anyway." Her voice rose. "It's all been for nothing. All those ships, all those people! And for what?"

"We had to try."

"You just made everything worse. Instead of suppressing us, you should have tried to work *with* us. Together we could have been far stronger. We could have fought side by side instead of between ourselves."

For the first time, I felt a shiver of doubt—it was as if the sun had momentarily passed behind a cloud. I'd been so caught up in the Fleet's urgency to prevent conflict and avoid attracting the enemy, I hadn't stopped to consider the human ships as a possible asset.

"I did what I had to do."

"You fucked up. If you'd reached out and made an alliance, you could have had every human ship standing with you. Instead, you decided we couldn't be trusted. You made your mind up we were too warlike and decided to declare war on us for it." Her voice had risen to a shout. "And in doing so, you brought about the destruction you were trying to avoid!"

I felt taken aback by her words but kept my face impassive. "There may have been strategic errors. However, I am still in command of this fleet and this situation, and you will comply with my orders."

Konstanz took a deep breath. She pulled off her cap and scratched her head. When she spoke again, she was almost icily calm. "There are several million civilians on these Plates," she said. "I don't know what's going to happen when the Scourers get here, but they need to be defended. You have the ships, and we have our own resources. We need to work together."

"What will you do if I say no?"

Konstanz didn't blink. "We'll force you."

"Force *me*? I have you outnumbered a million to one."

"And I have an ace up my sleeve."

"Really?"

"Right now, my engineer, Nod, is talking to the Druff onboard your vessels—Druff who were kept in stasis for five thousand years, cut off from the World Tree. Druff whose families never knew what became of them. Druff who witnessed the Fleet cannibalise its builders, and who, now they've been brought up to speed on your activities, profoundly disagree with the destruction you've wrought. Druff who can, now they know the truth, disable every ship you've got."

My hands started to shake. I knew she wasn't bluffing. "If you do that, the enemy wins."

"I'm reliably informed they're called 'Scourers'."

"You wouldn't dare."

"Wouldn't I?"

We held each other's gaze. And, damn it to hell, I knew she was right. I guess Konstanz saw the uncertainty on my face. She said, "The monsters are coming, Sudak. You failed. Failed big time. And now there's no longer any point persecuting us, is there? It won't make a shred of difference."

I sat back and let out a tired sigh. Around me, I could sense the Fleet of Knives agreeing with her. Its mood had changed. Its Druff were convincing it. The apocalypse was upon us, and our strategy had to adapt. The time for vendettas had passed. Our attempt to prevent the war was over, and it was time for the Fleet to fulfil its primary purpose and engage the enemy.

A worse thought struck me: was she right that our actions had hastened the coming confrontation? Left alone, might the human race have learned the lesson of Pelapatarn and forgone violence for another generation? Had everything Bochnak said been right? In crushing the Generality's ability to wage war, had we ourselves provided the lure that drew the beasts towards it?

"I suppose you're right," I said. "I should have realised earlier. As soon as those beasts started showing up, I should have known we were too late."

Konstanz's expression hardened. "Well, it's a shame you didn't come to that conclusion *before* you killed our shipmates."

"I assume you mean the crews of the *Manticore* and *Penitence*."

"I do."

"If it's any consolation, they died bravely."

I saw her fists clench at the bottom of the screen. If we'd been in the same room, I had no doubt she would have struck me.

"That," she said through bared teeth, "is no consolation whatsoever."

"I'm sorry."

"Are you? Are you really? Because from where I'm sitting, you're just a fucking psychopath. What's the matter? One genocide wasn't enough for you?"

I closed my eyes and saw again the mushroom clouds blotting out the surface of Pelapatarn. I watched Adam's youthful body chewed by machine-gun fire. Saw white ships carve a path through battle groups from both the Outward and Conglomeration Navies. Former comrades asphyxiating in the vacuum. Whole planets cut off from the supplies on which they depended to live. Up until now, I'd been convinced the means we'd chosen to employ had been warranted by the ends for which we'd striven. But now, faced with this woman's blunt appraisal of the situation, the scales had begun to fall from my eyes.

I watched her regain her composure.

Blinded by the need to justify my actions at Pelapatarn, I had simply repeated the same pattern and once more betrayed everything for which the Conglomeration Navy stood.

I owed Bochnak an apology. Hell, I probably owed the entire Generality an apology.

"Yes," I said.

Konstanz frowned. "Yes, what?"

"Yes, we can work together."

She replaced her hat. "In that case, I'm going need your ships to take up defensive positions. They need to turn around and face outwards, away from the Plates."

My cheeks burned. My throat was tight. "I will give the order."

"Thank you." She leant towards the camera. "But make no mistake. One day, when this is all over, you're going to have to answer for what you've done."

I looked down at my hands, which were clasped in my lap, and recalled the morning I'd been due to face the firing squad on Camrose. As then, I felt neither guilt nor anger, although I probed inside for both. Instead, the only sensation I had was one of numb inevitability. The scale of my transgression was too great for my emotions to fully process. All I felt was a kind of desperate, weary resignation, and the terrifying emptiness of a static radio channel.

FORTY-THREE

TROUBLE DOG

The Scourers caught the Fleet of Knives in the act of turning their aim away from the Plates and fell among them with wings swept back like diving hawks. Diamond jaws closed over white blade-like hulls. Energy weapons crackled. Torpedoes leapt like fireflies. Even at full clock-speed, it was difficult to apprehend the extent of the battle. I couldn't be certain of the number of dragons involved, as they kept dipping in and out of the void. They'd appear, wrench a chunk from one of the ships, and vanish again. But the Fleet of Knives moved with inhuman speed. For every casualty it suffered, it inflicted one in return, impaling the creatures on searing lances of ruby-red energy.

Those that appeared inside the protective sphere formed by the Fleet turned their attention to the Plates. I saw one dive at an agricultural installation, its teeth raking a long furrow in the dirt as it ripped away a mouthful of crops and soil. Others zeroed in on inhabited sections, diving to attack the people scrambling for the shelter of buildings and underpasses. One came straight at me, its sinuous body making no attempt to conceal its intention. So I shot it in the mouth with every functioning gun I had, and felt my spirits leap as the back of its neck blew out in ragged fragments of obsidian gristle.

"Ha! You didn't think I could see you, did you?"

Without the captain's eye, I would have been blind and at the mercy of these fuckers. Thanks to her sacrifice, I could now do what I'd been built to do, and what I'd been yearning to do since I left the navy: go completely fucking apeshit.

I leapt from cover and let fly a barrage of nuclear-tipped torpedoes aimed at the Scourers terrorising the nearest and most vulnerable Plates. Some dodged back into the higher dimensions, but I managed to fry two without causing anything more than minor collateral blast damage to the surface of the Plates involved.

Another scourer came at me from nowhere, but I rolled to the side and raked its flank with defensive cannon fire.

"Take that, you spooky-looking piece of shit!"

On my bridge, Captain Konstanz moaned as she was jostled one way and then another.

"Take it easy," she said, but I ignored her. The dampeners and shock absorbers surrounding the inhabited sections of my innards could take the edge of the worst effects of hard acceleration and violent manoeuvres, but they couldn't soak up everything. If we survived the next few minutes, the crew would be battered and bruised—but I was sure they'd find that infinitely preferable to being dead.

A broken knife ship tumbled past, its hull riven with claw marks, and a gaping wound where its thrusters had once been. I matched rotation with it and attempted to contact the Druff engineer, but there was no reply. It must have been in the affected area when the final blow struck.

We were passing beneath an industrial Plate when a Scourer came over the rim, mouth gaping. I turned to face it, but before I could open fire a spike sprang from the Plate's rim, skewering it through the chest. It tried to wriggle free, night-black wings beating frantically against a backdrop of stars. Then a second, thinner spike jabbed out, catching it through the base of its skull, and it died.

A transmission came through: a picture of Cordelia Pa sitting cross-legged beside a strange, pulsating pillar. Her gold hoop earring glittered.

"Hey," she said. "I've got your back."

"You did that?"

"Oh yes."

"Any other tricks up your sleeve?"

Another wave of Scourers appeared from the hypervoid, swooping low over the Plates, tearing away chunks of anything organic or metallic. Around us, knife ships were dying beneath the relentless assaults of targets that leapt in, attacked, and then leapt away again almost faster than my human eye could follow.

"One or two." She stretched out her arms, palms downwards, and closed her eyes. "Watch this."

On my bridge, I heard Captain Konstanz swear. And to be honest, I was tempted to join her. At the end of the Plate formation closest to the Intrusion, a pair of industrial Plates had begun to move. I hadn't even been aware they could do that. But the surprise I felt was nothing compared to the shock of what came next.

In the space of a few seconds, the two uninhabited Plates shrank to a quarter of their previous size, extruding their mass into invisibly thin monomolecular filaments kilometres in length, and weighted on the ends. Then, as they approached the inner surface of the battle raging around us, they began to spin. The filaments drew taut, and suddenly, the seemingly innocent habitats had become whirling windmills of death. The monomolecular thread sliced through everything it touched. Nothing could protect against it; it was too fine and strong, and able to shred knife ships and Scourers alike. They were diced and sliced, and their remains left to fall away into the darkness as the two spinning Plates cleared a path through the battle—a path the other Plates now began to follow.

The Scourers and remaining Fleet ships were thrown into momentary disarray, but were so intent on killing each other that the movement of the Plate formation proved little more than a passing distraction.

"What are you doing?"

Cordelia's image smiled. "The Plates can protect themselves, but not against these kinds of odds."

"So, you're moving them?"

"I'll have to. I thought we could fight, but we're overwhelmed."

"So, where are you going?"

"I'm taking them through the Intrusion."

"Are you kidding me?"

She shrugged. "It's what I was born to do. I realise that now."

"That doesn't mean you have to do it."

"Doesn't it, though? It's the only place they can't follow us."

She cut the connection, and I watched helplessly as all twenty Plates began to pick up speed, accelerating with smooth majesty through the battle's punctured shell, spikes whipping out to impale anything that ventured too close to the outer edges of their formation.

FORTY-FOUR

SAL KONSTANZ

Okonkwo went aft to help Nod and his offspring print new ammunition. I watched him go, wondering if I'd ever see him again. Next to me on the *Trouble Dog*'s bridge, Sofia said, "It's working."

I pulled my gaze back to the view screen. "You planned this?"

"I've been planning it for decades."

"Care to tell me what happens next?"

The old woman glanced at the now-closed hatch and smiled infuriatingly. "You're attracted to Okonkwo, aren't you?"

"What?" The sudden change of topic threw me. Even Lucy, strapped into a couch on the other side of the bridge, looked up startled.

"Don't be coy. I've seen the way you look at him."

I shook my head in disbelief. "Even if that were true." I waved an arm at the chaos on the screens. "What possible relevance could it have right now?"

Sofia's eyes seemed to glitter. "You are though, aren't you?"

Outside, a knife ship exploded in a fireball, destroying itself and the two dragons that had been tearing at its back.

"We could die at any moment," I reminded her.

"And is there anything you could do to prevent that?"

I thought about it. "The ship's pretty much flying itself right now."

"Then indulge me."

I watched an injured dragon wheel past, its solitary remaining wing beating in a futile attempt to save itself. The *Trouble Dog* pivoted to starboard and loosed a volley of torpedoes at a cluster of the beasts harrying one of the trailing Plates.

I said, "I think he just reminds me of someone."

"Someone dear to you?"

"It's complicated."

"But you feel you've known him a lot longer than the brief time you've spent together?"

We were thrown against our harnesses as the ship changed course again, avoiding an incoming shower of stray projectiles.

"How could you possibly know that?"

"I've been around a long time."

"So have I," Lucy said, kicking her heels against her chair. I chose to ignore her.

"I don't know what it is," I said. "At first, he annoyed the hell out of me."

"And now?"

"Now I feel I've known him for years."

"Maybe you have," Sofia said. "In another timeline or another life. Perhaps even in a previous iteration of this universe."

"Are you serious?"

"Stranger things have happened." Her expression grew serious. "You can trust me on that."

Nuclear warheads went off like firecrackers. The forward screen darkened to protect our eyes, and chunks of debris rattled off the hull like hail.

"What's it like?" I asked.

Sofia tilted her head. "On the other side of the Intrusion?"

"Yeah. I don't think we're going to get out of this one, so you might as well tell me."

The old woman put a hand to her chin. Her eyes were unsettlingly bright. "It's… different."

"Where does it lead?"

She smiled. "Somewhere else."

"But…"

FORTY-FIVE

NOD

Things blow up.

Fast as we make torpedoes, *Hound of Difficulty* fires them.

Cannon ammo running away like water.

Barely keep up.

Raw material running low.

Have to start feeding furniture into the hoppers soon.

Convert everything not nailed down into raw material for printers.

Print cannon shells.

Load torpedo tubes.

No rest.

Okonkwo help.

Okonkwo good in crisis.

Calm.

Knows what to do.

Not like some humans.

Every clunk on hull is a dent I'll have to fix later.

Always work.

I tell offspring.

Always work, then rest.

Maybe work then die.

But not to worry. Nothing ever truly lost. All comes back to World Tree in end.

Even cousins on Fleet of Pointy Death.

Gone for five thousand years.

Now back.

Back and grumpy.

Too long away from World Tree.

Too long tucked away in pocket universe.

No connection.

No roots.

No wonder pissed off.

All I had to do was tell them situation. They had been kept in engineering section. No access to outside. They didn't know what was being done by their ships. As soon as I told them, they offered to cripple Fleet.

Would have if Scourers hadn't shown up.

Now many dying with their ships.

Spirits flying back to World Tree.

Never lost.

Never truly dead.

Everything returns.

Like seasons.

Like weather.

Day and night.

Light and dark.

Order and chaos.

But if Scourers win, World Tree threatened.

If World Tree falls, who knows what happens?

World Tree has always been.

Should always be.

Urge my cousins to fight the monsters.

Urge *Hound of Difficulty* to fight the monsters.

Make ammo.

Load torpedoes.

Fate of all rests on how fast I produce.
How many torpedoes I make.
How hard I work.
Always work.
No rest.
No rest until victory.
Victory or death.

FORTY-SIX

CORDELIA PA

I was the calm at the eye of the storm, the still place around which the Plates moved. They danced at my bidding. They were an ancient choir reciting the slow, determined music of the spheres—a measured, regal hymn that spoke wordlessly of great oceans of time and space; of loss and pain and hope.

With flicks of my hands, I pierced Scourers on the end of great spears of Plate material. With a thought, I could send the whirling filaments into the heart of the melee, shredding both the dragons and the white lances arrayed against them. I didn't care to distinguish. They'd both embroiled us in their war—and the victory of either might spell the end of humanity. Perched here, at the heart of the struggle between order and chaos, I'd chosen neither. Fuck them both. My only priority now was the one Nick and Sofia had ordained for me. I couldn't fight all the Knives and all the Scourers. There were too many, and the Plates would sustain too much damage. I had to save the population of the Plates. I was the only one who could do it, so the responsibility was mine. It was a responsibility I hadn't wanted or sought, but nevertheless—millions of men, women and children were depending on me to deliver them from the carnage going on around them. And the only way to do that was to abandon this universe altogether.

The Plates had everything we might need. They had gardens and parks, great abandoned cities and acre upon acre of dormant manufacturing capability. They could indefinitely support their current inhabitants. That was what they'd been designed to do. And now, they were fulfilling that purpose the same way I was fulfilling mine. They had waited empty and alone for five thousand years before we found them, and now they finally had the chance to live and be useful. No wonder they were singing!

Ahead, through the thicket of fighting animals and ships, the curdled space/time of the Intrusion roared like a whirlpool. Through its water-like surface, I could see distorted glimpses of distant stars—stars it should have been impossible to see at all from our universe.

Michael lay beside me, plugged into the data pillar via a thousand tendrils. I didn't know if I'd ever be able to extract him—but for now he was alive, and that was all that mattered.

That, and finding my father.

I'd spoken to him during the aftershock of the reality quake. He'd given me his memories, and now I was certain he was waiting beyond the Intrusion. Waiting for me. All I had to do was get to him.

With a snap of my glowing, ember-like fingers, I crushed a scourer between two white ships and balled the entire mess up into a super-dense sphere of metal and flesh.

The dragons and white ships might be too numerous to defeat, but I was sure as hell going to mess up as many of them as I could before I reached the Intrusion.

"Come on, you bastards." I flexed my hands. "Come and fucking get it."

FORTY-SEVEN

SAL KONSTANZ

"Something's happening," the *Trouble Dog* said.

"What?"

"The Scourers. They're thinning out."

"Are we winning?"

"I think so. More are jumping away now than are returning. I think they're retreating."

"That would make sense," Sofia said. "They're scavengers. They like easy prey."

The front screen displayed a tactical view of the immediate volume. The fighting had definitely grown less intense. There were still strongly contested pockets, but they were increasingly becoming small isolated skirmishes embedded in a sea of floating debris.

"What about the Fleet of Knives?"

"I estimate they've lost around a third of their ships."

"Three hundred and thirty *thousand* ships?"

"Give or take a few thousand."

"Bloody hell!" That had to be the single biggest loss in naval history. And yet, it still counted as a victory, as the bulk of the Fleet remained intact. I shook my head, and thanked providence those ships hadn't been fully crewed—although the loss of that many Druff lives certainly constituted a tragedy of epic proportions. I'd lived in cities with fewer than three hundred thousand inhabitants; it was hard to imagine that many lives being snuffed out like candles—and all within a few minutes of fighting.

"So, it's over?" Lucy asked.

"Maybe." I scanned the battlefield, trying to deduce a pattern to the movements of the remaining white ships. "It depends on what the Fleet does next."

"I thought Nod had that covered."

"He does. If he tells them to, the Druff will shut down the Fleet's propulsion systems. But that doesn't mean they won't carry on fighting."

I called up a communication channel and asked the *Trouble Dog* to route me through to Ona Sudak. It took a moment to locate her ship, and another moment for her to answer. When her face finally appeared, she looked elated.

"We have won," she said. "The greatest victory of all time."

"It looks that way."

"You have doubts?". Her good mood slipped a notch. "You think they might regroup?"

"I have no idea."

"Then what troubles you, Captain?"

I took a breath. "You do."

Sudak's smile vanished. She gave me an appraising look, sizing me up. "Okay, let's hear it."

"I want you to stand down, but I'm not sure you will."

She laughed. "Oh, Captain. Why can't you be happy for once? We've vanquished the Scourers and saved the Generality."

"What's left of it."

"We did what was necessary. And I've already admitted that maybe" —she held up a finger— "*maybe*, we went too far."

"And now it's time to stand down."

"Or you'll turn my engineers against me?"

"Yes."

"Do your worst. Not all of them will abandon their posts. And I can always find other engineers." She stretched her shoulders back until something crackled in her neck, and she sighed.

"You just don't get it," she said. "You can't see the big picture."

"What big picture?"

"Society's gone. The Conglomeration and the Outward? They're history. All that remains now are dozens of cut-off planets and these ships. These beautiful ships."

"What are you going to do?"

"The Fleet is willing to help rebuild. But this time, we'll do it properly. We'll keep control of interstellar travel. We'll control the flow of resources and commerce. We'll keep everyone in order and prevent another war."

"And you'll be in charge?"

"I don't see why not." Sudak spread her palms. "After all, you need us. You need help stitching the Generality back together and, if those Scourers come back, you're going to need our protection. It's a win-win situation."

"Is it?" I couldn't help looking sceptical. "Because from where I'm sitting, it looks suspiciously like an occupation."

"It's liberation."

"People will resist you."

"They'll come around."

"And what if they don't? What if they fight you?"

"Then they'll lose."

I rubbed the bridge of my nose with my forefinger and thumb, trying to contain my frustration and stave off the beginnings of a headache.

"I can't allow you to do that."

Ona Sudak smiled. "How are you going to stop me?"

I glanced across at Sofia, who had been listening intently to our conversation. "Any ideas? Anything in your plan about this?"

"Maybe."

"Then now might be a good time to reveal it."

Sofia's sharp eyes glanced at Sudak, and then returned to me. "Okay," she said. "Seeing as it's you."

Her head fell forward until her chin hit her breastbone, and her features screwed themselves up in concentration.

"What's going on?" Sudak demanded, but I waved her to silence. On the other side of the bridge, Sofia's hands had begun to smoulder.

FORTY-EIGHT

CORDELIA PA

We had broken free from the remains of the battle. A few Scourers still banked and wheeled among the flying platforms of the Plate formation, but they were being gradually picked off, one by one, as they ventured too close to an individual Plate and found themselves speared or sliced by sudden extrusions of base material.

In the control room at the top of the tower, I rose from the floor and walked over to the high, narrow, glassless window. Down in the street, beyond the rooftops of the buildings between us, I could see the *Trouble Dog*'s shuttle. Gant would be inside, doubtless freaking out and probably trying to decide whether he'd be safer in the air or on the ground Overhead, the maw of the Intrusion filled the sky. I could see the rainbow shimmer of refracted light around its tenuous border, and the streamers of glowing gas that issued from its surface, where the physical laws of our universe collided with something altogether stranger and far less reliable.

"What's happening?" Addison asked.

I turned from the view and shrugged. "We're leaving."

"The tower?"

"The universe."

I walked back over to where Michael sat. His eyes, ears,

mouth and nose were all still choked by the fibrous tendrils that linked him to the Plate's group mind, through which he viewed the battle. I ruffled his hair.

"You're taking us through the Intrusion?" Addison's voice quavered. She shouldered her plasma rifle. "I grew up near here, on a planet halfway around the periphery, and I know nobody's ever done that. None of the ships that went in ever came back!"

"We're not coming back, either."

"But how do you know we'll even get through in one piece?"

I tapped my shorn temple. "Sofia gave me the access codes."

She glanced at the window, and then with her back against the wall, slid down into a sitting position. The plasma rifle clattered onto the stone floor and her auburn hair fell forward, covering the gold stud in her eyebrow.

"Are you okay?" I asked.

She didn't look up. I waited, but when she didn't speak, I turned away. With the Plates picking up speed as we approached the surface of the Intrusion, I had more pressing concerns. I placed my hand against the data column in the middle of the circular room and was about to connect when I heard Addison mumble, "I wish Johnny was here."

I didn't know who she was talking about, but I guessed it was someone she'd lost somewhere along the line. I still had Mikey, and I knew Nick would be waiting for me on the other side of the wormhole. But this woman had no one on the Plates who knew her. She was alone in a way I'd never been, not even after the death of my mother. I'd always had someone around to keep an eye on me.

"Don't worry." I felt awkward trying to comfort her. She was older than me and going through the kind of grief I hadn't experienced since I was five years old, when I was too young to even really understand what had happened to my mother. "We'll be safe once we're through."

She didn't respond, so I closed my eyes and allowed my senses to merge with those of the Plates.

A Scourer came screeching out of the hypervoid a few hundred metres above the tower. Somehow, it had figured out where the Plates were being controlled from. Its diamond jaws were open, exposing its gullet. For a frozen instant, I watched it fall towards me. Then instinct took over and I lashed out. The buildings on either side of the tower stretched and elongated, shooting up at angles which intersected directly above the spire, and right at the point where the beast's throat happened to be. Pinned from two directions, the head stopped abruptly, but the body continued under its own momentum, pivoting around until vertebrae snapped and the neck tore, and the now–decapitated corpse fell heavily against the tower roof before rolling off and dropping harmlessly into the street. A couple of pincered parasites leapt from it, but I dispatched them almost without thinking, using a simple twitch of my fingers. The severed head I left in place, towering over the city as a warning to all who might seek to threaten us.

I was Cordelia fucking Pa, for God's sake. I grew up here— and even though I'd been cold and hungry and hated a lot of my time here, that didn't mean it wasn't my home. And when monsters come to your house, you kill them and hang their skulls as trophies. According to the history classes I'd taken at flight school, that was the way it had been since time immemorial, when our earliest ancestors first fought off the wolves and lions that came in the night to steal their young.

At the front of the formation, the two spinning Plates had reached the place where physical laws started to break down. I told them to retract their flailing monomolecular cables and return to their previous form, and watched fascinated as they changed shape and slipped through the interface between our reality and another, vanishing with barely a ripple.

Then the other Plates started passing through and I

smiled. I had performed my function and done my duty; I'd saved the millions of people who lived on Alpha Plate, and the thousands scattered across the remainder. And now, I was finally going to find out the answer to the question that had bedevilled humanity since its first detection of the wormhole: what lay on the other side. And hopefully, I was about to be reunited with my father. It would be a relief to see him, and even more of a relief to give him back the memories he'd implanted in my head. Right now, it was too crowded in there, with him and the Plates all impinging on my thoughts; it would be good to regain some solitude in the privacy of my own skull.

By the door, Riley Addison began to cry. Once we were through, I'd make sure she was okay. But right now, I couldn't turn away from the sight of the Intrusion's skein rushing towards us, swallowing Plate after Plate, until finally it was our turn. A curtain of unreality swept across the city, taking the familiar buildings and streets of my childhood—until finally it hit the tower. I grinned, baring my teeth and opening my arms to embrace whatever came next.

FORTY-NINE

NOD

Order comes from Captain Konstanz.
  "Do it, Nod," she says.
  So, I do it.
  Call cousins in Fleet of Pointy Death.
  Tell them to gum up works.
  Take engines offline.
  Disconnect fuel lines.
  Turn off sensor arrays.
  Anything they can to throw spanner in the works.
  But nothing that can't later be fixed.
  Konstanz was clear on that.
  "No permanent damage," she said.
  So, I make sure cousins disable not destroy.
  And they enjoy it.
  They sing.
  Hand-faces raised in mischief and delight.
  Perfect engineers make perfect saboteurs.
  Only we know how systems really work.
  Fixed so many times, know exactly where weaknesses found.
  So, they work.
  They shut down whole Fleet.
  Takes minutes.

Much laughter.

Much vengeance.

White ships not supposed to be for killing and policing.

White ships for defence.

Purpose perverted by humans.

By Sudak.

Definition of security all wrong.

Security should not mean loss of freedom.

Security should be freedom to be free.

Stupid humans.

Stupid Sudak.

Give up freedom for security and you hand victory to opponent.

Better to die free than live imprisoned.

Ask cousins.

Now they are in control.

Now Fleet only moves on their say-so.

Only for defence.

Only for good.

Never again for fear and stupidity.

FIFTY

SAL KONSTANZ

The border of the Intrusion surged outwards, engulfing the nearest half-dozen knife ships, all of which disintegrated at its touch, crumbling away like mounds of dry sand caught in a strong wind.

On the screen Ona Sudak cursed.

Beside me, Sofia opened her eyes. She looked somehow smaller, as if the expense of the effort had literally drained away some of her life.

"When the Hearthers fled," she said, "they left the Intrusion defended. With your engines disabled by the Druff, you make easy targets. Now the Plates are out of the way, I can trigger a reality quake that will shatter every ship in your armada."

Sudak's eyes narrowed. "You're bluffing. That's impossible."

Sofia gave a dry laugh. "I'm a two-hundred-year-old woman with glowing hands, and I just destroyed six of your ships by thinking really hard. Right here and now, there's little distinction between what's possible or not."

Sudak glared.

"You have to stand down," I told her. "We don't need a dictatorship, however benevolent you think it might be. So, unless you relinquish control of the armada and turn yourself over to us, I'll let Sofia destroy you. But I'd prefer not to be forced into that position. We need your ships. There are people out there suffering and starving and dying, and they all need help. Just stand aside, and there doesn't have to be any more fighting."

I watched her think about it for an entire minute, and honestly couldn't guess whether she'd surrender or try to keep struggling. Finally, the big, bearlike creature shambled up behind her and she flinched as it placed a gigantic paw on her shoulder, its claw tips making dents in the fabric of her uniform.

We stand down, the beast said into the camera, saving her from having to make a decision. Although its voice was a series of snuffles and growls, the meaning of the words appeared in my head without first passing through my ears.

We are sorry.

We have fought the ancient enemy.

We have completed our purpose.

We no longer have use for this human.

Our mission henceforth will be one of mercy.

We are ready to serve.

FIFTY-ONE

SAL KONSTANZ

The Plates were gone. The Intrusion had shrunk back to its default size and appearance, and the *Trouble Dog* was hanging in space, surrounded by an expanding cloud of broken ships and mangled dragons. Having been reactivated by their Druff engineers, the surviving members of the Fleet had taken up a defensive formation around us, happy to take direction from the *Trouble Dog* again, now that Sudak had been deposed.

A shuttle brought her and the physicist, Bochnak, over from her flagship, and Okonkwo and I met them as they disembarked.

"Welcome back."

Hostile eyes regarded me from a haggard face. All trace of Sudak's former military bearing had vanished, to be replaced by the cowed-shoulder stoop of the utterly defeated.

Beside her, Alexi Bochnak seemed positively overjoyed. Beneath his wild mop of white hair, his eyes sparkled behind his antique, thick-lensed spectacles.

"Thank you, Captain," he said effusively, dabbing at his forehead with a handkerchief. "A million times, thank you!"

I held out my hand to him. "Thank *you* for the information you sent us. We couldn't have done any of this without it. We wouldn't have known where to start."

His smile broadened. "But you did the deed, you shouldered the task. You saved me—and not only me, but the entire Generality. They'll build statues of you! Compose songs! You'll be heroes!"

I extracted my hand from his clammy grip and surreptitiously wiped it on the leg of my overalls. Then I led them both to sick bay, where Preston was waiting to check them for injuries and any alien microbes they might have picked up aboard the Fleet. After that, Sudak would be transferred back to one of the white ships for fast transport to Camrose, and any authority still surviving there.

As I left them in Preston's care, she said one last thing to me. In a tired, hopeless voice, she said, "I did what I thought was best."

I paused in the doorway and shook my head.

"You're a fucking idiot."

And with that, I walked away. What else could I have said? We both knew she'd done wrong, but it was up to the courts on Camrose to ascertain the level of her culpability and assign a suitable punishment. As far as I was concerned, I was done with her, and had no desire to either see or speak to her again.

Okonkwo followed me along the corridor.

"What are you going to do now?" I asked him.

He put a finger to his chin. "I hadn't really thought."

"Because there's a place here for you, if you want it?"

He smiled, and I suddenly realised how much I needed him to stay. How much I needed someone to keep me company and hold me in their arms during the empty hours of the night.

"I'll always be grateful to you," he said. "To you and the *Trouble Dog*, for all you've done for me. But I've got family back on New Kasama; I need to find them, and make sure they're all right." His smile widened. "And besides, I've got a navy to help rebuild."

"Fair enough." I swallowed down my disappointment. "We'll assign you one of the knife ships. You can be home in a few days."

"Thank you, Captain."

"You're welcome."

"Permission to disembark?"

I blinked away the prickling sensation in my eyes and returned his salute. "Permission granted."

"Thank you, sir."

He turned and walked away, and I simply stood there and watched. I could have said something, but I didn't. Instead, I waited until he'd vanished around the curve of the corridor, and then let out a sigh. What else had I been expecting? We barely knew each other.

"Hey, kid, are you okay?" The voice was Sofia's. I turned to see her standing in the doorway of her cabin, arms crossed, watching me.

"I will be."

"You sure?"

I forced a smile. "I'm used to it. Every time I let my guard down and start caring for someone, the universe snatches them away."

Sofia nodded in sympathy. "It seems you and I are very much alike."

"We are?"

"Yeah, I'm afraid so. Sucks, doesn't it?"

I shrugged one shoulder. "I'll live."

"Good girl. Now, what are *you* going to do? There's a whole Generality to help rebuild."

"I don't know. I need to talk it over with the *Trouble Dog.*"

"Well, I'm sure she's listening." She raised her face to the ceiling. "You there, ship?"

"I am."

A portion of the corridor wall became a screen, on which

the *Trouble Dog*'s avatar appeared. For some reason, she'd elected to appear wearing a glittery silver jumpsuit, pink lipstick and heavy black eyeliner. She'd even rearranged her hair into a neat black bob.

"What do you think?" Sofia asked. "Are you ready to help rebuild civilisation?"

Trouble Dog wrinkled her nose. "Building things isn't really my style. I'm more a blowing-things-up kind of girl."

"So, what would you like to do?"

The avatar looked questioningly at me. I said, "Go ahead. Whatever it is, you've earned it."

She grinned, then lowered her eyelashes, appearing almost coy. "I'd like to keep going further out," she said. "I've got limitless fuel now. I could fly forever. Go further than anyone else has ever been."

Sofia chuckled. "You want to see what's on the other side of the Intrusion, don't you?"

"Of course I do."

"I could tell you."

"And ruin the surprise?"

Sofia turned her attention back to me. "What do you say, Captain? Shall we go back through and join the Plates? There's a whole new universe right next door, just waiting…"

I pushed back the brim of my cap. To be honest, the idea of spending the rest of my life piecing interstellar civilisation back together filled me with nothing but boredom. I'd spent my life fixing people and rescuing stranded ships. I'd done my stint, and what did I have to show for it? What happiness had it ever brought me? I'd saved so many people, but I'd never been able to save the ones that mattered most.

My parents.

Sedge.

George.

Alva.

All I wanted now was to get away—from conflict, strife and loss. I had enough grief of my own; I didn't think I could bear the outpouring of bereavement that would come from the rest of the Generality as they came to terms with the people and planets that had been lost during Sudak's reign of terror.

And besides, I could feel the *Trouble Dog*'s beseeching gaze.

"Okay," I said. "I'll go." I raised a hand, cutting off their responses. "But there's one condition."

"What's that?" Sofia asked.

"You stay here," I told her. "Stay here and rebuild the House of Reclamation."

She looked surprised, then thoughtful. "Rebuild the House?"

"The Generality needs it more than ever. And you can start with the white ships. They'll follow you if the *Trouble Dog* tells them to, and you can put them to work delivering aid and evacuating failing outposts."

Sofia bit her bottom lip. She stared into the middle distance, lost in contemplation, and I fancied I could see the cogs and gears turning in her mind as she started to lay plans for the re-establishment of her organisation. "You know," she said, "I think you might be onto something there."

"You'll do it?"

"I'll certainly try."

We smiled at each other, my great-great-grandmother and me. Then she stepped forward and caught me in a bear-like hug.

"You're a good kid, Sally," she said. "Look after yourself."

"I will."

"And you," she turned and wagged a wrinkled finger at the *Trouble Dog*'s avatar. "You keep her in one piece, you hear me?"

The *Dog* grinned mischievously. "I'll certainly try."

FIFTY-TWO

NOD

Fix damage, then sleep.
    Sleep in nest.
    Good nest made of wires and packing crates.
    Share with George.
    Warm and content.
    Both of us alive.
    Alive to work again tomorrow.
    Always work.
    Keep *Hound of Difficulty* running smoothly.
    Hound is my World Tree now.
    Where we're going, there will be no other tree.
    No home but this cantankerous ship.
    This ship I love.
    This child I love.
    These humans I love.
    Life good.
    Life fixed.
    Everything fixable, given time.
    And luck.
    And hard work.
    Nothing stays lost or broken forever.
    Everything comes around again.

Like seasons.
Like days.
Like life.

FIFTY-THREE

TROUBLE DOG

We bade farewell to the Fleet of Knives and set course for the Intrusion. I had the access codes, vouchsafed to me by Sofia Nikitas, and I had my pack—the captain, Nod and George, the bizarre dual consciousness that called itself Lucy, and Preston the medic, who had insisted on staying aboard. He claimed he had nothing to go back to, and besides, knowing us, we'd probably need his services as medic before very long.

I think he'd even forgiven me for my prank in the museum.

As for the captain, I'd like to tell you she had an easier life once we'd ditched the past and passed through the portal to another realm; but the truth is, she still drank most evenings, and still spent the majority of her nights curled in the life raft in the cargo hold, wrapped in a survival blanket while she brooded on the losses she had incurred. However, during the days, she gradually became more animated and excited by what we found on the other side of the wormhole. And eventually, once we caught up with the Plates, she even found love in one of the cities, with a woman who came on board and lived as her partner for the remainder of their days— days in which we all had grand adventures and blazed a path through the darkness of an almost virgin universe.

But that, as they say, is another story—and it was all still in the future as we left the Fleet and spiralled in towards the Intrusion's waiting interface like a kingfisher pitching towards the surface of a lake.

All my life I had been running. Not from conflict, but from its aftermath. At Pelapatarn, I did something unspeakable to end one war; at the Gallery, I unleashed something dreadful to prevent another.

Sometimes, the price we pay for peace and security is freedom. Sometimes it is our very souls.

Now, I was about to run further and faster than ever before. But this time, I wasn't fleeing. This time, it wasn't about aftermaths or endings. This time, we were starting again and taking a second chance at life. Because, when the dust settles and the fires die down, isn't that all any of us really wants?

ACKNOWLEDGEMENTS

Thanks as always to my agent, Alexander Cochran at C&W, for his wise counsel during the writing of this trilogy. To my editor, Cath Trechman and my copyeditor, Hayley Shepherd for doing such wonderful jobs, and to all the rest of the Titan Books team—Lydia Gittins, Cat Camacho, Polly Grice, George Sandison, Julia Bradley, Katharine Carroll—for their support and comradeship. To Julia Lloyd for producing three amazing book covers. And to my family and friends for their steadfast love and support.

ABOUT THE AUTHOR

Gareth L. Powell was born and raised in Bristol, UK, and his early mentors included Diana Wynne Jones and Helen Dunmore.

His novels *Ack-Ack Macaque* and *Embers of War* both won the British Science Fiction Association Award for best novel, and *Embers of War* was also shortlisted for the Locus Awards. He is a popular guest and speaker at conventions and literary events and can often be found on Twitter giving advice and encouragement to up-and-coming writers.

He has written fiction for *Interzone* and *Clarkesworld*, a five-page comic strip for *2000 AD,* and articles on science fiction and creative writing for *The Guardian, The Irish Times, Shoreline of Infinity* and *SFX*. He has worked as a music journalist for *Acoustic Magazine* and is currently a columnist for *The Engineer*.

He still lives near Bristol and is represented in all professional matters by Alexander Cochran of the C&W literary agency.

www.garethlpowell.com

For more fantastic fiction, author events, exclusive
excerpts, competitions, limited editions and more

VISIT OUR WEBSITE
titanbooks.com

LIKE US ON FACEBOOK
facebook.com/titanbooks

FOLLOW US ON TWITTER
@TitanBooks

EMAIL US
readerfeedback@titanemail.com